By Larry McMurtry

Lonesome Dove
The Desert Rose
Cadillac Jack
Somebody's Darling
Terms of Endearment
All My Friends Are Going to Be Strangers
Moving On
The Last Picture Show
In a Narrow Grave: Essays on Texas
Leaving Cheyenne
Horseman, Pass By

THE DESERT ROSE

A NOVEL BY

Larry McMurtry

WITH A NEW PREFACE

A TOUCHSTONE BOOK
Published by Simon & Schuster, Inc.
NEW YORK

This is a work of fiction. Names, characters, places and incidents either are the product of the author's imagination or are used fictitiously. Any resemblance to actual events or locales or persons, living or dead, is entirely coincidental.

First Touchstone Edition, 1985

Published by Simon & Schuster, Inc.
Simon & Schuster Building
Rockefeller Center
1230 Avenue of the Americas
New York, New York 10020

TOUCHSTONE and colophon are registered trademarks of Simon & Schuster, Inc.

Designed by Irving Perkins Associates

Manufactured in the United States of America

10 9 8 7 6 5 4 3 2 1

10 9 8 7 6 5 4 3 2 1 Pbk.

Library of Congress Cataloging in Publication Data

McMurtry, Larry.
The desert rose.

I. Title.
PS3563.A319D4   1983   813'.54   83-4687

ISBN 0-671-46143-5
ISBN 0-671-55537-5 Pbk.

For Leslie,
for the use of her goat.

PREFACE

Writing a preface to a book only published a year ago seems faintly ridiculous. Once I finish a book it vanishes from my mental picture as rapidly as the road runner in the cartoon. I don't expect to see it or think about it again for a decade or so, if ever.

If one should agree to attempt such a preface, as I have, the first necessity is to avoid all thought of Henry James, whose rich, ruminative prefaces to the New York edition constitute a model of self-criticism which has so far not been surpassed, or even approached. Those prefaces are to novelists as the *Poetics* are to tragedians; we have no more intelligent body of commentary on either the theory or the practice of fiction. Writing in their shadow leaves one feeling no keener than Mortimer Snerd.

John Barth observed long ago, in a fine interview, that writers, like athletes, work by trained instinct. After a game or a book they may wax eloquent about why they made such a move or struck such a stroke; but when they are in motion such decisions are seldom consciously made. They come unprompted from the training and the instincts.

In my own practice, writing fiction has always seemed a semiconscious activity. I concentrate so hard on visualizing my characters that my actual surroundings blur. My characters seem to be speeding through their lives—I have to type unflaggingly in order to keep them in sight. I have no time to refer to manuals, particularly not dense, poorly indexed manuals such as the James prefaces.

Mention of the speed with which fiction can sometimes get written is especially appropriate to a discussion of *The Desert Rose*, which was written in three weeks.

I had been laboring away on a long novel about the 19th-century West called *Lonesome Dove*. Some twelve hundred pages were in hand at the time; the narrative was not exactly stalled, but it was slowing. My characters seemed to be moving at an ox-like pace up the great plains. They still had a thousand miles to go, and, worse yet, there were two parties of them, one proceeding out of Texas, the other meandering indecisively west and north from Fort Smith, Arkansas. Would they ever meet? And, if so, would it happen in Ogallala, where I needed them to meet? I didn't know, and in fact was growing a little bored with their slow trek over the plains. I needed a vacation.

Opportunity beckoned, as it usually does, from the West Coast. A Hollywood producer wanted to have a film script written about the real life of a Las Vegas showgirl. Would I write it, or at least go take a look? I had passed on the same project only a few months earlier, but then I hadn't been so bored with my cowboys. I said I'd go take a look.

As it happens, I am peculiarly ill-equipped to observe the real life of a showgirl. I like to sleep at night—preferably all night. But the showgirl's work is nocturnal. I dutifully tried to attend a few shows, but found it a heavy chore. My researches were not helped by the fact that I was allergic to something in my hotel room, probably the rug; I couldn't breathe in my room, or stay awake outside it. After a day and a half I had not been closer than a hundred feet to any showgirl; the charms of my trail-driving novel were beginning to reassert themselves.

I had been supplied with a long list of contacts, most of whom proved uncontactable. But, in the course of ticking them off, I actually met a showgirl. She was living in comfortable retirement, and she raised peacocks. We met only briefly and mainly talked about how I might find a legendary former showgirl who had retired less comfortably than my hostess.

This legend I never found, though everyone in Las Vegas seemed to know her. Not only that, they all seemed to love her. She was said to be somewhat down on her luck; it was rumored she was working as a barmaid.

Meanwhile, I was intrigued by the peacocks. Tits and

feathers were the staples of the Las Vegas shows, as they had always been. Peacock breeding as a retirement career for the beauties who had worn the feathers seemed wonderfully appropriate.

My hostess told me, as others had, that showgirls were a dying breed in Las Vegas. Showgirls are large, full-breasted women who neither sing nor dance. They are on stage to wear gorgeous if skimpy costumes and be beautiful. But fewer and fewer producers want to use them; today's producers wanted dancers. Only one or two of the larger shows still used showgirls to any extent—the future belonged to small-breasted women who could dance.

I have always been attracted to dying crafts—cowboying is one such. It became clear that the showgirls were the cowboys of Las Vegas; there were fewer and fewer jobs and they faced bleak futures, some with grace, and some without it.

I left Las Vegas on the morning of the third day and told the movie producer I would attempt to write the film. I suggested, however, that I start with an extended treatment. Dying breeds aren't the only thing I'm attracted to. I also like mother–daughter stories. Why not a mother–daughter story in which the daughter replaces the mother on her own stage, in the show in which she had been a star for some years? It's the old-matador-going-down-vs-the-young-matador-coming-up motif, except with a family twist.

I had written a number of original screenplays over the years, always with the feeling that I was going about it wrong. I work in textures, and the kind of details that bring a character to life (at least for me) seem excessive (or merely weird) when packed into a scene. They need to bob up in the flow of prose, then sink again, to live in the undercurrents. But in a film the director and the actors account for most of the undercurrents, not the writer. The screenplay is a kind of blueprint, and there are few undercurrents in blueprints.

The producer agreed to let me try an extended treatment, and before I had written a paragraph I knew I was writing a novel. Harmony's voice won me at once; I felt I had rarely, if ever, made a happier choice of point of view.

Finding Harmony was a great relief to me, in as much as I had just spent nearly ten years writing books that I didn't really like as I wrote them, day to day. I *did* like writing Harmony and her friends, and was rather sorry when she strolled out of hearing in Reno three weeks later.

I believe the energy that enabled me to write the book so rapidly was the result of the switch from *Lonesome Dove*, a long, third-person novel about men. The switch from third person to first, if you like the voice you switch into, can itself be energizing.

I didn't anticipate that Pepper would be such a monster. It was hardly just that she should find someone as considerate as Mel, but there you are, for now. Pepper is very young, and her story deliberately left unfinished. Sooner or later, rainy days come in one's artistic life, and when they arrive it is nice to have a character available in whom one's interest is not exhausted.

I'm happy, though, to have spent three weeks with Harmony and Jessie and Gary, Myrtle and Maude and Wendell. One of the nicest things that can happen is to have one's characters teach you something: that optimism is a form of courage, for example. It's Harmony's theme, not one she sings, just one she practices.

In retrospect I'm glad I never found the legendary showgirl who had drifted down. If I had found her, I wouldn't have had to invent her, and Harmony and her optimism would not have graced my life for those three weeks.

—Larry McMurtry
October, 1984

I

HARMONY IS driving home, eastward out of Las Vegas, her spirits high, her head a clutter of memories. Harmony loves to remember bits of her life, it makes her feel well, anyway, it's all been interesting. One of the memories that pops in is something Ross used to say, which was that they ought to call Las Vegas Leg City, or else Titsburg. Ross was always thinking up funny names for things, he had kept her laughing right up until the time they had Pepper, plus about a year more, and then she and Pepper took him down to the bus station behind the Stardust one day, he was going to check on a job doing lights for a show up in Tahoe, and had sort of just never come back, although Pepper was as cute a little girl as anyone could want and Harmony herself at the time had been said by some to have the best legs in Las Vegas and maybe the best bust too, although that was long before she had ever done topless, so that only Ross and a few of her old boyfriends really knew the whole story there.

Ross did think she was great-looking though, there was no doubt of that, and their sex life had been okay—maybe not va-boom-karoom, which was the phrase Gary always used about people who had a big attraction for one another —but definitely okay, and they had almost had enough money to make a down payment on a house with a swimming pool. Didn't happen, Pepper had to take swimming lessons down at the Stardust pool with the other kids whose parents worked in the show.

But then Harmony had always sort of known that legs and a sex life and a little girl and a house with a swimming pool hadn't meant that much to Ross—he had told her right off he liked to change lives once in a while and he was such a good light man he could always get work.

It was just that Ross could always make her laugh, that had been the cute thing about him, she still smiled when she thought of Ross although he had started going bald and wasn't even thirty when he left. She didn't mind his going so much, Ross should get to change lives if that was what he liked, and he did send money, not too regularly but sometimes he would send a lot if he had a run at the craps tables, he had never been unkind, so if he liked to change lives that was okay. The only sad part was that Pepper was beautiful from the time she was about three, it seemed kind of wrong that Ross wasn't getting to see it. By the time she was five Pepper could sing well enough that she could have probably even got on the radio if Harmony had ever had time to investigate that angle, somehow she never did. Once in a while she would dream that Pepper did sing on the radio and would maybe dedicate a song to her Daddy and Ross would hear it, that would be a nice thing for him. He was up in Reno, still working lights.

But then dreams, they weren't too real—or maybe real but not too likely to happen. Pepper had got more interested in dancing than singing, although she still sang beautifully, Harmony thought—others too, particularly Myrtle, who owned the other half of the duplex they lived in.

Harmony had always wanted to sing—it was something she envied Pepper—but she had just never had much of a voice. The one time she auditioned people couldn't keep from laughing, after all her name was Harmony but she couldn't sing, who could blame them for laughing? "Harmony, accept your fate, just be beautiful," Bonventre said —that was at the Dunes and he was a young producer then.

10

Still, once in a while she sat on the back steps and sang to her peacocks, they were about the only audience she could get to listen, them and Myrtle's goats.

Meanwhile, driving out Sahara Avenue, as the night was into its finale, Olivia Newton-John sang to her, on the car radio, a song from *Grease*. Harmony had loved the movie, plus she truly did love driving home just as the day was beginning. Already dawn had sketched the outline of the mountains to the east in light gray. Usually after the show she and Jessie and Gary would go sit in the little keno bar at the Stardust and drink beer and wind down for a couple of hours. Mainly it was just listening to Gary talk, he was the wardrobe manager and if there was anybody who could talk more than Gary Harmony didn't know who. Gary was an old friend, plus he had his own point of view, sort of an interested-in-everything point of view.

Jessie liked him a lot and once confided in Harmony that she still hoped Gary would stop being gay and fall in love with her, which was a hopeless wish of course, Gary couldn't stop being gay just for Jessie's sake, but he did spend most of his nights sitting around talking to two showgirls rather than hitting the discos or having dates, he was an unusual man, Gary, unusual for sure, if you were depressed or in any trouble there was no one better to talk to, not in Las Vegas anyway.

But usually it was Jessie who got depressed, and it was happening more and more lately. Even if the specific depression was over nothing worse than that one of the dancing nudes had told her her ass was getting dimpled, something normally bitchy like that, Jessie would just about sink out of sight she would be so unhappy. She would sit right in the keno bar and cry, with her stage makeup on, then she would just fade out and go to sleep with her head on the table, with Harmony and Gary both trying with might and main to cheer her up.

11

"It's the end, I know it is," Jessie always said, when she was sinking out of sight.

"No it *isn't!*" Gary would insist, "it's just that that little French girl told you your ass was dimpled. *She* certainly has no room to talk, her hips are wide enough that she could have had about five kids. Besides, she uses body makeup, which I *hate* because it turns the costumes orange and if it ever gets on the feathers you can just forget that costume, those feathers won't come clean."

By that time Jessie would usually already be asleep anyway, Gary's case against the French girl was mostly overkill but body makeup was one of his pet peeves and he went through his little tirade anyway. Then he would get real concerned about Jessie and drive her home to make sure she didn't have a wreck.

Once in a while Harmony let him drive her home too, not because she was usually tired or depressed or anything but mainly because it gave Gary a chance to see Pepper, he admired her so and thought she was so beautiful and talented.

Pepper loved it when Gary came, she thought he was the most knowledgeable man in the world and they would chatter away about clothes and hairstyles and makeup and dancing all through breakfast. Whereas Pepper would just about never have even a how-do-you-do for any of Harmony's boyfriends, no matter how sweet they were or how nice they tried to be to her, except with Denny it was not just ignoring it was kind of more like hate, Denny wasn't a guy you could just ignore, he was something but probably sweet wasn't a good word choice for what Denny was.

Gary always brought Pepper beautiful clothes for her birthday, or sometimes just if he was coming out on Sunday or something he would bring Pepper clothes and she would model them for him. She had started modeling teen fashions at Goldwater's when she was only ten—mainly she just liked trying on the clothes, the actual modeling bored her. Even real young, Pepper thought of herself as a dancer, she didn't really care for modeling apart from the makeup and getting her hair done and stuff.

The only thing not so very great about Pepper talking clothes so much with Gary was that it made her more critical where Harmony herself was concerned. Pepper did have the sense that she sort of absolutely knew what was good when it came to clothes—as she got older it got so Harmony could just about never find anything to wear that Pepper approved of. Harmony thought she dressed all right, after all she had always been thought to be one of the most glamorous showgirls in Las Vegas, she got to do all the publicity shots for the Stardust and met all the celebrities that came to town if management wanted them to meet a showgirl, and yet she could not seem to dress well enough to please Pepper.

"Couldn't you just buy a plain white blouse sometime?" Pepper had said only the week before—Harmony had been cleaning out her closets. "Every single blouse you've got is tacky."

Harmony didn't pay the remark any attention at the time, but later it came back to her when she was in a low mood anyway because of some things Denny said when he was drunk, and those things plus Pepper thinking her blouses were tacky were too much and she went out and sat under the little lawn umbrella and cried so hard she couldn't see the peacocks. Although it was silly, Pepper was just sixteen, she didn't really know everything there was to know about clothes even if Gary did brag on her taste all the time. It was just that the word had been wrong —tacky, it was the word that was hurtful, it was the one thing Harmony had always tried to avoid being and if your own little girl said it about you then it had to arouse some doubts. Though mainly it was just that Pepper always stuck to basic colors, she was very insistent about it, whereas Harmony liked clothes that were a little more un- usual, she liked gold blouses or maybe blouses with a little purple in them, something you'd notice.

After all, wearing those costmes every night, being a feathered beauty as Bonventre used to call her, sort of changed your attitude toward clothes. After the costumes it was sort of hard to know you were there if you didn't wear clothes with a little color in them. Pepper just didn't realize that, she was so beautiful she didn't even need makeup yet.

Harmony turned off the pavement onto a little dirt road that was the last road there was to turn off on, if you were going east out of Las Vegas. She rolled the window down —it was good to smell the desert in the morning, even in the winter she liked to get some air when she was driving home. After all the smoke in the casino just the clean air and the dry sagey smell made her feel lively. Now the outline over the mountains was gold instead of gray and the stars were beginning to die out in a cloudless sky.

Seeing the line of sun over the mountains made her hopeful, it just about always did, for another beautiful day was about to get started, which meant to Harmony that things could really be fresh and there could be a lot to hope for if you took the trouble to notice, instead of getting depressed, as Jessie did.

Harmony kept wishing Jessie had taken her advice and got a little house out closer to the desert, she had an apart- ment a block off the Strip, which was handy it was true but still didn't offer the great sights Harmony had to look for- ward to every day, such as the desert and her peacocks and the streamers of sun creeping over the mountains—though of course Jessie was scared of peacocks along with about everything else, but still, just to get farther from the Strip and see a real morning once in a while might have at least taken her mind off bad comments she heard in the dressing room. Genevieve, the French girl, wasn't that bad really, it was just her little boy had a learning disability and she got upset sometimes and said bitchy things, plus at the moment all Jessie had that might take her mind off her various problems was Monroe, not exactly the world's greatest prize in the boyfriend department, at least not in Harmony's opinion.

When she turned off the pavement onto the bumpy dirt road Harmony looked back at the Strip, eight miles away. It looked so miniature, like a wonderful toy place, with all the lights still on, whereas on her other side there was a bright band of sun behind the mountain, from horizon to horizon. It was one of her favorite things, to turn onto her own road with the air smelling so good and be able to see the Strip, with the Trop up at one end and the Sahara at the other, and besides that have the sun coming up just as she got home. With sights like that to see every day, who could complain?

Pretty as the sunrise was, though, it wasn't enough to keep her mind off the fact that Myrtle's car was acting like it meant to konk out. Harmony had been having to borrow it ever since Denny totaled their Pontiac, three weeks before. Myrtle was generous in emergencies, which was a good thing because it was definitely an emergency, since Denny had taken off the day after he totaled the Pontiac. The insurance check hadn't come yet either, though Harmony had been told several times it would come any day. Myrtle's car was an old Buick station wagon which was sort of manageable on the highway but got cases of the jerks when you had to go slow. There was no way to keep from going slow on the dirt road, to go fast meant probably knocking the bottom out, which Myrtle no doubt would not appreciate, she didn't consider Harmony a good driver anyway.

15

The more she slowed down for the bumps the worse the Buick jerked. Also, it could not be said that it smelled so great, mainly because Myrtle was in the habit of stuffing Maude, her main goat, into the car, so she'd have company while she roamed around Las Vegas or went to Boulder City to check out garage sales. Myrtle had very little to do except go to garage sales or else hold them in their mutual garage. The car had so many goat hairs in it that Harmony had to spread towels on the front seat in order to keep from being covered with them when she got to work.

Well, this car's not going to make it home, I guess we're down to no cars, she concluded, about five seconds before the Buick konked out.

She tried the ignition but all that did was make about fifteen little red lights flash on the dashboard, plus some white smoke was pouring out from under the hood so Harmony grabbed the newspaper she had bought Myrtle and took off down the road, it was just maybe a quarter of a mile on home and she enjoyed a nice walk anyway.

Before she had been walking two minutes she heard her peacocks calling, she only had three now, Joaquin her favorite, the most beautiful of them all, had somehow gotten out of the yard and fallen prey to coyotes, but the three that were left were beautiful too. She knew some people didn't like to hear peacocks but she loved to hear them in the still morning, across the quiet desert, it could almost make her cry if she was feeling lonely.

Particularly since Denny had left she was spending more and more time with the peacocks, though Pepper thought it was creepy and Mrytle argued that peacocks weren't survivors, like goats. Myrtle was hipped on survival and anyway Maude was every bit as spoiled as a peacock, if not more so. Harmony loved to sit and have the peacocks come and eat kernels of corn out of her hand, they were quite delicate and hardly ever pecked her. Then they would get through and go spread their beautiful feathers and parade them around the yard, which would have been just an ugly little yard in the desert if the peacocks hadn't been there.

Harmony liked to think the peacocks called just at dawn because they knew it was time for her to be getting back, maybe that was romantic but she had never seen anything wrong with being romantic, it just meant you were a little more tender about things and liked to think about the good kinds of things that could happen rather than the bad kinds of things, which there were enough of, there was no point in dwelling on them. Anyway she loved the peacocks and sometimes did her exercises for them, they seemed to take an interest, at least feeling that the peacocks were on the same wavelength as she was made coming home sort of better now that Denny had taken off. She just liked to feel in her heart that the peacocks were glad.

2.

WHEN HARMONY walked up the driveway carrying her bag and the newspaper, Myrtle had already laid out her garage sale for the day and was sitting in the only lawn chair she hadn't already sold at previous garage sales eating a bowl of Cheerios and waiting for customers. Sometimes customers came early, too—a lot of the keno runners and even a few dealers, older women mostly, were into the garage sale scene and would grab a morning paper and hit a few sales before going home to bed. It was Myrtle's theory that any sane person would rather buy things than sleep and the steady parade of would-be customers proved her right, although Myrtle actually had nothing left to sell except cheap glassware, cheap costume jewelry, some *Reader's Digest* books, and a few bedraggled blouses that had hung for months on a rack in the garage, long since picked over by every bargain hunter in the area.

Myrtle had set a bowl of dry Cheerios on the driveway for Maude, but Maude—a little black goat not much bigger than a dog—was sniffing around Myrtle's old card table as if she would rather nibble the costume jewelry—mostly imitation pearls, Myrtle's one area of expertise.

Myrtle was a tiny readhead in her early sixties who had no intention of letting age or anything else get in the way of pleasure. She lived on Cheerios, except on the rare occasions when her boyfriend Wendell could be persuaded to take her to a fast food feast. Wendy's was her favorite feasting place, but Wendell was not a big spender and would only pop for Wendy's about once a month, which was, for that matter, about as often as Myrtle had any intention of popping for Wendell.

"He's too oldt and anyway he's got that tricky back," Myrtle said, in her own defense.

Wendell was on the pool-maintenance crew at the MGM Grand, which, in Myrtle's view, contributed to his sexual discontent.

"Sure, he sees them gals with their floppies hanging out, what else would he come home thinking about?" Myrtle said.

Harmony's private opinion was that Myrtle took advantage of Wendell, a sweet gray-haired man with a big belly and sad eyes who had never meant to stay in Las Vegas but had come out and gotten stuck. His son had killed himself because of gayness, at least that was Gary's angle on it, and Wendell's wife had divorced him and married a cop. It had left Wendell with such a sad look in his eyes that Harmony could barely stand it.

The sadness of men, once it got into their eyes, affected her a lot, she sort of couldn't bear it and would usually try and make it go away if the circumstances permitted her to, often they didn't but sometimes they did, it was mainly a desire to kiss their sadness away that had caused her to bring so many of them home, a habit she knew Pepper didn't appreciate but then Pepper wasn't even old enough to notice the sadness in men or if she noticed she wasn't too sympathetic.

Harmony was though, sad-eyed men just got her, she could rarely keep it from happening and might not could even have kept it from happening with Wendell had it not been that Myrtle was usually sitting there in the cool of the garage in her lawn chair, waiting for one last customer to come by and snap up some imitation pearls. Wendell didn't talk much, he mostly just stood around looking down at his feet unless Myrtle was in such a good mood that she brought out one of the kitchen chairs for him to sit in.

Harmony would look out her window and see him standing and think oh Wendell, she couldn't help it, unhappiness just made her feel tender, when she saw a guy looking that way she wanted to maybe just lay her palm against his cheek, or maybe a kiss, something to let him know her heart did sort of go out to him even if she didn't understand precisely why he looked so sad. Old or young, fat or thin didn't matter so much although definitely fat rather than thin if she was given a choice, she was not so drawn to the skinny guys, it was just that she sometimes got the sense that she overwhelmed them, after all she was pretty tall and had a good bust and a few of them had sort of seemed to feel that they were being smothered.

Also her preference for the husky ones might have had something to do with Didier, who had given her her first job, at the Trop, when she was only seventeen but looked a lot more mature. She had always thought Tropicana was a wonderful name, when she was younger just saying it or hearing it mentioned on the radio made her feel romantic, so that when she got off the bus in Las Vegas the first thing she did was walk right up the street and look at it. And about three months later, just when she thought she was going to have to be a waitress all her life there was an audition and she got up her nerve and Didier hired her right away, and then fell in love with her, although he was sixty-four at the time and was the producer of the show and very busy. She had even got to live in his suite at the Trop, which was a pretty big change from life in Tulsa, where she grew up.

Probably it was Didier who got her to liking fat men, he was French and used to good food and was so fat he was dangerous to himself, which was proved for sure about six months later when he died in bed one morning while Harmony was downstairs unwinding with some of the girls.

It was her first death, she was not experienced with it at all, she had come in meaning to give Didier a kiss and saw that he was dead, only she couldn't admit it right away, couldn't admit it one bit and went on and took her makeup off and looked and Didier was dead okay though she still couldn't admit it, maybe not for an hour until she thought well I guess now I'll order some breakfast so she did and Jimmy came up with it. They always sent Jimmy because Didier was fussy about his food, he was fussy about everything actually but particularly about his food, and Jimmy came in with the breakfast and stood around waiting to serve it until she just said "Could you go look at him," which surprised Jimmy, that was a little unusual, and he looked and came back and said "Harmony, he's dead," which was when she admitted it and started to cry.

Years later Jimmy's wife, who by his own admission had been a hooker once, went back to her old habits, only she took it further and stole some guy's wallet and he turned out to be pretty big time and the wallet had like a few thousand in it so she got sent to prison and Harmony was driving along the Strip one day and happened to see Jimmy

20

standing at the bus stop in front of the Circus Circus looking so sad that she just immediately took him home, only the problem was all they could ever find to talk about was the morning Didier died, it was not a basis for a relationship they concluded, though Harmony had no regrets about it, she had for sure tried worse than Jimmy, he was from San Francisco and dressed nice and would definitely spend his last dime if it was something she and Pepper needed for the house, or doctor bills or whatever.

Still, it was Didier she remembered every time she saw Wendell standing in Myrtle's driveway looking down at his feet, it had to be the big belly that caused her to be reminded, they were otherwise not alike. Didier had been a happy man, at least he was as long as the show was okay and his food cooked the way it was supposed to be and he had a girl with an absolutely perfect bust to be his mistress, fortunately hers *had* been perfect when she was seventeen, Didier had stressed that fact a lot—on the other hand Wendell looked like he would like to stick his head in the pool he helped maintain and keep it there. He moonlighted at the all-night Amoco station and Harmony always felt a throb of love because he was such a gentleman and cleaned all her windshields and even her mirrors, even the rearview mirror inside the car which of course in a desert got dust on it too, she could tell he couldn't get over his son losing his life like that because of the gayness, or his wife and the cop and who knew what else, Wendell probably had sorrows she didn't suspect; after all he was in his late sixties and she had only known him for a year or two.

Myrtle looked up from her Cheerios and saw Harmony but no car, which was a shock but secondary to finding out if there were any garage sales on that day that offered goodies she had urgent need of. Harmony pitched her the paper and squatted down to say good morning to Maude, knowing full well Myrtle wouldn't even say hello until she'd checked the sales. Maude was nibbling the bottom of the card table and when Harmony made her stop she gave an annoyed little bleat and ran back in the garage to sulk.

"Oh, Maude, don't be mad, it's such a pretty day," Harmony said.

The want ads were a cruel disappointment, all the garage sales being continuations of ones Myrtle had already been to at least once if not several times. She tossed the paper aside and began trying to get resigned to sitting and waiting.

"If that goat was to have to wait for a cloudy day to get her feelings hurt she'd be out of luck," Myrtle said. "I hope you didn't forget the vodka, this one's gonna be a long one."

"I didn't forget it, I just left it in the back seat," Harmony said. On her days at home Myrtle had a tendency to get looped, after which, if a customer irritated her by trying to bargain, she might capriciously double the price of everything in the sale. Myrtle had worked as a checker at the Safeway for twenty-five years, during which time she had often had the desire to double the prices when a snotty customer came along.

"So where's the car, I hope you didn't knock the oil pan off again," she said.

"It just konked out between here and the highway," Harmony said. "I was driving real slow when it happened."

"Well, there ain't no interesting sales I could have gone to anyway," Myrtle said. "Only Pepper's gonna be pissed, if I know her."

That was for sure—if there was one thing Pepper hated it was being told she had to hitch to school.

"If Wendell comes with the tow truck maybe she can hitch a ride with him," Harmony suggested. Since her Pontiac hadn't been exactly reliable even before Danny totaled it Wendell was frequently required to come out and tow in one car or the other before he went to work at the Grand.

"Maude didn't eat her Cheerios," she added. Maude had wandered down the driveway and was staring at a weed.

"She's holding out for Captain Crunch. Likes the sugar," Myrtle said. "You call Wendell. I'm going down and get that vodka before some alcoholic comes along and happens to look in the back seat.

3.

HARMONY WAS a little late, mainly from having to walk the last part of the way but also partly because Gary had been explaining his views on the end of the world, which always got him sort of keyed up and meant that she hadn't left the Stardust as early as she usually did. A lot of people in Las Vegas seemed to think the end of the world was probably going to come in about a year or two, Jessie certainly had the feeling there wasn't all that much time left but Gary said all those views were nonsense. It wasn't that he didn't believe in God, he just felt there was no reason to suppose the end of the world was at hand particularly, which Harmony agreed with, it seemed to her why should it be?, maybe the people who thought otherwise were not reading the Bible right or something.

Gary's main point about the end of the world was that most of the people who felt that way were dancers who were so sick of the show they happened to be in that they would welcome any change, even one that was real drastic. Since Gary knew the whole life story of every dancer or showgirl working in Las Vegas once he got to explaining it could take a while, but also it was interesting, kind of amazing really when you stopped to think of all the things Gary knew. The one point she couldn't agree with him on was that there was very little happiness, he mainly got off

23

on that when he was drunk but it was a viewpoint Harmony couldn't bear to listen to, she just would usually leave when Gary became pessimistic, it made her worry too much that Pepper's life would turn out wrong or something.

For herself she didn't worry too much, she still loved being in the show, plus there was a lot to like about life if you could make a little effort and look on the bright side. Even a nice morning was a form of happiness, plus having a sweet guy around for a while was another form, a major form actually, major even if usually sort of brief in her experience.

She and Jessie agreed that one reason Gary was so pessimistic at times was that his own sex life seemed to be kind of a blank, though certainly he had a million friends. Even Jessie had *somebody*, if only Monroe, no great lover Jessie was frank to say but at least he was not mean and he did own his own business, Monroe's Muffler Shop, out on the north edge of town. In the course of time he had put three mufflers on the Buick, since Myrtle would kind of drive at breakneck speed whether it was a terrible road or not if she was trying to beat the crowd to a garage sale she was always knocking holes in her mufflers and had gotten if anything more reckless since she knew Monroe would give her a good price on a new one.

But listening to Gary's end of the world spiel had contributed to making her late so she started cooking breakfast without stopping to take her makeup off, which caused Pepper to make a face when she came dawdling in.

"Pepper, why did you make that face, I'm just trying to hurry," Harmony said, not particularly offended, it just always seemed Pepper made a face if she caught her with her makeup on.

Pepper yawned and sat down at the table. She had the blank look of a child who was still sleepy, and was wearing a T-shirt Harmony had been given one time when she was in a bicycle race just for showgirls down at the Sands. She had come in about ninetieth, she was a little afraid of bicycles and just tried to keep on the outside and not wobble into the path of one of the French girls, all of whom were sort of like demons once they got in a bicycle race, not that they were always totally polite even in the dressing room but there was no doubt that they became very competitive if you stuck them on a bicycle.

Pepper was just so totally beautiful, Harmony stopped to look at her for a second and almost burned the toast, she had a face that made every photographer want to take a picture of her. Even Denny had taken quite a few pictures of her—a number of them were stuck on the wall over the table, Pepper practicing dance steps mostly. It hurt Harmony that there had never been the slightest bit of love lost between Pepper and Denny, but how could you make two people like one another if they just didn't?

Denny was quite a good photographer, much too good for the job he had, which was just taking pictures of houses that were for sale, for a real estate company. That seemed a waste, considering the wonderful pictures he took of Pepper despite saying constantly she was such a little bitch.

Every time he said it Harmony said okay, move out, she wasn't going to live with a man who would say such things about her child, although to be fair Pepper said even worse things about him, maybe because Gary had not been all that discreet and had informed Pepper about the trouble Denny had gotten into when he was a lifeguard at Caesars Palace, it was a tragedy Denny would have to live with all his life, because a child had drowned while he was screwing a woman in the towel room.

Pepper hadn't needed to know that but Gary had told her. Sometimes Harmony suspected that Gary wasn't totally and absolutely gay, at least there were times when he did things that made it seem like maybe he was just a little bit jealous in some way. There were times, thinking about Gary and Denny and Pepper and how complicated life could get when Harmony would feel a sinking, she would start getting low and then it was like something was falling, like she couldn't keep a high heart anymore no matter how much she tried, and she would end up out under the umbrella, usually in the heart of the day, pitching little handfuls of corn to the peacocks and not even being able to see them because of her tears.

At times even before he totaled the car she almost wished Denny would go because for the life of her she couldn't understand what it was with Denny and Pepper, after all she loved them both and yet they said such tearing things about one another, Denny said terrible things and Pepper just totally ignored him, treated him as if he wasn't there.

"I wish you wouldn't cook eggs in that makeup, it's grotesque, you know," Pepper said, after another yawn. Pepper's hair was coal black and cut very short, which she felt was the height of fashion just then, also it was handy, three strokes of a brush and she was ready for school or whatever. She stretched out a leg and flexed it a time or two. Her legs were so much like Harmony's that every time Harmony noticed she thought well that stuff about genes has to be true, she's even got my kneecaps. Only since Ross had been kind of a shrimp maybe Pepper wouldn't get quite so tall, which would mean she had a chance to really go somewhere as a dancer, Madonna, her teacher, had already let everybody know that Pepper was the most talented young dancer in Las Vegas.

"Well, the car konked out and Wendell was fixing a flat for somebody and didn't know exactly what time he could make it with the tow truck," Harmony said. "I wanted to hurry up breakfast in case you have to hitch."

"Forget it, I'm not hitching," Pepper said, without changing expression. She had such a crisp voice, some-

26

times it startled Harmony, she just delivered her statements with such authority it seemed there could be no denying them.

"Pepper, you can't just not go to school because the car konked out," Harmony said. "Life has to go on, even if we don't have a car right now."

"Who said anything about life?" Pepper said, looking at her in that way she had which was so cool Harmony often felt a little unnerved, just at the thought that her own daughter could be that cool.

"Well, school is part of life," Harmony said, feeling it wasn't entirely an adequate remark as she sat a nice plate of scrambled eggs and toast in front of Pepper. She had already squeezed the oranges and was pleased to see there was nothing at all wrong with Pepper's appetite. She killed the orange juice in about four swallows and started eating the scrambled eggs, despite the fact that Harmony had cooked them with her makeup on.

"Make Denny pay for a taxi if you want me to go to school," Pepper said between bites. "He did ruin a perfectly good car that wasn't his in the first place."

"It wasn't *perfectly* good," Harmony said, wishing she had got to the point where she could stop taking up for Denny, he didn't deserve it, the fact was he had probably totaled the car on purpose just because he was mad at her for refusing to call in sick the afternoon he wanted to go to the lake and do cocaine. Before he had come to Las Vegas he had done stunt driving in L.A. and had bragged any number of times that he could total a car and walk away without a scratch should the mood strike him, which it had and which was exactly what he did.

"Look, it *ran* and I could have taken my driver's test in it if your fucking idiot of a boyfriend hadn't destroyed it," Pepper said. "I could have taken it in Myrtle's car only now you tell me you've ruined that one too."

"It's not ruined, Wendell just needs to work on it a

27

little," Harmony said, trying to be reasonable. Pepper had the advantage of being able to sound more reasonable than anybody else, even Gary got defensive once in a while when Pepper chose to really challenge one of his theories or something.

"Anyway, it's a station wagon and you know how hard they are to parallel park," Harmony said.

Pepper finished the eggs and sort of cleaned out her jaw with her tongue before she took on that comment.

"You're the one who's paranoid about parallel parking," she pointed out. "I can parallel park the Buick perfectly well."

It was true—the test would undoubtedly be a pushover for Pepper, who had been driving her boyfriends' cars since she had begun dating at about age eleven. She just had absolute confidence behind the wheel, it was another facet Harmony envied, she herself got nervous driving sometimes but not Pepper, she would instantly honk at people if they made what she considered a driving error.

As for her own problems about parallel parking it had resulted from hearing a horrible story on the radio many years before about a little baby who had gotten squashed by a woman who was parallel parking. The mother had just stepped into a store to buy something leaving her little boy to watch the baby which was in a stroller and the little boy got distracted and let the stroller roll off the curb and a woman who was parallel parking ran over it.

For years the story kept coming back into her mind and upsetting her, the thought of a helpless little baby being squashed, and all the anguish it must have left in all those lives, the mother feeling guilty and the woman who was driving feeling guilty and then the little boy growing up and feeling guilty too. Harmony just knew she would never have been able to live with herself if she had been involved in a tragedy of that kind, which she easily could have been, it happened not three blocks from the Stardust and except for luck she could have been backing into that parking space. For two or three years it kept coming back into her mind, before that she had not been a worrier particularly or an overprotective mother, but once in a while the thought of the helpless baby would come back to her and she would almost feel dizzy for a second just from realizing how it could be such a near miss that kept you from being in a tragedy. And it had had a permanent effect on her parallel parking, she just would not back into a space without getting out of the car and checking to be sure there was nothing alive in it that she could run over—it often made people behind her pretty angry, along the Strip people did expect you to get on with the business of parallel parking.

"Maybe we could rent a car for you to take the driver's test in," Harmony said. "Budget's right there and they have real nice cars."

The minute she said it she realized that wouldn't work either, they had canceled her Visa card and there was no way anymore to get a rent car without one. Denny had been supposed to get a raise and had talked her into letting him put six hundred dollars' worth of scuba-diving equipment on her Visa, it was when they were spending a lot of time at the lake so she did it, and when the big Visa bill came and she tried to get him to at least pay part of it he had acted quite brash, the way he always did if you actually asked him for something, he told her he had considered the scuba-diving equipment a present, which flabbergasted Harmony, six hundred dollars was nearly two weeks' wages. So she ended up losing her Visa, which was a big inconvenience.

Pepper knew all about the trouble with Visa, she didn't even bother to destroy the suggestion about the rent car.

"Bonventre told me when he took his driver's test he

29

stole a car to take it in and the cops didn't even catch him," Pepper said. "Maybe I'll just do that."

"Oh, Pepper," Harmony said. "Now why did he tell you that? Bonventre's my age."

"So? He still did it," Pepper said.

"Yeah but that was before they had computers," Harmony said. "It's easier to catch people now. Anyway, what were you talking to him for?"

"He was at Madonna's the other day," Pepper said.

"Well, he and Madonna used to be involved, when she was lead dancer at the Trop," Harmony said. "Maybe they'll get back together."

Pepper curled her lip at that suggestion. She had a beautiful lip too, but Harmony would have rather she didn't curl it quite so often.

"He told her she had an ass like a prune, so I don't guess they'll get back together, Momma," Pepper said. "How come you're such a dreamer?"

Harmony didn't know, you were or you weren't so far as that went, the prune remark was nothing but typical Bonventre, he was known throughout Nevada for his horrible comparisons. Personally Harmony thought Madonna had a great ass, considering she had to be pushing sixty, though Bonventre would naturally be the last person to give her any credit.

"For a man who's not exactly the best-looking I ever saw he certainly feels free to criticize," Harmony said.

"Well, he's in the body business, that's the way he describes it," Pepper said. "It's his show, there's no reason he should have people in it who look bad."

"I don't want to argue with you, Pepper, I've known Bonventre a lot longer than you have," Harmony said, sitting down at the table to have her coffee.

"That doesn't mean you know all about him," Pepper remarked, stretching out her leg and curling her toes.

"It wouldn't kill him to say something nice to Madonna," Harmony said.

"He just came by to see my lesson, Momma," Pepper said, standing up and stretching. Even when she was being catty, it was hard not to be proud that your child was so beautiful, she had a nice little bust and basically looked wonderful, even just in the T-shirt.

The peacocks knew Harmony was there and were pecking impatiently at the back screen, they wanted their breakfast too.

"Of course Bonventre's not handsome enough for you, we all know what terrific taste in men *you* have," Pepper said.

"Why'd he come to your lesson?" Harmony asked. Bonventre was not one to drop in on ballet classes unless he had something in mind.

Pepper shrugged. "Wants me to audition," she said.

"Au*di*tion?" Harmony said. "Audition for what?"

"To be Monique's understudy," Pepper said, setting her plate in the sink.

Harmony was so stunned by that one that she left her coffee and got up and walked right out the back door, not even noticing the peacocks. All of a sudden she had too many different feelings working in her to even try to sort them out. She had known Bonventre for over twenty years, he was her boss, she saw him every day, what did he mean by trying to audition her daughter to be Monique's understudy without even saying a word about it to her? As if it were none of her business?

Harmony went and stood by the back fence, feeling more anger than anything. Bonventre just never stopped, the very first words he had said to her the day she met him had been a lie. He claimed to be a producer when in fact he was just one of Didier's assistants, he didn't even care if you found out about his lies five seconds later, he would

31

just look you in the eye and pretend you couldn't understand plain English or something. And if there was the slightest ground for criticizing someone for physical flaws Bonventre would spot it instantly. For two years after she had had Pepper he told her practically every day that her breasts didn't match anymore, it was true they didn't one hundred percent but even Gary who had a good eye for such things said it was something you would only notice if you happened to be looking from a very peculiar angle, like you would have to be in the light booth or somewhere to even notice, it was just Bonventre reminding you that if you worked for him your body was his to condemn.

While Harmony was standing by the back fence trying not to feel so upset she noticed the tow truck down the road, at least Wendell had come. She started to go back and tell Pepper but before she could Pepper came out the door, she was wearing jeans and a black blouse and had her books and was off down the road without saying goodbye. Of course she had to hurry if she wanted to catch a ride, Wendell was such an expert at towing the Buick that he could latch onto it in about half a minute, but it didn't help Harmony's confusion that Pepper had left before she could ask a few questions about Bonventre, maybe he had just been teasing?

The peacocks could tell she was upset, they tipped around her nervously, bending their long necks this way and that and not making too much fuss about the fact that she hadn't fed them, though one did reach through the fence and peck one of the brown goats that Myrtle kept in the backyard month after month, hardly paying them any attention at all.

The reason she had them was because she loved animal acts probably more than anyone alive and had once had the idea she could work up a goat act and in no time be making the kind of money Bobby Berosini made with his orangutan act up at the Grand. But in fact all that had happened was that Myrtle fell totally in love with Maude and developed total apathy toward the other three goats, who had never learned a single trick, although goats *could* be trained. Once there had been a rather sweet Hungarian who did a goat act at the Trop, Harmony had even gone with him a time or two, kind of a wistful guy with yearnings that he couldn't talk about in English, which meant that Harmony never got to find out about them exactly, though some of them turned out to be for a boy who left to go to work at Harrah's, where the guy eventually took his goat act, too.

The sun was well up and beginning to get hot, Harmony suddenly felt an urge to get her makeup off. She didn't really have the falling feeling that came before crying, she just felt confused and angry at Bonventre for not at least mentioning it if he thought he had plans for Pepper. Anyway Pepper was contemptuous of practically all the dancing in Las Vegas, Madonna had assured her that she could probably get a scholarship or be apprenticed to some regional ballet. It was absurd for Bonventre to suddenly audition her for a show her own mother had kind of been a star in for twelve years, not that she was a dancer, she had always just been a showgirl, but still she was at least as well known as Monique, except maybe strictly in dancing circles. It would certainly be a big move for Pepper, whose only job so far was taking orders for fried chicken at the Gino's down the road.

By the time she got her makeup off she had decided it was probably a joke, she had more serious things to worry about, such as whether the insurance check was ever going to come so she could get some kind of car and get to work without having to call Gary and make him go several miles out of his way. Also she was tired, the fatigue had begun to hit her. It was already too hot to sit on the back steps and let the peacocks eat out of her hand, she just scattered some food in their tray and put it under the little shade that Wendell had been nice enough to build for her so the birds wouldn't die of the heat.

Then she put on her nightgown and pulled the shades and turned the air conditioner up high and got her sleep goggles and crawled into bed. She liked to sleep in total darkness, which was not easy to achieve in Las Vegas on a sunny day, even with the shades pulled all the way down the room was just barely dim. Finally someone told her about sleep goggles and she became immediately addicted. With the goggles on it was so black it was like being in another world, much darker than even the cloudiest night, it made for very good sleeping, which was important, Harmony had always been a healthy sleeper and if she got the right amount there was hardly a day that she didn't wake up feeling cheerful.

Only if Denny happened to be around when she put the goggles on sleep wasn't what was going to happen first, for some reason the sight of her in the goggles was a terrific turn-on for Denny, he liked it that she was in pitch blackness and couldn't see him.

At first before he got so crazy that had been okay, making love in total blackness had been kind of a novelty, it had a pretty strong effect a few times. But then sometimes she would rather have seen him, after all Denny's worst enemies couldn't deny that he was a very good-looking guy, she loved the way his jaw looked and his mouth, but the one time she had yanked the goggles off just in order to see him he said she had spoiled it and got furious. She said I'm sorry and offered to put them back on, it didn't seem like that big a deal, but Denny got dressed and left and she didn't hear from him for three days.

Then once he began to get crazy the goggles became too big a thing. Once he had made her take them to the lake, which was when she began to think once in a while, what's wrong with this guy? Then he got sweet and conned her into wearing them in the boat when they were right out in the middle of the lake and the result was anything but sexy in her view. It was just a small motorboat anyway and though Denny could swim for miles she herself couldn't swim that well so it was more a frightening experience than anything. Denny got mad again and told her she was a coward which could well have been true but being in pitch-blackness in the middle of a lake and knowing she wasn't a good swimmer hadn't been anything she had bargained for.

Now she was in her bed and yawning and very tired but she didn't get right to sleep, it was getting so just putting the goggles on and laying there brought Denny to mind. With all his faults she did love him a lot and kept thinking maybe it was just a little period of craziness he was going through, maybe one day he'd come back and be sweet again like he'd been the first few weeks.

There was no telling, sometimes people went through periods, even Gary had days when he looked like the end of the world couldn't come too soon for him. Although Gary didn't approve of Denny at all, once he even acted a little superior and told her she was like a beautiful car, a Mercedes or something, that had everything it needed except brakes. Then the next day he apologized and claimed he had been in a bad mood and listened to all her troubles and was on her side again, but she never forgot the remark because it was sort of true, in the love area she didn't have such great brakes, Generally when a guy left her love would be going at full speed, she would be feeling great and not have even a remote suspicion that the guy was about to vanish, and then he would vanish and she would have no way at all to stop the love, sometimes it would just zoom right on, sort of like Myrtle racing to a garage sale only pointless of course, maybe it would run for several weeks or even a few months before it finally sort of coasted to a stop.

Actually with the goggles on it was more than Denny that came into her mind. Probably the stuff about Pepper and Bonventre could have been some kind of mistake, it was not unknown for Pepper to have little fantasies about her dancing, Pepper did spend a lot of time thinking about her career. Maybe all that had happened was that Bonventre had been behaving himself for once and said something to be polite and Pepper had turned it into a fantasy about having an audition and being famous overnight.

Anyway, Madonna would know what the story was. It was Denny that her mind just couldn't turn loose of, her feelings just hadn't started slowing down at all where he was concerned. She didn't want to cry under the goggles, it made her feel silly to have to sit up and empty tears out of her sleep goggles, but despite herself she did anyway, not a whole lot of crying, just a little, enough that the goggles were pretty damp. She would just think oh Denny why can't you just come back and be nice, knowing he wouldn't probably but still hoping anyway.

4.

BY THE time Harmony woke up and showered and had some strawberry yogurt, she loved it, Myrtle was so disgusted from having taken in only seventy-five cents all day that she was looped to the gills. She was sitting there holding Maude in her lap, looking like she was about ready to fall out of the chair.

"So what was the seventy-five cents for?" Harmony asked, sitting down to drink a little iced tea. She had brought Myrtle a glass but Myrtle took two big swallows and then poured in vodka until the glass was full again.

"A pair of dumb earrings," Myrtle said. "I think the woman I solt them to must have been color-blind, she said they matched her pants and they never matched a thing she had on."

"Maybe she just liked them," Harmony said. She could never quite understand why Myrtle was so critical of her customers—she was equally insulted if they bought anything or if they didn't.

"I think Maude's pregnant," Myrtle said, scratching Maude between the ears. Maude had just about nibbled through one of the canvas arms of the last lawn chair.

"Oh, Maude, I can't believe it," Harmony said. "What did Wendell say about the car?"

"Ain't called, I guess he's too busy fishin' turds out of that dumb swimming pool," Myrtle said.

"Well, it never has seemed like the right kind of work for Wendell," Harmony said. "Maybe they'll make him manager of the Amoco station or something."

"What'd you put in this tea to make it taste funny?" Myrtle asked.

"It's just mint tea," Harmony said. "Maybe it doesn't mix with vodka."

The day was hot but sort of hazy, sort of a thin haze over the mountains to the west. There was so much heat coming off the ground that you couldn't really see the Strip, just the tops of one or two hotels.

"Myrtle, has Pepper talked to you about auditioning or anything?" she asked. Pepper and Myrtle spent so much time talking it was sometimes easier to find out what was going on with her daughter by asking Myrtle.

Maude suddenly hopped out of Myrtle's lap and went racing down the driveway like she was going to run for a mile. She was so little it was comical to see her run, but before she even got to the end of the driveway she stopped abruptly and began to cat a weed, as if getting to the weed quick had been the only purpose in running.

"See, pregnant behavior," Myrtle said.

"Well, Maude never has behaved like other goats," Harmony said.

"All Pepper talks to me about these days is how much she hates Denny," Myrtle said. "She thinks he's a jerk, only that ain't the word she used."

"I think I'll get my hat and go see if the insurance check came," Harmony said. "We got to get us at least one car out here."

But she didn't just right away leave. Myrtle was squinting off into the distance. Harmony kept wishing she would drink less and eat something besides Cheerios, she was just skin and bones.

"She didn't say anything to you about getting a job?" Harmony asked.

"Harmony, I ain't telling you any of Pepper's secrets," Myrtle said. "One of us has got to keep the lines of communication open to that girl."

"Well, I'm her mother, Myrtle," Harmony said, a remark Myrtle just ignored.

Harmony decided just to go on and take a walk to the mailbox, there was no point in arguing with Myrtle when she was depressed over a failed garage sale. She went in the house and got a big straw hat to protect her in case the sun got hotter all of a sudden and started walking down the gravel road only to discover after she'd gone too far to go back that Maude was following her.

"Maude, go back, you know you're not supposed to come," Harmony said, Myrtle practically lived in terror that someone would steal Maude as it was, and if she let her follow and something happened Myrtle would probably never get over it.

Still, there was not much to be done about Maude, Harmony didn't have the heart to take really stern measures such as throwing rocks at her, so they walked along together. Harmony had worn shorts, she liked to feel the warmth on her legs, after a little bit of a walk she forgot her worries and began to enjoy the day. It was wonderful to live out of town and have so much sky around you, probably half of Jessie's problem was that when she stepped out her door all she got to see was city buses and the adult bookstore across from her apartment building.

The mailboxes were out by the highway, just a nice walk for a person who enjoyed outdoor exercise. Too far for Maude though, she began to run around in front of Harmony and bleat and get right in her way, which meant that she wanted to be carried. Harmony walked around her several times but Maude was very persistent, she just kept doing it, so Harmony finally picked her up to keep from being tripped, thinking if Myrtle suddenly missed her she would go into a panic in two minutes. Three times so far she had called the sheriff's department to demand they put out a dragnet to find her goat when all that had happened was that Maude had run down to the next street where there were some children she liked to play with.

Just as Harmony was nearly to the boxes she happened to look up and there was Denny, sitting in what looked like a brand-new blue car right by her mailbox. It was such a shock she nearly dropped Maude, she had sort of half-noticed the car earlier but it never occurred to her Denny would be sitting in it.

Before she could get any closer or do much of anything he grinned and waved a piece of paper out the window at her.

"Hello there, Harmony," he said, and then pulled back on the highway and drove off, still grinning and waving the piece of paper out the window at her.

Harmony suddenly felt just sick: there was no doubt in her mind about what the piece of paper was. She put Maude down and walked to the mailbox, so weak for a moment she had to lean on it just to stand up. Seeing Denny in the first place had been a shock, but then instead of being nice like she was still imagining him he had to do something like steal her check. She thought maybe it was a joke, even Denny wouldn't do that, maybe he was just pretending to steal it to tease her or something, maybe he meant to turn around and bring it back and they could have a chance to make up.

But when she looked down the highway there was not a single car in sight, the highway was hot and empty, which was awfully discouraging. Before she could start to cry she heard a little click click and it was Maude running across the highway, Myrtle would have a fit if she saw that. Harmony had to go get her, but then she gave up on it being a joke and Denny coming back and just wanted to sit down by the road and cry until someone with a little kindness came along and stopped to help her, though how could anyone help her if Denny had really stolen the check? It was thirteen hundred dollars and just about the only hope she had of being able to buy some kind of used car or for that matter even pay Madonna all she owed her on Pepper's lessons, not to mention that she still owed Visa and quite a few other bills.

Of course the check was made out to her but that wouldn't matter to Denny. One of his claims was that he had been a handwriting expert for the Miami police, she didn't believe it but still there was no doubt he would forge her name and figure out a way to get the check cashed.

When she looked in the mailbox there was nothing except a flyer from Western Auto announcing a tire sale, plus the envelope from the insurance company that the check had been in. Denny had scribbled on the back of it: "A big hello in case I miss you, hope you don't mind extending me this little loan and if you do tough shit."

Harmony started to just leave it in the mailbox but then

she thought she might need the number of the insurance company. They might have some suggestions, plus maybe Myrtle would want to know about the tire sale, the week seldom went by that she didn't have two or three flats.

It was not a nice walk home, she couldn't help crying that he would do that, plus there would be no way to hide it from Myrtle or Pepper or Gary or even Jessie for that matter, all of whom started telling her she was crazy practically the minute she fell in love with Denny. Jessie would probably soften up the quickest, she never held it against anyone when they made mistakes and got in love with the wrong people. Of course Jessie might have had the least room to talk considering that Monroe was probably the best boyfriend she had ever had, some of Jessie's had not exactly been prizes, either.

Harmony still kept thinking maybe it could be some kind of joke, her birthday was coming up on Saturday, maybe there was at least an outside chance he was planning to buy her a birthday present or something, she tried to think of good possibilities but it didn't really work, she kept remembering the way he smiled when he waved the check at her. It was not the way he smiled when he was being nice.

Myrtle had been in a fret about Maude, but when she heard what had happened she forgot about that and came right over looped as she was and started offering advice, all of it having to do with calling the police and getting criminal charges started. Harmony thought of calling Gary but he seldom got up before four in the afternoon and it wasn't four yet, so instead she let Myrtle call Wendell to get his opinion. But he was on his coffee break, nobody could find him, which for some reason caused Myrtle to assume he was having an affair with a bathing beauty, she often got a little insecure when she was drunk and imagined that Wendell was having affairs with women he had practically never

41

even met. Harmony got the phone long enough to call the insurance company and ask them to please stop payment on the check, but the girl she got was cross with her because she didn't know her policy number, though she could have probably found it, given a little time.

Then Myrtle got on the phone again and somebody at the Grand finally located Wendell, but instead of asking his advice Myrtle spent fifteen minutes grilling him about how he had spent every second of his coffee break and then totally forgot to ask him what he would do if someone stole an insurance check from him. Though it was clear that Wendell had been completely innocent it didn't have the effect of getting Myrtle in a better mood.

"Myrtle, you ought to be glad he's faithful," Harmony said, forgetting her own troubles for a second to marvel at the fact that Myrtle had managed to get angry at Wendell for not having an affair with a bathing beauty during his coffee break.

"Well, he don't even have guts enough to get in trouble, I think I'm losing interest," Myrtle said. She went back over to her house to get her drink and apparently went to sleep, because she never came back. Harmony sat on her bed with the phone in her lap for an hour, crying and thinking about calling the police, but she never did.

5.

THE BEST thing of all about Gary, the thing that made him such a wonderful friend was that when you were really in trouble it never entered his head to criticize. Sometimes if you just bought some pants he thought were ugly or went to a hairdresser he had a low opinion of or were a little slow with a costume change he could be snippy for five minutes.

It was more likely to occur over clothes than anything, he was as bad as Pepper when it came to his preferences in clothes, but when Harmony called and told him Denny had stolen her insurance check he just said, "Oh, sweetie, I love you, I'll come right out and we'll talk this over."

That made her feel better so she got dressed and decided to be brave, then the minute Gary stepped in the door she forgot about brave and cried like a faucet for about five minutes, with Gary shushing her and telling her not to ruin her eyes, she was going to have a show to do after-while, insurance check or not. Then while Harmony was freshening her face he went over to see what had become of Myrtle. Gary thought Myrtle was a hoot and always liked to exchange a few words with her when he came out, but this time he was out of luck, Myrtle was asleep on her little daybed and Maude was on the couch eating the stuffing out of one of the cushions.

"I knew goats had a bad reputation but I didn't know they'd eat foam rubber," he said, and complimented Harmony on her blouse, maybe just to cheer her up. Gary was a little dumpy man about the size of Ross but he had real warm eyes, brown ones, and gay or not he liked to hug her and hold her hand sometimes, which Harmony appreciated, she had come from a hugging family and was glad Gary wasn't so gay he didn't want to touch her at all.

They got in his camper and drove up Paradise Road to a bar they liked called Debbie's and Marty's, whose owner had run the baccarat room at the Imperial Palace for about twenty years. His name was Giorgio. For baccarat you had to wear a tuxedo and he had gotten pretty tired of it and wanted a place that was no frills as he put it, so he just bought an old bar and called it Debbie's and Marty's, in honor of the couple who went in with him.

Harmony still felt a little shaky and would have liked maybe a vodka tonic, but Gary said forget it, he had seen her put away vodka tonics before when she was upset and was afraid she might fall off her disc or something if he let her drink. In the opening number she and Jessie, they had always been sort of paired, were the showgirls who came down from the ceiling on discs and of course in the finale went back up again. Harmony had no fear of falling off. She had been riding down on the disc twice a night for over twelve years—it was such a popular thing that the producers kept it in every show—but then it was true vodka tonics went down awfully easy so she contented herself with a couple of beers.

"Well, basically, it's just a matter of do you want Denny in jail or don't you?" Gary said.

But Harmony just didn't really want to be involved with that question. She looked around the bar hoping maybe someone from the show was there who might sit down and chat with them. She didn't know if Gary really knew about Denny being in jail twice before, not for anything real serious, once just for hot checks and once for stealing a car from his father-in-law not thinking he would call the police much less press charges, but the man had apparently never liked Denny being married to his daughter, so he did. Mainly the jail things were just things Denny bragged about, just a little bit of wildness, he did like the idea that he was wild, sort of in the sense of always seeing how far he could go or doing things like making love in the middle of the lake.

"You see, I don't think he realizes," she said. "I mean, his mind doesn't work like yours and mine, Gary. He probably just thinks I know somebody who will loan me the money if I really need it."

"Only you don't," Gary said, not being harsh, just pointing it out.

"Yeah, but Denny just thinks about scuba diving and betting on basketball and doing coke and stuff like that,"

Harmony said. "He's not like you. It's not like he ever understood my life."

Not like I do either, she thought, holding up the empty peanut bowl so Giorgio would bring some more. She kind of had to wave it around to get his attention but when he saw her Giorgio came right over and filled it up, giving her a grin with his very white teeth. She had always sort of thought probably Giorgio would ask her out someday but so far he hadn't gotten around to it, just expressed his affection by being liberal with the peanuts.

Gary meanwhile was being very patient and kind but Harmony knew him well and could tell that he thought her attempts to excuse Denny's behavior were total horseshit, which was probably true.

"He understands that you live eight miles from town, which is too far to walk," Gary pointed out.

Then Harmony remembered the unusual business about Pepper and Bonventre, which was a good thing to change the subject to since Gary was fascinated by anything that smacked of intrigue in the world of the shows.

"Hey, could we go to Madonna's?" she asked and told him what Pepper had said. He didn't look the slightest bit surprised, which made Harmony feel like she must have been living on another planet or something, because Gary seemed to think it was normal whereas she had never given the possibility of Pepper dancing at the Stardust one moment's thought.

"Would you let her if he makes the offer?" Gary asked.

"No, she'd have to be topless," Harmony said, realizing that was a strange answer since she herself had been on stage there topless for twelve years. Another funny thing was that when the pressure to be topless had got real intense, which had been fifteen years ago almost, it was Gary who had persuaded her that it was right to do it. Previous to that she had always been covered and had never supposed she would work topless but Gary of course had seen her breasts, he had to dress her, some of the changes were so quick modesty was the last thing on anybody's mind, and he had made it seem like basically an artistic thing, told her her breasts were truly beautiful and what was the point of the show if not to show people beauty, mainly people who never got to see very much of it at any one time.

So she agreed to work topless, not being so sure at all that she really wanted to, plus Bonventre made it worse by telling her practically every day that her breasts didn't match. But finally she began to feel that Gary was right, it was just beauty she was offering, and after all most of the people in the audience were married couples, older ones mostly except for the honeymooners, and a lot of them came from small towns and they just ran grocery stores or had car dealerships and sort of led ordinary lives so it was true they didn't get to see all that much beauty. Often if a couple who had seen the show happened to see her in the bar afterward they would almost always come up and tell her how beautiful they thought she was and how much they enjoyed the show. They were so sweet about it usually and seemed so thrilled to meet her that Harmony more and more realized Gary had been right.

But Pepper was just sixteen, at that age she would never have uncovered her breasts on stage, probably not even if Didier had asked her and she had loved Didier a lot.

"Anyway, Madonna says Pepper can easily get a ballet scholarship if she keeps working," Harmony said.

"Why would she want a ballet scholarship if she can be lead dancer at the Stardust?" Gary asked.

Harmony didn't really know the answer to that, she was suddenly getting the peculiar feeling that everybody understood her daughter better than she did. It was bad enough that all her friends felt they had to just immediately tell her what she could expect from every boyfriend she managed to get—they were usually right, too, it was a big thrill for her if a boyfriend turned out not to be as bad as everybody said he was.

But that was just boyfriends, Pepper was her daughter. For presents Madonna always gave Pepper subscriptions to all the good dance magazines, she had always encouraged Pepper to set her sights high. Not that being the lead dancer at the Stardust was nothing, it was quite an honor really, but still it wasn't like getting into ballet in New York or somewhere where you would have to dance a lot of different roles, at the Stardust Pepper would just have to do the same routines five or six thousand times depending on how long they ran the show. For a girl who got bored easily it didn't make a lot of sense.

Plus there was always Bonventre to consider. Since Denny loved video games on Sundays they sometimes went to one of the arcades, one day it occurred to Harmony that Bonventre was like a human Pac-Man, he sort of beeped around the casino eating up whoever he bumped into. It might be a blackjack dealer or it might be a showgirl, it didn't matter to Pac-Man.

"What do you think, does Bonventre just want to go out with her or what?" Harmony asked.

"Harmony, you just live in your own world," Gary said, as if it sort of made him sad. From behind the bar Giorgio was smiling at her with his big white teeth again. He was quite a nice-looking guy really, very Italian. Now that he was out of baccarat he always wore bright shirts, they looked like silk, with the sleeves rolled up to show his muscle, he was always sort of smiling and showing off his muscle, it was kind of charming really, you could just see him thinking how could any woman resist me. Harmony loved it when some guy sort of preened like that for her, it was sweet and also more fun usually than actually going out with him. The Continental types who looked so great in silk shirts usually got stiff as a fish once they put a suit on. They would even forget how to do the sexy smiles, much less conversation, and would sit there looking sort of worried and drinking lots of drinks until some sort of meal had been gotten through and they finally figured it was time to make the pass. Their behavior would become so hopeless it was kind of winning—unless they had terrible breath or something Harmony would usually let herself get won if only to see if she could sort of get them to remember how irresistible they had felt when they had just been sort of lightly coming on in a bar, or maybe letting her watch them shoot craps. It was definite that Giorgio was attracted, she had the notion he was a little afraid of her or something so she gave him a smile back, maybe he would get over it. She was trying to remember whether Giorgio was actually married or not, meanwhile Gary was not really doing much to clarify the situation with Pepper, he was just sitting there sucking ice cubes and waiting for it to be time to go to work.

"I think we ought to pick up Jessie, she's got her own problems," he said. "You know she had the dentist appointment today."

"Oh, God, I was gonna call her," Harmony said, ashamed that she had become so engrossed in her own miseries that she forgot to call her best friend on a day when she had a trauma to face.

Jessie had a very low pain threshold, any dentistry, even just a cavity, worried her for weeks, she couldn't stop thinking about the novocaine needle. Gary might point out very gently that having novocaine wasn't really that major but it didn't ease Jessie's mind at all.

Jessie lived in a sand-colored apartment building across the road from the Desert Inn. Sure enough when they got there Jessie was in tears, she was sitting out on her tiny balcony in her bathrobe, crying and then dropping wet Kleenex beside her chair.

"Look at that, a pyramid of wet Kleenex," Gary said, trying to joke. "You girls will be lucky not to both get fired, you've both certainly ruined your eyes."

Jessie was a beautiful woman, an inch taller than Harmony, but not confident, it was actually not diplomatic of Gary to mention firing since that was what Jessie lived in dread of. In all she had three operations on her breasts, one of which was a disaster, they had done a tuck wrong or something and when it was over her nipples pointed straight down. Fortunately that was correctible or Jessie would have never worked another day. Even so she was paranoid about her scars, which were up under her breasts and hardly noticeable even in the dressing room, much less from the audience.

"What's the matter, did the novocaine hurt?" Harmony asked.

"Yes but that's not the terrible part," Jessie said. "He says I have to have two root canals."

That was pretty sobering, a root canal for Jessie would be the equivalent of open heart surgery for most people, she was just not up to dealing with much pain.

Jessie's apartment was a mess, she got around to basic matters like making the bed only about once a week. The sight of it always brought out the housewife in Gary, he went around picking up beer bottles and emptying ash trays, Jessie didn't smoke but Monroe was seldom without a cigar.

Harmony didn't know what to say about the root canals, when it happened they were all going to have to be very supportive, for sure. While she was trying to think of something a little bit cheerful she could say to Jessie she wandered into the bedroom to see if Jessie had bought any new stuffed animals recently and woke up Francois, Jessie's miniature black poodle, who had been napping beside a stuffed raccoon. Jessie was totally vulnerable to stuffed animals, she would buy any species not already in her collection. She had about a hundred arranged along one wall of the bedroom plus several on her bed.

A stranger just walking in probably would have thought Francois was stuffed too but in fact he was a live dog and the minute Harmony woke him up he began to yip and jump around on the bed wanting to be picked up and cuddled. Jessie loved Francois more than she loved Monroe or anybody else—naturally he was extremely spoiled and got very outraged if he didn't get whatever he wanted instantly. Fortunately he was cute, Harmony enjoyed cuddling him herself and took him over and sat him on top of the stuffed hippopotamus, supposedly a third life-size that was by far the most expensive of all Jessie's stuffed animals. Once for about two weeks Jessie had gotten a boyfriend who was sort of a high roller, he was from Texas and very excited about the fact that he had actually seduced a show girl. He had been generous enough to buy her the hippo, which cost $600, before he went back to his wife.

Now Jessie had her heart set on a stuffed polar bear that was about as large as the hippo but there was widespread agreement that she would be lucky ever to get the polar bear, certainly Monroe wasn't likely to pop for it.

Francois was not wild about being on the hippo. He began to yip so Harmony took him back into the other room. Gary was holding Jessie's hand but had evidently not come up with too many cheering words about root canals because Jessie still looked frightened and actually paler than usual.

"Okay, but I didn't even tell you the *really* bad part," she said, totally miserable as only Jessie could be. "The really bad part is he wants me to have braces."

"My goodness, you're a grown woman," Harmony said, "you don't need braces."

"Well, he said that at my age your gums get soft and mine are real soft and they're letting my teeth begin to move around. I do have a space, see?" And Jessie opened her mouth so they could see the tiny space that had developed between Jessie's front teeth and the ones just to the side of them.

"Well, so what, nobody has to look at your teeth under a microscope or anything," Gary said.

Except the human microscope, Bonventre, Harmony thought, she had never known anybody with such an appetite for flaws as Bonventre, he could look at you as you walked down a hall in street clothes and say "Harmony, you look like a chub-ette," or "This is the Stardust, not the Fat Follies, Harmony, how come you gained three-quarters of a pound?" and when she actually got on the scale it would probably be three-quarters of a pound exactly. Some girls became so paranoid about it they suspected Bonventre must have a secret scale set in the floor, maybe out by the check-in sheet or somewhere so that he knew everybody's weight to a hair before they even got to the dressing room. Harmony's instinct was that one reason Bonventre treated her so sullenly was because all these years he kept expecting her to gain and she hadn't, she was only maybe two pounds over what she weighed when she came to Las Vegas as a girl, mainly because right off Didier had told her what to eat and impressed upon her that the very worst thing was to turn to food when she was depressed. She might not have any control in the love area but she didn't just sit around and eat because she was blue.

It was a big frustration to Bonventre, nothing would have made him happier than for her to walk in with a couple of new pounds on her midriff, but she hadn't let it happen. If she had Bonventre would have demoted her long ago or else fired her altogether.

It did seem though that Jessie's dental problems were more major than usual, even having to have novocaine wouldn't make her cry up a whole box of Kleenex, which she had practically done.

"On top of that my overbite's getting worse," Jessie added. Harmony gave her Francois to hold, hoping that would cheer her up.

Gary was looking like he had had a little too much depression for one day.

"Nobody ever died of an overbite," he said. "Nobody ever died of having an insurance check stolen, either. What we need around here is a little perspective."

"I've already got a prescription," Jessie said, misunderstanding completely. "Who stole the insurance check?"

"Well, Denny, I'm hoping it's a joke," Harmony said.

Both of them looked at her as if to say who do you think you're kidding, she didn't particularly think she was kidding anybody, maybe she just didn't want to admit he was a total criminal yet.

Jessie had never been able to work up much outrage. Her view was that Denny probably needed to see a minister. She herself had been brought to Christ a few months ago and had been baptized in the swimming pool of a little motel whose owner was quite religious, but she was timid about trying to get other people to find Jesus, she felt it had to be a personal need and had never pressed Harmony or Gary very much about it.

Then Gary noticed it was nearly seven, they all had to get to work. It was not until they were driving along the Strip that Harmony remembered to tell Jessie about Bonventre offering to audition Pepper to understudy Monique. Jessie was a lot more surprised by the information than Gary had been.

"Goodness," Jessie said. "Then if Monique quits Pepper might be making more than you."

That was an aspect of the matter that had not so much as dawned on Harmony, it would certainly mean Pepper would have a lot more money to spend on clothes. That didn't necessarily make it a good idea, though, Pepper had plenty of clothes.

Meanwhile the sun was setting but they were only a block from the Stardust, she wouldn't get to see the whole sunset. She loved driving and looking out the window, it was too bad there wasn't time for a little drive, she had sort of a tiny fantasy which was that Denny was waiting for them in the parking lot in the blue car, he gave her back the check and they made up. Harmony took her time walking in, giving the fantasy every chance to happen, but it didn't, basically she was just out thirteen hundred dollars and late for work too. She could only take about three seconds to flirt with Billy, the sweet young cop who sort of kept the traffic moving in front of the Stardust. Gary practically cried every time he saw Billy, Billy was so beautiful, but he was married to an English girl, a dancer at the Trop, Gary was just out of luck in that instance.

Still, Billy was sweet, he gave Harmony one of his wonderful little shy smiles that you had to look quick even to catch, but she caught it, he was a beautiful kid and it was pretty cheering, by the time she got backstage her spirits had risen, she was feeling okay and was not the least affected by the fact that Rodney tore into her for checking in five minutes late.

6.

WHAT WAS actually more bothersome than Rodney was the fact that the backstage smelled of elephant fart, probably for the very simple reason that one of the elephants had recently let one. A couple of younger stagehands waved brooms around pretending it would make the smell go away, but it didn't.

"Rodney, is the elephant sick or what?" Harmony

asked. Rodney was one of Gary's protégés, he was only twenty-two and seemed to think it was his duty to bitch if anyone in the show was a few minutes late.

"Do I look like an elephant doctor?" Rodney asked, he always liked to have a comeback. In fact he just looked like a slightly pimply kid from L.A. who had probably been gay from the moment he was born.

"Rodney, I just asked," Harmony reminded him and went on to the dressing room. Probably the trainer had been trying to make the old elephant learn something new. It didn't like to and farted a lot on those occasions.

Harmony waltzed into the dressing room to discover Jessie standing there in her G-string showing the other girls the little space between her teeth, though about the only one who was trying to be sympathetic was Cherri, the other three girls were basically more interested in getting their makeup on. Cherri was the youngest showgirl, she was only nineteen and by her own report had pretty much been happy all her life. Consequently she was sort of awestruck by the number of miseries Jessie came up with day after day. Cherri was from Houston and her breasts were sort of the envy of everyone, including people from other shows, they weren't small and yet they stuck straight out, without the tiniest suggestion of sag. Even Bonventre, who had seen his share of breasts and had had horrible remarks to make about most of them, hadn't been able to come up with an immediate criticism when he saw Cherri's.

"Well, I sympathize if you have to have braces, I had to wear mine till two days before I graduated," Cherri said, leaning over and smiling at the mirror to make sure she wasn't developing gaps.

The dressing room was tiny, converted from a wardrobe closet actually, but Harmony didn't really mind, she got undressed and got her G-string on and a bathrobe and sat down to do her makeup, something she had done so many

54

times she was convinced she could probably do it okay even if she suddenly went into a coma or something. Jessie's space was next to hers at the makeup table and when Jessie had done her eyes she sort of practiced smiles for a while, obviously trying to come up with a way to smile that wouldn't show the gap between her teeth or maybe her braces if she actually had to have them. Of course it was ridiculous for Jessie even to fantasize that she could be a showgirl and wear braces, after all wonderful smiles were part of what made the show a gay spectacle. When Bonventre really wanted to fire somebody but didn't want to bother to even think up a good excuse he would usually just say a waiter had told him the girl wasn't smiling enough, or it could be a boy, Bonventre didn't like men any better than he liked women.

"Jessie, you're getting on my nerves doing that, just put your makeup on," Harmony said.

"This is gonna give me bad dreams, I know it is," Jessie said.

In fact the dressing room was kind of gloomy. Linda, who was next to Jessie, was three and a half months pregnant and was going to have to quit in another week or two, plus Beryl who was English finally thought she had found a boyfriend only to have the guy inform her he had decided to be gay, after all. When Jessie got tired of looking at her teeth she turned around and began to look at her ass, having remembered that Genevieve had told her it was dimpled. Nobody in the dressing room was speaking to Genevieve except Harmony. Genevieve had even alienated Cherri, who was a perfectly friendly girl, by laughing sarcastically just because Cherri hadn't understood about having to shave her pubic hair before she could wear a G-string. She had been very embarrassed, but Genevieve had just laughed and not been at all sympathetic.

But then Genevieve's lover, who was on the order of

forty years older than she was, had recently lost his job and become a taxi driver, plus her child had learning disabilities, she tended to carry a lot of unhappiness from her home life into the dressing room. Even Murdo the ventriloquist hated her because she kept pointing out that she could see his lips move every time she happened to glance at his act. She wasn't particularly pretty and the consensus was Bonventre only kept her in the show because he liked to have someone around who was as critical as he was.

When Harmony was satisfied with her makeup she stepped out of the dressing room hoping to spot Bonventre and did spot him, only he was talking to Monique, obviously an argument, Monique's face looked very tight. She was almost Harmony's age only she was thinner and had a narrow face which showed whatever strains Monique happened to be suffering from. Harmony didn't dare interrupt, particularly not to ask Bonventre what she had been going to ask him, she sort of gave him a wide berth. When Bonventre argued he kept squirting a nasal spray up his nose to keep his mucous membranes from drying out, he hated a dry nose. In the twenty years she had known Bonventre the only real change was that at first he had worn white suits and now he wore black suits, he had decided black suits were more sophisticated or more in keeping with the sinister image he liked to cultivate or something.

Gary was backstage checking out all the costumes, he looked frazzled but things were no more out of control than usual, that Harmony could tell. She and the rest of the showgirls were in feathers for the opening number. The feather outfits were so large you couldn't just put them on, they had to be lowered by a little hoist, which was another reason Harmony usually came out a little early, that way Gary could always adjust hers himself and help her get the huge headdress sitting right. That was very important, the headdresses were really heavy and if you didn't carry them right you could really screw up your back. Another wonderful thing Didier had done for her was to educate her about posture, which was all-important if you had to walk around in heavy headdresses six nights a week.

"Bonventre's on Monique's ass," Harmony said as she was standing with her arms out, waiting for the feathers to come down around her, they were pink in the first number and she did sort of love it, being a feathered beauty, they were gorgeous costumes and the people out front sort of gasped when the curtain finally went up and they saw them for the first time.

"Harmony, lean this way or at least move your tit," Gary said, adjusting her position a little. Once the headdress was on she turned her neck a time or two, making sure it all felt right. The other girls were lining up, all except Jessie, who would invariably be last. She would get insecure about her makeup or something and go back to check it which meant that if a hoist didn't work or the costume slipped or a zipper stuck Jessie would be the one it happened to. Gary's two little assistants spent hours pleading with her to line up a little sooner but Jessie couldn't help it, she was sort of doomed to be last. Half the time they only got her into her feathers and up on the disc about ten seconds before the curtain went up.

"He's not on her ass, he's after her ass, everybody knew that except you," Gary said and then hurried off to do Linda, leaving her with the living-on-another-planet feeling, she was experiencing it pretty often lately. Maybe it was just Denny that had caused her not to notice things like Bonventre being after Monique. It had been a while since love had hit sort of totally, like it hit when Denny came along—people could warn her all they wanted to, love had hit and before he started coming up with the bad surprises like not paying her back for the scuba-diving equipment she had tended to get to work feeling fairly dreamy and had not been tuned in to backstage gossip all that much. In fact she had never paid all that much attention to it. Knowing Gary, it was easier just to get it from him, that way she could just think her own thoughts and not have to try and keep up with every little anxiety in the whole company.

When the dancers began to line up Harmony went slowly up to her disc, being careful not to snag the feathers on anything, and then just waited, doing a little deep breathing. She wasn't really nervous, she just liked to feel composed and sort of ready when the curtain went up.

Down below she saw Bonventre still in the wings, still arguing with Monique, although it couldn't have been more than three minutes to curtain. She could hear the audience sort of rumbling and the clink of lots of plates and glasses being stacked none too gently. The waiters hated to work after the curtain and were probably grabbing plates of coq au vin or trout amandine out from under the noses of people who still thought they had a few minutes and were sometimes kind of indignant at not getting to finish eating, after all they had worked for their money and paid for their dinners. Fortunately they still had their drinks or their champagne and once the show started would soon forget about all those uneaten English peas.

As usual both of Gary's assistants were working with Jessie, her headdress was on at a tilt but finally they got it right and hustled her up on the disc. Harmony heard a curse from way backstage, evidently just one of the magician's pigeons getting loose. Then the announcer announced the show, he was a very handsome guy named Jerry Fowler, Harmony had dated him awhile just about the time she was leaving the Trop. Jerry really wasn't very enthusiastic about anything except the sound of his own wonderful voice, that and occasionally blackjack, but he had done her the favor of introducing her to Ross, who at

58

the time was too shy even to speak to her, she was just really getting famous then and was pretty sought after. As a light man Ross didn't suppose he could aspire to date a showgirl, particularly not a famous one like her. Ross had had a very slight opinion of himself and for that matter probably still did. Harmony had done her best to convince him he was cute, even going so far as to marry him and have Pepper, but she soon had to admit that the slight opinion wasn't going away. One of his main lines was "This is too good to be true." Gary had explained to her that some men just practically couldn't accept being loved, they didn't feel worthy at all.

Standing on the disc, with the show finally assembled down below her, all the dancers in place, Harmony felt a little pang. In some ways Ross had been the sweetest of all, maybe that was why he was the one she actually married. The funny thing that only a few people in Las Vegas knew, just Gary and Jessie and a couple of others, was that they weren't even divorced. In the eyes of the law they were as married as ever. People kept saying Harmony get it and a couple of times she had thought well, maybe I should, but she had just never gotten around to it. There had been no one else she exactly felt like marrying, and apparently Ross hadn't found anyone that would apply to either, if so he hadn't mentioned it in the little notes he wrote when he sent the money. She had never even discussed the fact with Pepper, it was sort of a forgotten thing, even she forgot about it most of the time, but the truth was she was married to a man she hadn't seen in fourteen years.

It didn't bother her, just once in a while something would bring him to mind and she would find herself wondering how bald he was by now. The little bald spot upset him almost as much as the thought of a dimpled ass upset Jessie. If Ross was ever late to work it was because he spent too much time trying to figure out ways to comb over the

59

bald spot. That too was kind of sweet, they lived in a motel then and it was memories of Ross standing in the tiny bathroom trying to comb hair over his bald spot that kept sort of giving her the pangs now and then. One definitely came as she waited on her disc, but then it was finally show time, the orchestra struck the first notes, the curtain began to come up, lights flooded the stage, the disc began to go down, and at just the right moment, when the brilliant light struck her legs, Harmony spread her arms and smiled.

II

THE THING about Madonna that Pepper wasn't too sure what she thought about was lately she had been acting very maternal. It was a little like having two mothers, it meant basically two people you had to dodge instead of one, although it was no big deal dodging her real mother, maybe she saw her for ten minutes at breakfast and sometimes on Sunday. She spent a lot more time with Madonna, five afternoons a week at least and usually Saturday and Sunday too. Madonna said if you want to dance you dance every day, then if you have the energy to do other things, fine. But dance first. Even when Pepper first started with her, at five years old, she made it real clear that if you wanted to get anywhere with her you had to give up some other stuff.

That was okay, Pepper did love the dancing, besides she could do whatever she wanted to at night, movies or dates or whatever. It was just that lately Madonna had gotten kind of possessive, and one thing that was clear was that she didn't care for Buddy. Usually when the lesson was over Buddy would be waiting for her in the little Cadillac his father had bought his mother for her birthday. So far as Pepper could tell it must be a funny marriage Buddy's parents had, his mother was usually in San Francisco and his father either in New York or L.A., they didn't hang around town a lot. Of course Buddy had a Mustang they had bought him to go to college in but as he said, why drive a Mustang when you can drive a Cadillac. The thing he didn't do was drive his father's Mercedes. His father would probably have killed him on the spot if he had even so much as scratched it—Victor was lenient about a lot of things but not about that car. According to Buddy his father had managed to talk his mother out of divorcing him because he didn't want to give up half his millions, but the price was she could stay gone as much as she liked and fuck whoever she wanted to, although Buddy said that probably just meant nobody. One morning standing outside their bedroom he had heard her tell Victor that she had had about enough of penises and didn't particularly want to ever see another one. Buddy had been kind of startled, he thought he was real cool where sex was concerned but hearing his mother say that had disturbed him or something, plus the remark had upset Victor so much he left and went all the way to Spain to think matters over.

So for about the next month Buddy was paranoid about whether she was suddenly going to stop wanting to fuck him. He worried about it so much that she was about in the mood to do just that, tell him the deal was off, so long it's been good to know you, it was exactly what he was expecting anyway although he tried to act like Mr. Confident.

Madonna had never said anything against Buddy, but then she had never said anything nice about him either, and Madonna was usually quick to comment if she thought a boy was unusually good-looking. Pepper thought Buddy was great-looking and kept waiting for Madonna to maybe slip in a compliment but she never did, she ignored Buddy and once in a while asked about a boy Pepper had dated for a while named Woods Weeks, a total genius with computers and video games but nothing to compare with Buddy in the looks department. Buddy after all had been a model too, that was where they met, at a session out at Neiman's. Buddy didn't need the money, it was just that Victor knew the owner of the store socially and the man had seen Buddy by the pool one day and suggested it, which pleased Buddy, he was pretty vain and proud of the fact that he photographed so well.

That was how it all started with Mel. One of the other male models was gay and told Buddy about a rich guy he knew who liked to make home movies, it might involve getting naked but it wouldn't involve any real action. The guy was grossly rich and if he liked your looks and the way you moved he would pay really well for just making a little movie of you walking around or standing on his diving board or something, plus he was very liberal with drugs, there was always lots of coke and just about anything else you wanted, and it was totally safe, the guy was a guy the cops would never touch, probably not even if he chopped up four or five people with an ax, he was *protected*.

So Buddy had done it a few times, with the other male model. Mel had given them a couple of hundred apiece and hadn't asked them to do any more than sort of model naked. Buddy had described him as real nervous but nobody to be scared of, just a little weirdo with lots of money. They assumed he was gay but he didn't come on or anything, just followed them around with his little movie camera.

Then about the third time he asked if maybe they knew any young ladies who might be willing to participate, he didn't mean hookers either, he could get plenty of them just by dragging Las Vegas Boulevard a few times, he wanted high school girls who were basically proper girls but maybe liked a little excitement now and then or wanted to make a little money for college. So without even telling her Buddy had shown Mel a few pictures of her, a teen fashion spread she had done for Neiman's, and Mel had been immediately interested.

Buddy had said come on, do it, maybe you won't even have to be naked, the guy's real shy, plus it's two hundred dollars a session just for walking around. Pepper immediately liked the idea, the thought was kind of exciting, after all Denny took hundreds of pictures of her and didn't pay a cent, plus living off her mother and fucking her constantly. Why not do it and have the money to spend?

Except even before she met Mel she had a sort of intuition or something that he was going to fall for her, he sounded at first like a guy who was just a pretzel waiting to be twisted, why not twist him a little?

So she said okay, but tell him it's three hundred and I'm not showing him my cunt, which freaked Buddy, he was so rich anyway he didn't have much imagination about things like that, they sort of had a fight about it because Buddy said come on, you should at least do it once before you start raising the price, you might scare him off, he's actually kind of nice, why make him mad? Then it came out that Victor knew the guy. At one time they had played bridge together, they belonged to some club in Palm Springs or something, the point was Buddy was nervous that his father might find out and Mel was nervous about the same thing, didn't want Victor to suddenly get wind that he was making home movies of Victor's kid. Buddy just wanted her to be polite and not cause any trouble, it sort of made her realize that Buddy was just gonna be temporary even if he was super good-looking.

Also they had never had a big test of wills, she sort of was interested in finding out what Buddy was made of and discovered that he was made of toilet paper. She proceeded to wipe her ass with him and of course she got her three hundred and even made Mel cough it up in advance, before he had even seen her in the flesh.

Mel wasn't exactly a pretzel, it was apparent from the way he looked at her and the way he spoke that he was an on-the-ball guy, but still the first time she modeled he was so nervous that when he stood still you could see his legs

66

shaking. He didn't even ask her to be topless, much less bottomless. All he got for his three hundred was that she walked around in her underwear for maybe ten minutes, looking at things in his house. The house was great, very tasteful, she had expected something pretty vulgar but on that one she guessed wrong. Mel was into Japanese design, he had an elaborate garden with a fishpond and a little bridge, plus all sorts of ferns and four or five little Japs to keep it all watered and green. Also he had a big collection of Japanese ceramics, which she had to admit were beautiful, and scrolls and other very tasteful stuff.

It was too bad his legs shook but otherwise he couldn't have been more polite and gentlemanly, plus it was easy to see he was sort of totally in love with her looks from the first minute. In fact Buddy and the other guy got a little jealous before the session was over, the minute she walked in Mel sort of totally forgot about them. Pepper found it laughable, these two vain guys totally naked, both of them standing around trying to get their cocks to hang in a way that might interest Mel, both of them seemed to feel that the fact that they had fairly large cocks was a phenomenon that would excite the world—exciting the world was a phrase she got from her old boyfriend Woods Weeks who did in fact claim the world's record Space Invaders score, somewhere in the billions, Woods was definitely a genius in terms of the arcade—but on that particular afternoon their two cocks weren't exciting anybody, though Mel finally noticed they were sort of pouting and turned the camera on them for a while. Still, it was pretty obvious his heart wasn't in it, he was just trying to be polite.

So she made the three hundred and went back the next week and made another for doing practically the same thing, just more posing in her underwear, though she did dance a few steps that time. Fritz, the other male model, refused to come that time or ever again, not that Mel wanted him—very definitely Fritz's vanity had suffered a blow. Buddy came but Mel sort of politely indicated he didn't really need to get undressed, it was basically just going to be a session involving Pepper although of course Mel was very grateful to Buddy for having made the introduction, and Buddy was welcome to whatever drugs might interest him.

So Buddy did a little coke and then got bored with it all and went out and sat in the car and played tapes until she came out. Then he threw a big fit because Mel hadn't paid him. Pepper said why should he you didn't do anything, and Buddy got so furious he was stopped for going 85 in a 45 on the way home. Of course Victor would fix the ticket so that didn't matter, but Buddy's behavior was still pretty irritating. He told her he was thinking about revenge of some kind, like maybe leaking the news socially that Mel was making kiddie porn or something, basically Buddy just couldn't stand rejection and got very bitter if it happened. She told him that if he said one word to anybody that was it, he would never touch her again, so of course he backed down within five minutes.

By the time she had been to Mel's three or four times she got the feeling she was sort of into something, it just happened to be something a little weird. Buddy never went again, she would just borrow his Mustang and go by herself and it didn't worry her, Mel was about the last person you could be afraid of. Often she would stay for quite a few hours, Mel would say do you want to go swimming or he would ask her if she wanted a sandwich or something to eat, which usually she did, mainly it was after her lessons that she went to Mel's. He would just have his servants bring out whatever she wanted, once she was starving and they brought a steak, it was delicious like everything else the servants brought out.

When Mel found out she had an appetite it became a

thing, she would model a while and then they would have dinner, usually out by the pool. He had a very expensive telescope set up out there, forty thousand dollars he told her it cost, and he showed her a few things about the stars which weren't too interesting, they still just looked like stars, but the moon was a different matter, the moon was wonderful through the telescope. It delighted Mel that he had been able to show her something she liked and he always made a point of getting her over if the moon was full or anything spectacular was likely to happen in the heavens.

He never stopped loving to take movies of her, to Pepper it was a sign of appreciation. Mel definitely loved her looks but the photography wasn't something he had to do every time, sometimes she would just get to eat some wonderful meal and they would sit outside and talk. Mel had been all over the world and had plenty of stories to tell.

Then one day he told her one of his secrets. He had once been a fashion photographer and as a result had become a lingerie collector, he had a whole closet plus drawers and drawers full of antique lingerie, would she try some of it on and model in that? Pepper had no objection, she had always liked to try on just about any kind of clothes, so they spent about twenty minutes in the closet picking out old bras and panties for her to try on. He had them in several colors, black and pink and white and light blue, it was a pretty amazing collection of lingerie. They experimented for a while and Mel discovered that what he liked her most in was lingerie from the early 30s, he had slips and half-slips and stuff she had never expected to see, much less wear. She could tell that Mel loved the way she looked in the old lingerie. He chewed Chiclets constantly and when he got turned on he chewed real fast, it was a little off-putting at first but then everybody had bad habits and otherwise Mel was so sweet and polite, unlike just about every male she had ever known except Gary, he was very polite too.

Meanwhile there was a problem with Buddy, who was growing sort of madly jealous. At first he had been jealous of Madonna who he was convinced was a dyke, he wouldn't let go of that one although Pepper told him he was an asshole and a prick and didn't know what he was talking about, Madonna had two children who lived in France. Anyway, what business was it of Buddy's? Then he got sort of insane about Mel, he was convinced things were going on she had never told him about, he had seen some of the movies Mel had taken of other girls and they had involved not merely toplessness, but also spread shots and a lot of disgusting stuff, or so Buddy claimed. Naturally Buddy believed she was exhibiting her cunt, he couldn't be convinced that all she was doing was modeling a few panties and bras plus eating excellent meals and getting the use of Mel's pool and his telescope and anything else she wanted. Pepper told him to stop being an asshole, she wasn't doing anything but he didn't believe her and it was becoming more and more of a problem.

Plus another problem, kind of a strange one, was that money was sort of piling up. Mel always insisted on paying her no matter what if she got there too late and they just ate dinner, he assured her he could afford it and got upset if she even tried not to take it. So she was raking in some six hundred a week, maybe more if she felt like going more often. Mel said anytime, Pepper, anytime, she could probably have gone every day if she'd wanted to, Mel was always there. He never seemed to leave his house. Of course he had a beautiful house, plus a satellite dish out back so he could get just about any TV program in the world, and naturally he had thousands of tapes and records and a great sound system, there was probably not a lot he needed to go out for.

70

Still, the money was piling up, more than she could possibly spend on outfits. In no time she had quite a few thousand hidden in her bedroom, if her mother found it she would probably die of shock, not that it was likely. Her mother hardly ever did anything except sit in the backyard feeding the peacocks, either that or she was in bed with some horrible man like Denny. It had been a big relief when Denny checked out, the car had been a small price to pay, in her view, she hated the way he looked at her, about all she could do was treat him with the utmost scorn.

Besides being a prick and an asshole, he had one thing on her, which was that he had seen her let Joaquin out of the backyard. Joaquin was always pecking her ankles, one day he did it once too often and she just opened the yard gate and drove him right out. Okay, Joaquin, go get eaten by a coyote she said, which was exactly what happened, but Denny was always turning up just when you didn't want him to and he turned up then, he had been in the shower and he came out on the back steps just in his Levi's, drying his hair and grinning that grin. Of course he didn't bother to get his shoes on and go bring the stupid peacock back, he just grinned and dried his fucking hair and let the peacock go off to get eaten, probably he hated Joaquin too. Myrtle had this theory that the peacocks were the main reason her mother couldn't keep boyfriends very long, she doted on the birds so much the men got jealous.

"What about Maude?" Pepper asked. "Isn't Wendell jealous of Maude?"

"No, 'cause he ain't got the brains to be," Myrtle said. "Anyway, all Wendell wants is to get in my pants, he ain't got time to be jealous."

The thought of Wendell and Myrtle fucking was a total yuk, Myrtle was old and dried up and Wendell had a belly like a tub. She had never fucked Woods sort of for the same reason, he was quite fat and she just couldn't see it, he was great to talk to and it was sort of fun to hit an arcade with him, he was definitely a hero to the arcade freaks, but to get in bed with him, un-uh. She was very spoiled when it came to looks but she didn't see any reason not to be, after all Buddy was extremely good-looking even if he wasn't ideal in other respects.

She hadn't thought all that much of Mel's looks when she first started doing the posing, but they were sort of growing on her. He was small and delicate and had very curly black hair, he wasn't bad-looking at all. The sort of interesting thing about him was that it was hard to tell what he was thinking, unlike Buddy, who told you every thought in his head about ninety times and there weren't that many of them anyway. But Mel, it was curious, there was no doubt that he loved her, it was just hard to figure where it was supposed to go, it couldn't just consist entirely of her walking around in the underwear, sooner or later he was going to want to see her topless, or bottomless, or fuck, or something, but he was so delicate about it all that she got a little bored waiting for the pace to change. Finally one day when they were looking at the lingerie, trying to come up with a new combination she got the feeling he might enjoy it if she kind of took it further. After all he was always very respectful of her choice of clothes, she never arrived at the house without Mel complimenting her on her outfit.

So maybe that was it, maybe he wanted her to run the show, so she said "Hey, Mel, what if I just wear the half-slip and no bra?" He said goodness, would you like to do that and speeded up with the Chiclets, so Pepper just took her top off, she thought he was probably going to fall down when he saw her breasts for the first time, it was like he had never suspected such beauty. They did a real long session, she went all over the house, which of course was surrounded by a wall, no danger of getting seen. Then after they had dinner he gave her five hundred dollars, although she said hey, you don't have to pay me so much. She was used to being looked at but the truth was there was something a little exciting about what she was into with Mel, he was not just your gawky guy, he was a very smart man and had wonderful taste, just about perfect in fact, so it was kind of flattering that he thought her looks were so great. She definitely liked it and felt some turn-on, once in a while he would sort of touch her arm or maybe brush against it, she would feel him shiver when that happened and it made her feel extremely confident, it was more interesting than the money in the long run. If she needed money she could always just steal it out of Buddy's billfold, she had done that a few times and he hadn't even noticed.

Then she got worried about having so much money around the house, she had about four thousand and Denny was a natural criminal. One day she dug it all out and asked Woods if he would keep it for her, Woods's father was a lawyer and things around his house were very orderly, there were no criminals like Denny to worry about. Woods was perfectly agreeable, he was totally in her power, as he often mentioned, only he was curious about where she got it so she told him about Mel and it turned out Mel was his godfather. It didn't seem to surprise Woods greatly that his godfather had given her over four thousand dollars to walk around in old underwear, Woods was basically a lot cooler about such things than Buddy. He took the money and said keep me informed, and after that she gave him three or four hundred a week to hold for her, she even offered to pay him for acting as her banker but of course Woods declined.

The only thing that worried her was Buddy, he was becoming so jealous he was apt to do anything. Usually she let him pick her up after her dance lesson which didn't wow Madonna exactly, when they drove away Pepper would see Madonna looking down at them from the window of the studio, Madonna didn't say anything but it was plain she thought Buddy was a yuk. Even if she went straight from the dance lesson to Buddy's house and fucked him it didn't really help matters, by the time she had taken a shower and borrowed the Mustang to go to Mel's Buddy would be sulking again. Pepper was beginning to decide she didn't need it, he wasn't the only good-looking guy in the world, in fact she would have gone for Mel in a minute if she could have got him to make a move. But Mel was complicated, she could stand a foot away from him topless and he wouldn't make the move.

Then one night he asked her if she wanted to see any of the films. "You mean of me?" she asked, and he nodded, he had a little screening room out by his pool and they went out and did a little coke and she got to see herself on the screen for an hour. It was sort of fascinating, she had seen lots of pictures of herself but never one of herself moving before, much less shots of herself in old underwear. The old underwear looked weird but she was amazed anyway, Mel knew what he was doing with the camera, she really liked the way he made her look. Also she could sense that the film was a big turn-on for Mel, the atmosphere had a kind of turned-on quality. She thought here comes the move, but instead when the films stopped running Mel sat there a minute chewing Chiclets and looking sort of depressed and then asked her to marry him.

Pepper had to admit that one was a total surprise, Buddy was always asking her to marry him, he would have dearly loved to have her legally his, but it was nothing she had expected to hear from Mel, after all it was weird, not even a kiss had happened. He hadn't even asked her to pose naked, which she would have done happily, not only had he spent thousands but there was something definitely exciting about the posing, it was a far cry from modeling at

Neiman's or Goldwater's. It was such a surprise she thought maybe he was drunk or high or something, but nope, he wasn't even shaking, he just wanted to marry her.

"Please don't say no," he said. "Just go home now and we'll talk about it next week."

"Are you serious?" she asked, knowing perfectly well he was.

Mel just nodded. He was funny, he might be odd but he could put things in a way you respected. It seemed definitely weird and yet Mel was not just some flaky weirdo, in his way he was an extremely together kind of man. At times, when they were laughing about the underwear, she would forget that he was a lot older. The simplest thing was just to do exactly as he said, go home and not ask any questions or make any moves. Somehow he commanded respect, much more so than Buddy, who could make fifty moves a week and still be hard to take seriously except at the level of looks.

Then two days later Bonventre showed up at the dance studio and sort of leaned against a wall and watched her, not saying a word to Madonna or anyone else. It was no secret who he was, everyone in the studio knew Bonventre had suddenly appeared, it was about as surprising as if the President had just walked in. A lot of the other dancers got immediately shook but not Pepper, she felt very confident and just went on with her class lesson.

Finally when the lesson was over Bonventre went up to Madonna and they had a few words. Madonna looked a little strained, didn't seem too happy that the great producer had walked in, but then she sort of nodded at Pepper and Pepper went over.

"Hi, Pepper," Bonventre said, giving her a grin out of the corner of his mouth. "Jackie Bonventre. I like your dancing."

Then without so much as mentioning her mother, who

had worked for him since before she was even born, he told her his lead dancer might be leaving in a few weeks, would she like to audition as her understudy?

That was the second big surprise of the week, Pepper had to glance at Madonna to see what was going on, but Madonna sort of deserted her, she was looking away as if her mind was elsewhere though Pepper could tell it wasn't.

Bonventre could be a little nerve-racking, his grin came from so far out of the corner of his mouth that he might have been grinning at somebody behind him. Of course it was pretty flattering that he would pick her of all the young dancers in Las Vegas, to understudy for the lead, flattering and sort of scary at the same time, she had only heard about five thousand stories about what a mean guy he was. But she didn't just kneel down and kiss his ass, after watching her mother be a pincushion for any man that came along all her life, if she knew anything it was that that wasn't going to be her style. People that looked at her like Bonventre was looking got treated with total scorn, so she just said, "Well, thanks, I'd like to think about it, I'm engaged you know," thinking how handy it was that Mel had made his offer just in time for her to use it.

That definitely took Bonventre aback, probably he wasn't used to young dancers not kissing his ass. He sort of gave her a look and switched the grin from one corner of his mouth to the other, and then all he said was, "Well, Pepper, could you let me know, we've got to get an understudy."

"Oh sure," she said. "Just let me think about it for a day or two," maybe it struck him as an amusing novelty or something because he got real friendly and told the story about stealing a car to take the driver's test. She decided he was not that bad, he was kind of attractive in a fat sort of way. On Woods it didn't work but on Bonventre it sort of did, it went with his meanness or something.

Then for some reason Madonna suddenly blew up and started yelling at him in French, and he said, "Well, you've got an ass like a prune, enjoy yourself," and slammed out. Madonna burst into tears, which annoyed Pepper, after all so what if he produced a show, it was just a tits and ass show in Las Vegas, it was not as if he were Balanchine. Madonna should have hit him or something instead of letting him make her cry.

Then it turned out part of the reason Madonna got so upset was because she thought she had got engaged to Buddy, of course it was a reasonable thought since she knew nothing about Mel, but still off the mark, like shit she would get engaged to Buddy.

"It's an older guy, you don't know him," Pepper said. "He's sweet and he's very rich. Anyway, I lied, I'm not engaged, but he did ask me."

Madonna was wiping her eyes, she was still beautiful even if her hair was half gray, but it didn't help her to cry. The news about the older guy definitely came as a surprise.

"I didn't know about this man," she said, sort of in a possessive tone, as if Pepper should tell her everything instantly. Then she sighed, as if Pepper had broken a promise or something. It was pretty annoying that she would get so possessive, even if she was almost like another mother it didn't mean she got told everything.

Madonna sort of stood there waiting for her to explain but Pepper didn't really feel like it, Madonna would just freak out when she heard about the modeling, she was not all that different from her real mother when it came to how she was supposed to behave.

"What do you think, should I understudy?" Pepper asked, thinking it was time to get back to the immediate problem, what to do about Bonventre's offer.

Madonna wiped her eyes with a towel and sort of watched the other students trail out.

"Maybe I should do it," Pepper said. "I could be getting some experience. Anyway, it's just understudy."

"No, it's the lead," Madonna said. "He is ready to destroy Monique. I knew it. Maybe he wants to destroy your mother too, so this is the way he chooses."

Pepper thought that was a little farfetched, even if the guy did have a terrible reputation.

"Who said anything about her?" Pepper asked.

"She is a star too," Madonna said. "As much as Monique."

"Come on, she's a showgirl," Pepper said.

"Who is this rich man who is so sweet?" Madonna asked, watching her for every clue she might give away. Pepper thought fuck, why am I standing here getting grilled so she ignored that question and left, maybe in a day or two when Madonna got a little more used to the idea—either idea—they could discuss it some more.

Then she told Buddy who was extremely impressed, it meant he was fucking somebody who was a lead dancer, at least he would be if he could hold onto her for a few more weeks, of course he wanted her to take the job. They went to his house where he wanted to do practically every imaginable sex act in order to keep her interested. She was polite but actually not that interested, which Buddy recognized, he was not totally insensitive. She didn't go so far as to tell him that Mel did more for her with a camera, he blamed Mel for all their problems anyway. Then he refused to let her borrow his Mustang, that was a first, usually he pretended to be sort of good-natured about it. It pissed her off but she had a pocketful of money she was about to give to Woods so it was no big deal, she just called a cab. Then Buddy said it's just cameras you like he knew some people who went a lot farther than Mel had the guts to go. Pepper didn't like the insinuation that Mel had no guts, she got rather cool when Buddy let that one slip. Naturally

it turned out the people made fuck films. "Oh great," she
said, "I bet I know what my part would involve, sucking
your fucking cock for about a week." Then he backed off,
he always backed off when she got angry, he even pretended he had been kidding about not loaning her the car
but she had already called a cab and went outside and
waited until it came, with Buddy trying frantically all the
while to get her in a better mood. He apologized so many
times she thought she might vomit if she heard him say it
one more time, and he said he had only mentioned the
fuck films because he thought it might be kind of exciting.
It was true they had talked about doing that once, most
people in fuck films were ugly and they weren't, they decided they could probably be the first couple of porn, but
it was just mainly joking, it was just stuff they discussed
when they were first dating.

Finally the cab showed up and she left, leaving Buddy
in a frenzy, on the road to town he passed them in the
Cadillac doing about ninety, he was on his way to collect a
few tickets if he didn't slow down. It was quite a relief to
get to Mel's. Right away she told him she had been under
a lot of pressure, of course he was completely understanding and just said, "Forget about modeling tonight, Pepper,
let's just go sit by the pool. Would you like some dinner?"
Sure, she said, she was starving, between the dance class
and Madonna getting upset and then the fucking and a big
fight with Buddy it was enough to give anyone an appetite.
So Mel ordered a steak for her and they sat and watched
the stars come out, another nice thing about Mel was that
he didn't pry, he didn't just ask her to tell him every secret
thing. He sort of listened to what she felt like telling him
and then he might give a little advice.

When she told him about Bonventre's offer he said right
away take it, which was a surprise, they hadn't even settled
the question of whether she was going to marry him. She

79

wondered if maybe it had been a joke about marrying him, after all nothing that had happened between them had been very normal, maybe he just got a turn-on from asking or something.

"Why do you think I should take it?" she asked.

"Oh, because it means you'd stay here," Mel said.

"Yeah, but I wasn't going anywhere," she said.

Mel just smiled, as if he knew things about her that she didn't know.

"I have a confession to make," he said. "Jackie Bonventre is an old friend of mine. I showed him a little bit of one of the films. The one where you're in the blue bra."

That was definitely a surprise, she didn't know if she liked it or not.

"He was extremely impressed, and he's hard to impress," Mel said. "He said you were more beautiful than your mother."

She couldn't help smiling at that one, after having heard ten thousand times that her mother was the most beautiful woman in Las Vegas. Pepper couldn't see it, her mother was very good-looking but the horrible way she dressed sort of spoiled it, all those loud blouses and shiny pants.

"I don't know about the job," Pepper said. "He's supposed to be mean."

"He *is* mean, but he wouldn't be to you, since he knows I like you," Mel said. "For one thing, we're friends, though he says terrible things to me too. For another, I have money in all his shows."

"Why, are you a gangster?" Pepper asked. That thought kept occurring to her, maybe he was a gangster, just one of the gentlemanly kind—there were supposed to be some.

"Sorry to disappoint you," Mel said with a grin, he thought that one was funny. "I just happen to be rich."

Once she had eaten the steak Pepper felt fine, things had certainly stopped being boring, at least. Instead of just trying to decide who she could go out with if she broke up with Buddy, right away she had a rich guy who wanted to marry her and a weirdo producer who wanted to star her. She felt a little excited just having it all to consider—she asked Mel if he wanted some coke and he said sure. One of the Japs brought some out. What she would have liked was maybe to hit a disco but it was hard to imagine Mel wanting to do that, in fact it was hard to imagine him going out of his house at all, it was definitely his world.

Then, to show what a perceptive man he was, he cocked his head at her and said Pepper, would you like to dance. It was a surprise, though of course he had a great sound system and thousands of records, which seemed to appear as if by magic. Often when she first came in there would be a new pile in the study and she would check them out before she got undressed, he had all the right ones immediately, which was pretty amazing.

Also he was nice to dance with, better than Buddy although Buddy thought he was John Travolta II or something. Mel wasn't flamboyant but he was okay, mainly it was an excuse to watch her, he definitely loved watching her move. They hadn't really discussed his proposal yet, and she hadn't mentioned it to Buddy yet either, there was no telling what kind of a freak-out it would have produced.

They danced until they were pretty sweaty, Pepper said how about a swim, of course Mel was agreeable. "I think I've got a suit for you," he said, but Pepper said forget the suit, she just went out to the pool and shucked and dove in, wondering if he would go naked with her or if that would upset him. In fact he did go naked with her, she had been beginning to wonder if he had something missing physically, no cock or something but from what she could see in the moonlight there was nothing wrong there. There were times when she loved to swim, almost liked it better than anything, so she swam a lap or two while Mel rested and watched.

"Pepper, you're so gifted," Mel said. "If my father could

have got hold of you at the right time he'd have had you in the Olympics."

"How come?" she asked.

"Well, he's a swim coach," Mel said. "But of course if you were a swimmer you'd just be peaking. Sixteen's the best year."

"Where was your father a swim coach?" she asked, that was an interesting piece of information.

"In New Jersey, at a high school in Trenton," he said.

It was sort of startling, she had assumed his family must be rich too, though actually she'd never spent that much time thinking about his family, obviously he didn't have any around very close.

"A swim coach?" she said. "So how come you got so rich?"

"I just happened to be good with money," he said. "Sort of like you're a good dancer. I'm that good with money. Or maybe a little better."

Her hair was dripping, he reached out and sort of sluiced the water off of it, he liked it that she cut it so short. It was unusual for him to touch her, but he did it and he didn't seem nervous, maybe it was the dancing or the coke. She wanted to kiss him, when were they going to get a better time? but he didn't, he had just wanted to stop her hair from dripping apparently. It annoyed her a little, enough was enough, she was normally willing to make a move if she felt like something but with him she felt it ought to be him, he was too much older.

"Pepper, I think you're getting impatient," he said immediately, as if he had just read her mind. Her bangs were stuck together, he sort of took a finger and gently smoothed them out. They dripped on her face again and at that point he did kiss her, not for long, sort of light, but still it was a kiss, plus he caught the drip just when it hit the corner of her mouth. It was a delicate move, not something Buddy

82

would have come up with, she liked it, but then Mel smiled and asked her if she wanted to go in the Jacuzzi, the night was getting cold.

She said sure, so they did, he had already turned it on. Mel had a nice little body, very trim, but once they got in the Jacuzzi he didn't renew the move right away, she didn't know what to make of it. Maybe he was so old-fashioned he thought you had to get married before you fucked. It didn't seem possible he was that old-fashioned, but something was weird.

"Hey," she said. "Did you mean it about getting married, Mel?"

"Yes, I did, Pepper," he said. "I'd like to marry you very much."

"What would it be like?" she asked. She felt a little cautious. He had always been extremely kind, but still, a guy who collected old underwear could turn out to have bad tendencies of some sort.

Mel chuckled, he seemed delighted that she had asked.

"Pepper, from your point of view maybe the best thing about it would be that I'm very rich," he said.

It was interesting he emphasized that, because she had been thinking that too, no more living in a duplex with a yard full of peacocks and her mother's stupid boyfriends. Plus she could stop modeling in order to get clothes and she would never have to do things like hand out fried chicken at Gino's, which she had done the summer before for practically no money.

"I have so much money that now it makes itself faster than I can spend it," Mel said. "That can be nice."

I bet, Pepper thought.

"That's the simplest part of it, you'd like the money," he said. "I guess you're thinking this is all weird, I could have just tried to sleep with you instead of making movies of you in old underwear. Though actually I find it exciting to make movies of you, and I suspect you find it a little exciting too."

Then he touched her breasts. "I do *want* to sleep with you, Pepper," he said. "Do you know what usually happens when I make movies of young girls?"

She didn't, she had kind of been wondering, maybe he had closets full of the real scuzzy stuff, little cunts to look at whenever he wanted to. After all she was only there a few hours a week, other girls could still be coming for all she knew.

"Usually I just dress them and photograph them a time or two and then I undress them and photograph them and that's usually it, I never see them again. Oh, maybe we fuck or maybe we don't but pretty soon they're gone."

"Why?" she asked, she just wanted to know what he made of his own behavior.

Mel shrugged. "I get bored so easily," he said. "If I get bored with someone visually then I don't even care if I sleep with them. I'm very visual. I like really complicated effects, but most people just aren't subtle enough, either visually or sexually. Sexual effects can be very good effects but mostly they don't vary *that* much. Usually there's a kind of time limit, before I get bored."

She could sort of follow it, already with Buddy the fucking could seem boring. He was so obsessed with himself that he tended to grind away, well past the boring point.

"Now with you that's not true," Mel said. "You're never boring visually, because you're never the same."

She knew it was a big compliment, he was looking at her sort of keenly.

"You're very beautiful, Pepper," he said. "A lot of beauty is static, but not yours. You never look quite the same to me. Whatever happens to you shows up in your

face or the way you move—there are always subtle differences. Like today it was a fight with your boyfriend, you
were angry but very beautiful."

She liked hearing that, it was interesting, what he was
saying.

"You don't understand yet how selfish I am," he said.
"I made all this money for myself, so I could enjoy myself
absolutely any way I want to. I'm very snobbish visually,
and very easily bored. I need someone like you, extremely
beautiful and very subtle. Also you're not scared of the
unusual. I think if we're adventurous the effects could
keep changing for a long time."

"I'm not saying no," she said. "So would we ever fuck?"

"We certainly would," he said. "For periods. Probably
there'd be other periods, when we wouldn't."

Then he grinned, sort of appealing, his looks were growing on her more and more, the curly hair certainly didn't
hurt.

"The problem is how to preserve some effects that we
both find exciting," he said. "Most things get monotonous,
you're too young to really know that yet. We want to try
and keep some kick."

The words made sense, so far as she knew, it was just
nothing she felt she had to worry about.

"I'm forty-five," he said. "You'll have to live nearly
thirty more years before you really understand what I
mean. I won't get bored with you because just looking at
you is exciting, but what's going to keep it interesting for
you?"

Pepper had no idea, she just wasn't too worried. At the
moment she was more interested in why he wanted her to
work at the Stardust.

"Why do you want me to take the job?" she asked. "It's
two shows a night."

Mel shrugged. "It'll keep you in town," he said. "Besides, you're a dancer, you're not going to stop dancing just for me."

Nope, sure wasn't. "Maybe I *should* leave town though," she said.

Mel grinned the appealing grin. "That's right," he said. "Maybe you should."

Still, where she worked wasn't the big issue, there was one for sure that was more important.

"So what about guys?" she asked. "What if we weren't doing much and I got involved?"

"Of course you'll get involved," he said. "You'll have many, many men. You'll draw them like moths and most of them you'll just burn up in a twinkling. I don't want to be one of the ones that's burned up."

She didn't know about that, why would he marry her if he didn't care about the other guys? That was one she'd have to check out with Myrtle, who claimed to be an authority on the complications of things like that.

"You're not even jealous?" she said.

"Oh yeah, I'm jealous," he said. "If I happened to catch Buddy standing on the edge of a cliff I might push him right off."

"I wish you would," she said. "He's an asshole anyway."

"Just bear in mind that jealousy doesn't preserve anything," Mel said. "My jealousy won't keep you from getting bored."

I don't know, maybe this is not for me, Pepper thought. It was stupid that Buddy thought he was so cool when he wasn't, but Mel *was* cool and that was definitely worse. It was hard to understand but it was worse.

"What about you?" she asked. "What if you find someone more beautiful than me?"

"That's not too likely," Mel said. "I couldn't believe it when you walked in."

"What if you do?" she said, it was a key point. Somebody could always arrive.

86

Mel grinned. "If I do you can divorce me and get a lot of my money," he said. "Then you could do whatever you wanted to do."

Pepper got out of the Jacuzzi, she'd had enough of talking about it, she was not sure she believed he wanted to marry her. Maybe it was just some kind of come-on that was more complicated than it needed to be, maybe it was too much to think that all that money could be hers. He had a room where he kept towels, some of them vast, as big as rugs, of course there was a sauna and a little room with a massage table in it, apparently he liked to get rubdowns. She was angry and ready to split, she felt he was just enjoying some game of some sort with her. All that talk about preserving effects was bullshit, plus she didn't like it that he was prepared to be so cool about the other guys. Then he came in, wet and naked, looking upset, maybe he had thought she would enjoy talking all night or something. What she felt like was leaving and figuring it all out later, but to her surprise he came right over and kissed her, she thought boy are you weird, but it turned out okay, they ended up fucking on the massage table. It took her anger away. Then Mel gathered up her clothes for her and they went in the house and she dressed. She would have been happy to stay the night but he seemed a little depressed.

She sort of got worried, maybe she had blown it somehow, he was actually a lot better lover than Buddy, it was just that she had been impatient with all the talk. He put on a beautiful blue Japanese robe, he still looked sort of low but while she was drinking some orange juice he disappeared for a minute and when he came back gave her a thousand dollars. She felt really worried for a second, maybe he thought she had hustled him or something, he had never given her that much.

"You don't have to give me money, I'm not a hooker," she said.

He gave her one of the little corner of the mouth kisses. He didn't seem mad, just a little sad, maybe he had been building up to a different effect or something.

"So why are you giving me this?" she said. "I don't understand you."

"No, you don't, it's the very thing that may save us," he said and felt her cunt for a moment, she would have stayed but it wasn't what he had in mind, what he had in mind was a light feel and a few kisses.

Getting the money made her feel slightly cautious, she wanted to know if she was suddenly going to have to earn it some way. Mel had nice skin, actually, he kept himself in good shape which was a trait she admired. It had been the big barrier with Woods, he just would not take any kind of care of himself, ate junk food and anything gross he could find and hit the arcades all night, he was definitely a mess.

But Mel's skin was very smooth, she sort of felt weird and would have liked to stay, which he sensed, he put his arm around her and held her a minute, that he had never done.

"The more I give you the more you'll have," he said. "I could always get hit on the head by a brick or something. Of course the probabilities are against it, but the principle is important."

She started to ask why can't I stay, she really wanted to but then she got scared to push him. After all he *had* fucked her, maybe she just better not push it.

"Do you really want to marry me?" she asked. At times it seemed a little hard to believe although she was right there and it was happening.

"Oh yes, Pepper," Mel said. "I would be very unhappy if you said no."

"Do you know my mother?" she asked, it was something she had built up a curiosity about and she always meant to ask him but she kept letting it slip her mind. Her mother had had this army of boyfriends, there was a chance Mel was back there in the ranks somewhere, after all he was about her mother's age.

Mel laughed, he thought it was amusing that she was so interested in that question.

"Well, everybody in Las Vegas knows who your mother is," he said. "I see her in the Safeway once in a while but I've never been introduced to her."

The weird part of that one was that he would be in the Safeway, she assumed he just sent the Japs to do everything.

"Oh, I go to the Safeway," he said, reading her mind again. "I love it, it's the one place I still go."

"Why?" she asked.

"I go to see the styles," he said. "It's the great American style show, the Safeway. The combinations women wear when they're just shlepping around buying eggs delight me. They wander around buying food and I wander around watching them in their outfits."

That was definitely on the outside edge of weird, as Woods would put it, going to the Safeway to see outfits.

"You must vomit when you see Momma's," Pepper said, he was a guy with very peculiar inclinations, in her book. "Everything she puts on is tacky."

"No, she doesn't exactly have your purity, when it comes to fashion," he said. "I will say you can't miss her though."

Of course not, she'd dress in neon if she could, Pepper thought. She watched Mel, but he didn't seem that interested in the question of her mother, just a little amused that she brought it up.

"I think we chatted at the checkout counter once," Mel said. "She seemed very friendly but I guess that's the only time I've spoken to her."

Sure, friendly, she would have fucked you in the grocery cart Pepper thought, but she let it go, he wasn't really interested.

"I really do want you to marry me," he said. "I don't want you to say no."

No way she was gonna say no, after all he himself said if it changed it changed and she would end up with a lot of his money.

"Okay, I will," she said, feeling let's just get it settled. She gave him a real hard kiss, thinking that would turn the tide so far as staying the night was concerned, but it didn't, though he did stop looking depressed, he looked glad and said maybe she could come by tomorrow and they could work it out. Then he walked her to one of the Mercedes and told the Jap driver to take her home. The last thing he said was you know I'm crazy about your looks. That was probably the whole story, he couldn't get enough of looking at her.

She was hoping Myrtle was up, though who she would really have liked was Gary, he would definitely have something to say about Mel, and probably some information. Plus Gary was discreet, even if he was hopelessly crazy about her mother he could still keep a secret, and so could Myrtle, both of them knew ten times more about her than her mother did, she had told Myrtle all sorts of things about fucking and drugs and stuff and Myrtle had never leaked. In fact, Myrtle had shared a secret or two of her own, one of which was that she was two-timing Wendell once in a while. Wendell had a big rival he didn't know about, an air-conditioning repairman who lived across town. According to Myrtle he was better-looking than Wendell but undependable. It was hard for Pepper to believe that Myrtle actually still fucked guys, that thought was definitely on the outside edge of weird, but maybe it was possible.

When the Jap drove up with her in the car Myrtle was sitting in the lawn chair totally sloshed. She had some bizarre habits, such as propping her little TV set in the window by the driveway so if she happened to glance over and see something she liked she would go in and turn the sound up and then come back out and watch it through the screen. She never bothered to watch TV except from out in the driveway, she practically lived in that lawn chair.

Meanwhile Maude was eating some Cheerios that had once had milk in them but it had dried up and the Cheerios were stuck to the plate. So Maude was slowly moving the saucer down the driveway trying to get the Cheerios off. Didn't bother the Jap, he got out and opened the door for Pepper as if he were delivering her to the Riviera or somewhere. He totally ignored Myrtle and Maude and they totally ignored him. Pepper sort of wished Woods were there to see that sight, he would appreciate it whereas Buddy would be lucky even to notice it was going on.

Myrtle considered herself an honorary grandmother and demanded lots of affection so Pepper gave her a kiss, which was okay, besides keeping secrets Myrtle had always been good about slipping her money if she suddenly saw a blouse or something she couldn't live without.

"Pepper, do you think an all-night garage sale would work in this town?" Myrtle asked. "Maybe that would be one of them ideas whose time has come."

"Forget it, nobody's gonna leave the casinos and drive out here at night," Pepper said.

By this time Maude had pushed the Cheerios bowl all the way out to the road.

"Oh, Pepper, you won't never let me have my illusions," Myrtle said. "I guess I'm just a dreamer, that's what Wendell says."

"You wanta keep a big secret?" Pepper asked. It was kind of peculiar she was feeling so good about being engaged, since she had always considered marriage a definite yuk. She had thought maybe she'd try it at about fifty if she got bored, and then Mel had just immediately changed her mind. She didn't know any kids who had a chance at a guy that rich. It left her mind feeling sort of crowded, since there was also the chance she'd be dancing the lead at the Stardust. At least that meant the end of school, why bother with it any longer?

"I'm engaged," Pepper said, which gave Myrtle such a start that she sloshed half her vodka onto the driveway. Naturally she assumed it was Buddy, she was on the same wave length as Madonna on that one.

"Forget Buddy, this guy is older, he's about Momma's age," she said. "What do you think?"

"Well, if he's rich enough to hire a Jap to drive you around, why go to it," Myrtle said. "Maybe you can loan me your chauffeur once in a while if my car breaks down."

Then Myrtle suddenly started to cry, she just sat there and cried, which was slightly disgusting, after all she had never even met Mel and there was nothing to cry about.

"Come on, cut it out," Pepper said. "He's a real nice guy, I wouldn't marry some asshole."

"Oh well, I get sentimental when I'm shit-faced," Myrtle said. "I remember the day your daddy left, I've known you all that time. Besides, I was watching a sad TV show before you come home. It's one of them days. Your momma went off crying because Denny stole the insurance check."

That was infuriating, it meant no car. Maybe she should just ask Mel to buy her one, undoubtedly he would if she asked. Which didn't make it any less revolting that her mother would bring home some prick who was virtually a criminal, it was hard to have any sympathy for somebody with judgment that bad.

"So is she gonna have him arrested or is she just gonna let him get away with it?" Pepper asked.

"I don't know, she left while I was taking a nap," Myrtle said. "So when's the wedding?"

Actually that part was sort of hard to imagine, a wedding, she couldn't see Mel being into much of a production, so far as that went. Maybe he'd just get some preacher from the Strip to come out and marry them and that would be that.

Once Myrtle started asking questions she realized she didn't know that much about Mel. She knew his father was a swim coach, he had been a photographer, he had lived in Japan several years, that was about all she knew. In his house whatever he did seemed to sort of make sense, even not trying to fuck her until she sort of forced the issue, he had his own notions of when he wanted to do things, so why not? He did give you the sense he knew what he was doing, even just proposing hadn't seemed particularly weird, not while she was there in his house, anyway.

But being back home with Myrtle and the goats made it seem a little peculiar that he wanted to *marry* her. After all, he could have just asked her to move in, she would have probably gone right home and packed. At the very least there would be servants to drive her to school so she wouldn't have had to worry about hitching if both the stupid cars broke down. Her mother had lived with more guys than she could remember and the question of marriage had never come up—why Mel wanted to make such a big deal right away was a puzzler. Truly a puzzler.

"Hey, I got a job offer too, I guess this is my week to fly," she said, though Myrtle was looking kind of around the bend, it was late and she had probably been belting it all day.

"I know, Harmony told me," Myrtle said. "She thought that was crazy, wait till she hears you're engaged."

"Don't you tell her, I'll tell her," Pepper said. "Don't get drunk and forget, either. I don't want her bothering Mel or anything."

"Okay, but if he's gonna be her son-in-law he's got to get used to it sometime," Myrtle said. "Poor Harmony, nobody tells her nothing. She don't even know about me and Bobby"—Bobby being the guy who fixed air conditioners.

As a favor Pepper went out and got the cereal bowl Maude had nosed out into the road, but Myrtle hardly noticed, somebody was on the "Tonight" show that she wanted to hear and she had gone in to turn up the sound. Pepper went on in and brushed her teeth, she sort of expected Buddy to show up, he often did after she'd been to Mel's. He would show up hoping maybe to get fucked. Little did he know that was the end of that, as she would cheerfully tell him, he had been a total asshole about loaning her the car. It was too bad, too: If she had the Mustang she might hit the arcades and maybe find Woods, if anything would freak Woods out it was being told she was about to sort of become his godmother-in-law. Even Woods, Mr. Supercool, would have to admit that was sort of weird. She should have had the Jap take her, was sort of annoyed she hadn't thought of it. Of course she could call Mel and tell him to send the Jap back, but then she had already brushed her teeth, she decided why bother? she could always hit Woods with it another time. She cleaned her face then went to bed and listened to the radio for a while, remembering how surprised Bonventre was to get a little scorn instead of his ass kissed. Maybe when she went to audition she'd just mention that Mel was her fiancé, she had never even expected to have one much less the very one that could make the famous Jackie Bonventre behave for a few minutes.

That would certainly put her one up on her mother, she had worked for the man nearly twenty years and had not managed to get herself ten seconds of respect. Pepper figured she wouldn't sleep, too much to think about, but then she yawned and the last thing she heard was Maude tipping around on the driveway looking for the bowl of Cheerios.

III

1.

AFTER THE first show Harmony was feeling pretty good, after all nothing fatal had happened. She was hungry and tried to get Jessie or Gary in the mood to go eat, but Gary was in the process of arguing with Rodney, some of the changes hadn't gone too smoothly and Gary was upset, he liked things smooth, plus Jessie had lost her appetite from worrying about braces. She didn't feel like even leaving the dressing room, so Harmony asked Cherri to come, Cherri was very sweet and a lot more childlike than Pepper. Sometimes Harmony felt a little motherly toward her and Cherri appreciated it, she had only been away from home a few months and missed her family.

They decided to walk over to the Taco Belle, Harmony was in the mood for a taco, but first they had to stop at one of the craps tables, it was something she did every night between shows, a sweet kid named Gene from somewhere in Arkansas was managing the dice during her break and he loved for her to come by, he always saw she got to roll. Gene had very sweet eyes. He was not much older than Cherri but he was quite good at managing the dice, he always sort of took care of her and would never let her get in too deep, not that there was much danger, it was only the two-dollar table. Harmony was sort of hoping for a run, maybe she would get wildly lucky and win back all the money Denny had stolen, but it didn't happen, she crapped out on only the third roll and lost seven dollars.

Cherri tried to figure it out but she was having no luck, craps was beyond her. Even though Gene tried to quickly explain to her what all the lines meant it happened too quickly for Cherri, she didn't get it. But at least she got it that Gene was sweet. Harmony didn't see any reason why there couldn't be a romance there, Gene actually had a big crush on *her* but she had controlled herself for once and not encouraged it, just a little light flirting at the craps table between shows was all she allowed herself. She had a feeling that Gene was too young, he might get overwhelmed, after all he was not all that much older than Pepper's boyfriend. Pepper would definitely be annoyed if she brought home a guy that young.

Still, it was fun to hit the casino for a few minutes, she did it every night between shows and the guys at the two-dollar craps table definitely expected her. She wheeled in bringing a little glamour, which they seemed to appreciate, they all rooted for her when she got the dice and kept telling her she was due for a run any time although she had been doing it for a year or two and the most she had ever won was about seventy-five dollars, she was just not lucky at the tables.

Actually it was where she had met Denny, he had noticed that she kept showing up so one night he intercepted her. Now that he had taken off the news had quickly got around. In particular there was a slot-machine mechanic named Dave who had begun taking his break just when she did. They had exchanged a few words a time or two, Dave had been a marine then a cowboy up in Montana but said the winters were too long so now he was fixing slot machines at the casino. He had a gray streak in his hair, kind of attractive. Harmony was just sort of keeping him on hold because she hadn't actually quite given up on Denny, although it was kind of nice to know Dave took the trouble to hit the table just when she was due.

Gene had figured that much out, he had a sizable crush and didn't look too happy to see Dave, although he tried to be friendly. This time Harmony hung around a little longer, to give Gene time to notice Cherri, who was quite beautiful and a lot closer to his age. Harmony did let Dave put his arm around her as he was walking them out of the casino. He deserved that much reward for rearranging his break, plus she could use a tiny bit of comfort, it had not exactly been one of her better days.

At the Taco Belle Harmony used the pay phone to call Pepper, who of course wasn't home—checking on Pepper was a good way to waste twenty cents. So she called Madonna to check on the Bonventre business and Madonna said, "Harmony, I'm worried, has she told you she's engaged?"

"What are you talking about?" Harmony said. "Pepper's not engaged, she's just going steady with Buddy." Madonna said maybe it was all a joke then, Pepper was secretive and got angry if you asked her anything, she sounded quite disturbed, after all she had worked with Pepper since Pepper was five.

"Bonventre still hates me, he criticized my ass," Madonna said. She sounded like she had been crying.

"Come on, cheer up, your ass is better than mine and I'm younger," Harmony said. She went back and had her taco, feeling a little distracted, though she tried to listen to Cherri talk about her family. It seemed she had a little sister named Patti who had an equally good bosom and might be coming out to try and get in a show. Harmony thought it would be good for Cherri to have her sister for company, but the fact was she couldn't keep her mind on what she was hearing, it was a little disturbing that there was a rumor going around that Pepper was engaged. She wasn't really enjoying her taco, though she had been hungry when she ordered it. Too many things were happening

at once, none of which she could honestly say she understood, such as Denny stealing the check. Why would he do
that? What had she ever done but love him and actually try
to do practically everything he had asked her to do, up to
and including making love in a motorboat in her sleep goggles when she was basically scared out of her mind.

Harmony did notice though while Cherri was going on
about her family that a bunch of guys were sort of giving
Cherri the eye, there were about five of them. They looked
like they had maybe saved their money and rolled in from
Texas or maybe New Mexico or somewhere for a little high
life. They were taking time out to eat a little Mexican food
and it was easy to see they were smitten by Cherri, they
kept stealing looks which Cherri didn't even notice in her
homesickness. Harmony had noticed because at first she
thought the looks were for her, that was usually the case if
it was four or five guys. She was about to give them a nice
smile, she had never seen anything wrong with guys looking, she liked to sort of repay them with a nice smile, not
flirting exactly just a smile to be friendly, but then she did
smile at one of them and he looked very startled, which
was when she noticed it was Cherri they were interested
in.

Well, why not? Harmony thought, they were all young
guys. Cherri was a beautiful girl and she was their age, it
was perfectly appropriate and if Cherri would just notice it
might cheer her up and take her mind off her homesickness. But it sort of went on for a while, the guys kept
looking and Cherri kept not noticing and Harmony found
to be honest that it kind of lowered her spirits, even though
she thought highly of Cherri and would have loved to see
her have a nice romance. Still, it made her feel a little blue
that the kid had been so startled when she smiled back, as
if she were an old lady or something. After all she had had
her share of young admirers, several of Pepper's boyfriends

had sort of had crushes on her. If it was just going to be a matter of having a laugh once in a while then age differences didn't bother her. But the guys from Texas or wherever they were from had accidentally hurt her feelings a little, they acted like they thought she was Cherri's mother. Basically all they wanted was the thrill of flirting with a showgirl at the Taco Belle, only Cherri didn't notice and the guys sort of ruled her out, totally unaware that she was probably the most famous showgirl in Las Vegas, they just ruled her out, whereas Cherri didn't even seem to be aware of masculine attention, she hadn't even noticed Gene.

They took their time walking back to the Stardust, after all they still had nearly an hour before the second show. It was quite a beautiful night, warm, nice to be outside. Harmony had meant to try and catch Bonventre but she didn't feel like it, Bonventre was not exactly what she needed in her present mood. Cherri wanted to go on in, she was taking a course in real estate at the university so she hustled on in to study and Harmony took a little walk up toward Caesars Palace, she felt blue and didn't want to just sit around the dressing room watching Jessie be paranoid about the space between her teeth.

Too bad Billy was already off duty, he was the sweetest security cop in town so far as she was concerned, a smile or two from Billy would have improved her mood but Billy was probably up at the Trop keeping his wife company during her break. Harmony could remember when Ross would run up to the Trop to see her for a little while although his job was at the Desert Inn. It was a sacrifice for him to come up there every night just so she wouldn't feel lonely during her break, but Ross didn't seem to mind, he just considered it part of being a good husband. It was funny that she was remembering Ross more and more often, there had been years when she wouldn't think of him at all unless he sent some money or maybe a birthday present for Pepper or something. He was very good about birthdays, his present had only been late once all the time Pepper had been growing up, and that time it had been an ant farm and the ants had to come all the way from New England.

Harmony walked nearly to Caesars before turning back. She was remembering all the things that had happened to her in her years in Las Vegas, Didier falling in love with her and then dying, and Ross marrying her and then leaving, and Pepper growing up and quite a few guys who had been around for different lengths of time, not such long lengths most of them, still, it added up, she just hadn't expected it to suddenly start to show in that particular way, like at the Taco Belle. Of course the Taco Belle was very brightly lit, it would be instantly obvious even with both of them in makeup that Cherri was a lot younger. If they had been sitting in the keno bar or somewhere a little dimmer the guys might not have noticed at all.

But then it was true—why shouldn't they notice? They were just thinking in terms of someone their own age. The sad part was that she didn't care, she wasn't after them, she just liked to smile at guys and have them smile back. That was absolutely as far as it went most of the time, unless some guy got a little more interested and made an effort, on the order of Dave rearranging his break to meet her at the craps table. Over the years it must have been thousands of times that some guys from out of town would steal a few looks and she would smile, that was all that would happen, it wasn't like she was trying to drag them off to the sack or get them in trouble with their wives or anything. After all, showgirls were supposed to give the impression of friendliness. It had never been hard for her because she really felt friendly, it just had never happened before that a guy had looked startled when she smiled at him.

It left her with a little bit of a hurt feeling. She had never spent too much time worrying about the future, but it was the sort of incident that could kind of make you wonder what the future held. Probably all it meant was that she would have to learn a little discretion and not smile at guys so young. Leave them to Cherri, only that meant leaving them without even a smile, because Cherri just didn't notice.

Harmony spent so much time walking around, not exactly thinking gloomy thoughts, just mainly walking and enjoying the warm air—a little down but not in any bottomless pit of depression or anything—that she was almost late getting back. Gary was frantic, he assumed she had been kidnapped or Denny had done something crazy, she was usually back at least thirty minutes before the curtain. Gary was quite orderly, he always had the schedule in mind and any little thing that didn't seem normal, like her going for a walk instead of just coming back to the dressing room made him quite anxious.

"Gary, I was just taking a walk, it's a pretty night," Harmony said. It had been smart too. Jessie was no less depressed and sitting around the dressing room was no fun when everyone was in a bad mood anyway. Rodney in particular was in a terrible mood and was giving Genevieve a bad time because two of her costumes had tears but she hadn't bothered to point it out and give Rodney time to get them fixed. Harmony just quickly got undressed and into her G-string and left, it took all of about a minute and she wasn't that late anyway, it was just that Gary liked to get her into her feathers early, so he'd have more time to devote to people who were really late, like Jessie, who had been right there all the time, taking a nap or talking to Monroe on the telephone—the muffler shop stayed open till midnight, except on weekends.

"Guess what the latest rumor is, Pepper's engaged," Harmony said, as the hoist was bringing the feathers down.

"Oh no, who told you that?" Gary said. He didn't take it particularly seriously.

It was only when she was up on the disc that Harmony sort of felt a little nervous. There was general agreement that Buddy did too many drugs and was not that stable. In her view one of his worst faults was that he had no sense of humor and was too possessive of Pepper, she was bound to get tired of it. Harmony didn't want Pepper to get into something like that at sixteen and get hurt. If it was true that she was engaged they were all going to have to make an effort to talk her out of it. Pepper would undoubtedly just get resentful if she said anything, the best thing might be to get Gary to talk to her, Pepper had a lot of respect for Gary's opinion and hardly any for hers or Jessie's or Myrtle's or even Madonna's. For a moment just as the curtain was going up she thought of Ross again, what would he think if he knew the rumor? Before she had time even to wonder much about Ross's reaction the lights hit and the audience broke into a big hand.

2.

SOMETIMES IN the second show things got a little slack, after all it was late and they had all done it before three or four thousand times. Maybe the audience would have too much to drink and would get a little boisterous, they tended to be more respectful at the first show. Some of the dancing was totally lifeless, plus the acrobats were having an off night, they missed a couple of times and even when they didn't miss the catches weren't too smooth, the audience was not impressed. Harmony did her best, she thought any audience deserved to get its money's worth, but then she wasn't a dancer or an acrobat, there wasn't that much she could do about it. But it was depressing to be in a show that had sort of fallen dead on its feet, all you could do was keep smiling and wait for it to be over, at which point Bonventre would be sure to throw a fit and threaten to fire everyone.

It was definitely not the best show they had ever put on but everybody did sort of rouse themselves and make an effort for the finale. They got a burst of energy at the thought that it might finally be over. Harmony was glad herself, it seemed sort of endless when it wasn't really working but at least the finale was lively, the audience started clapping, it wasn't a total disgrace. Harmony gave them her best smile as her disc started up and was holding the smile when she got a big shock, someone in the audience screamed. The lights were so strong she couldn't see anything and didn't know if there was a murderer loose or what. Once at the Trop something like that happened. A guy evidently got so bored with the show that he pulled out a pistol and started playing Russian roulette. Nobody noticed except his wife, who thought it was a big joke until he suddenly blew his brains out. Fortunately he had been at the back, so Harmony had not really seen the blood and gore, but the cigarette girls and the waitresses were definitely shook up.

But the screams kept coming. With the lights in her eyes it was very confusing, it seemed like most of the people were clapping but a few were screaming. She had no idea what it could be until she got a little higher and looked down and had a horrible shock, there was Jessie lying on the stage sort of crumpled up between the two lines of dancers. It was such a shock that she thought for a moment it wasn't real. It was like a very bad dream that you wake up from and feel relieved. Only it wasn't, she looked over and saw that Jessie's disc was broken, it was just dangling from a couple of wires. She looked down and saw that at

105

least Jessie wasn't killed, she was sitting up, with the dancers all around her. It was the very end of the finale and the dancers couldn't stop, they had to keep dancing and singing, it was only about ten seconds to the curtain. At least Jessie wasn't broken to bits, she was definitely sitting up. Meanwhile Harmony could see Bonventre in the wings having a fit that his finale had been spoiled. He was waving at Jessie as if he wanted her to get up and hop off or something. Poor Jessie either didn't hear him or didn't want to, she just kept sitting there trying to smile. It had to be horribly embarrassing to have to sit in the middle of the stage during the finale. She would probably never get over it even if she wasn't really hurt.

Then the curtain finally dropped and Gary and a couple of stagehands ran out and sort of lifted Jessie off, but of course the audience was worried, they didn't know what to make of it. Harmony saw Bonventre talking to Jessie with Gary sort of shaking his head and looking more and more distraught. Then the curtain went up again for the curtain calls and somehow Bonventre got Jessie on her feet, or at least on one foot—she teetered for a moment and waved and gave the audience a smile to show she was all right. Of course the audience gave her a big hand. It was not exactly a standing ovation since most of them were leaving anyway but it was a big hand. Then she fell right into Gary's arms.

The minute the curtain went down again she got off the disc and hurried down the steps and out of her feathers, and got across the stage just in time to hear Bonventre yell at Gary.

"For Christ's sake, she only fell six or eight feet, will you stop making it into an Ann-Margret situation?" Bonventre said, he sort of looked bored.

But Jessie was one of Gary's pets and he was definitely disturbed.

106

"Listen, she didn't need to stand up, undoubtedly her ankle's broken—you could have just made an announcement!" he said.

It was no big argument though. Bonventre just walked off, probably he was disgusted because the accident happened just when he was ready to launch into a tirade about the poor quality of the second show.

Jessie was lying on a little cot backstage. She was crying which was no surprise and Rodney was trying to get her out of her feathers. She wasn't skinned or anything. Harmony hurried to the dressing room and got her her robe.

The showgirls and quite a few of the dancers were standing around looking sort of paralyzed. Three or four stagehands were examining the disc, to see what might have happened. There was a crowd gathered but no one was saying much, it was like they were all sort of a little bit in shock. Even Murdo the ventriloquist was standing by the cot and Murdo didn't mix with the group much. He was sort of unpopular with the gay dancers because though he was known to be basically gay he kept refusing to come out of the closet. Some said he was about the last person in the closet in the whole city of Las Vegas, and the boy dancers resented it fiercely.

Harmony helped Jessie get into her robe, it was hard to tell if she was in pain or just crying because it had been a shock and she was embarrassed.

"Do you hurt?" Harmony asked. Gary came and sat on the cot and held one of her hands.

"I did when I stood up, I got a real sharp pain," Jessie said. "I just wish I could take my makeup off, I don't want to go to the hospital in it."

"Well, it'll just be to the emergency room so they can take some X-rays, maybe it's not even broken, you actually didn't fall all that far," Gary said.

"Yeah, look on the bright side, kid," Murdo said. "If

107

the fuckin' disc had slipped when you were way at the top you'd have broken every bone in your body."

"Murdo, I don't think she wants to hear that," Gary said. He was irritated because the ambulance hadn't come, although it had been called almost the second Jessie fell.

Murdo got his feelings hurt at that. "I was only trying to cheer her up," he said. Probably he had meant well but the fact was that the mere mention of having every bone in her body broken only caused Jessie to cry a lot harder. She had a vivid imagination when it came to accidents and disasters of any kind.

Harmony didn't think she looked too damaged, though, maybe it was just a bad sprain. She told Jessie she'd go to the emergency room with her and hurried to the dressing room to get dressed.

As she was going back Bonventre suddenly popped out of his office and grabbed her elbow, it was just like him to suddenly appear just when it was a bad time to talk.

"Come in a minute," he said.

"What is it, Jackie, I've got to go with Jessie to the emergency room," she said.

"Far be it for me to detain you while you're on a fuckin' errand of mercy," Bonventre said, with a smirk. The fact that Jessie had at the very least a bad sprain wasn't going to cause Bonventre to lose any sleep.

"I'd like you to go down to the sheriff's office tomorrow and sign a work consent form for Pepper, since she's under age," he said.

"Jackie, I wish you'd talked to me about that, I don't know if Pepper ought to work here," she said.

"Who's the guy she's engaged to?" Bonventre asked. It was really pointless to say anything to him because he just completely ignored it and asked another question, he didn't even pretend he hadn't heard you he just ignored all words except his own.

"Pepper's not engaged, maybe her boyfriend just spread that rumor," she said. The ambulance had arrived, a couple of guys in white were wheeling a little ambulance bed backstage, sort of a stretcher on wheels.

"Well, Pepper spread it to *me*," Bonventre said. "It may be that you're not particularly well informed about your daughter's plans, which would not surprise me."

"I think I'd know if she was getting married," Harmony said, although she was not too confident really, maybe she wouldn't. Pepper was not one to confide, at least not in her.

"Harmony, if they ever decide to hold a Miss Vacant contest, I'll back you all the way," Bonventre said, and grinned at his own humor. It was just the kind of remark he seemed to think was funny. "Meanwhile just do me the small favor of signing a work consent form so we can audition your daughter," he said.

Harmony didn't have time to argue about it, they had lifted Jessie out onto the little bed and were already wheeling her out.

"No, I don't want Monique to hate me. Anyway, Pepper's still in school," she said, she had to hurry to catch up with the ambulance, the guys who were wheeling Jessie out were really fast. Bonventre was frowning, he was not pleased, she knew perfectly well she hadn't heard the last of that one but at least she could put it off.

She showed up just as they were about to shut the ambulance doors. Gary was already inside, but when she showed up he decided maybe it made more sense if he brought his car in case it wasn't as bad as it looked and Jessie got released right away they would have something to ride in. The ambulance drivers didn't care, they just said make up your minds. So Gary climbed out and she climbed in. By that time a crowd had gathered, mainly just couples who had been walking up and down the Strip and stopped when they saw the lights flashing. They were wondering if it had been a murder or somebody with a heart attack or what.

"I'm scared," Jessie said, gripping Harmony's hand tightly. It would have been good if she could have got her makeup off, it was a total mess from the tears. The guys in the ambulance didn't regard it as a life or death emergency. They left on the flashing lights but didn't bother with the siren except once or twice at intersections when the pedestrians didn't get out of the way quick enough to suit them.

"Maybe it's just a sprain, don't look on the dark side," Harmony said, though expecting Jessie not to look on the dark side was like expecting the desert not to be dry or something.

"No, I felt a real sharp pain when I stood up, I just know this is the end," Jessie said.

"Please stop talking about the end, even if it's broken you're not gonna die," Harmony said, "Besides, they have real light casts nowadays, remember when Jennie broke her wrist?"

"I mean the end of my career," Jessie said. "If it's broken Bonventre will never let me come back, he thinks I'm too old anyway."

Harmony started to point out that after all Jessie was nearly three years younger than she was, but then she didn't say it. In fact, Jessie looked at least as old, probably from worrying constantly about everything. Only the fact that she was basically a very beautiful woman was in her favor, certainly her attitude wasn't in her favor. Even so Jessie was thirty-six and there was no point in getting into one of those how-long-can-I-last discussions with her, those discussions went on practically constantly in the dressing room anyway. She herself tuned them out whenever possible. It was Didier who pointed out to her right away when she was practically the youngest girl in town

110

that you either have to die young or else get old. He said just take first-rate care of yourself, and that means mentally too, and don't worry all night and that's all you can do. Everybody in the business was aware that even the best bodies got a little less good eventually, though it was certainly a sad thought, it meant you had to quit sometime. Whenever those discussions came up Harmony would just sort of give them a pass, she would go down to the keno bar or else put in her earplugs and take a nap. She was grateful for the invention of earplugs, since it meant you got to miss a lot of conversations of an upsetting nature. She didn't like to invite bad thoughts into her mind. Who cares if they're true, it doesn't help you to think about them.

The difference between her and Jessie was that she gave the age question a pass, or at least she usually did, once in a while in low moods or if Denny acted like she was a grandmother just because she didn't want to do something or other he had in mind the age issue might get into her mind without being invited, she might have to go sit with the peacocks for a while until she felt happier, but it wasn't like she marked the calendar every day or anything. Half the time she would forget her own birthday unless Ross or one of her aunts or somebody sent a card.

Still, it was very hard to argue with Jessie about age, Harmony just sat and held her hand. Then one of the young guys on the ambulance got bored and decided to come back for a chat. It was probably not every night he got to haul two showgirls around. He was sort of fat and had a jolly grin, his name was Jerry and he told them about various disasters he had been to the scene of. He said he had grown up in Barstow and had started being an ambulance driver when he was still in high school. He told them about one particularly horrible car wreck in which a person had been totally decapitated, the head was never found, he made such a good story of it that it took Jessie's mind off the end of her career for a few seconds at least.

Meanwhile they were just driving slowly up the Strip, the driver didn't seem to be in any hurry. Harmony could see out the back window, lots of couples were strolling along enjoying the pretty night. She sort of felt a pang, it would be nice to be part of a couple, at least have someone to hold hands with if you were taking a walk. Of course she had been part of a couple quite a few times, it was not as if she had lived like an old maid, it was just that the guys kept slipping on by—the day would come when there would be nobody in bed, or even to hold hands with on a walk if it was a nice night.

"If they give me ether will you call Monroe? Nobody did," Jessie said.

"Why would they give you ether, it's just your ankle?" Harmony asked. One of Jessie's problems was that she had never gotten over having her tonsils out, it had been a difficult tonsillectomy, she had had to have ether twice and it left her with a horror of things put over her nose.

"Now don't you worry, pretty soon they'll have artificial ankles anyway," Jerry said. He said it was amazing what they could do with plastics, one woman who had been in a disaster he had handled even had a plastic hip. Jerry said he subscribed to a magazine that was totally devoted to artificial limbs and organs and stuff, he said he liked to keep up with recent advances, sometimes it was a comfort to people who had just been mangled if the ambulance driver could inform them that it didn't mean the end of their life just because they lost a limb or had an organ a little damaged, they really could do amazing things with plastics. Harmony began to sort of wish Jerry hadn't bothered to come back. Not only was he not making Jessie feel any better he wasn't improving *her* mood either, plus it was clear he was a guy who was easily turned on. Harmony

112

decided he was about to ask one or both of them for a date, he definitely had that look but luckily they got to the hospital before it could happen. Jessie was worried too, after all Jerry was sitting right there over her and she just had on her bathrobe over her G-string. It was sort of close quarters in the ambulance and Harmony decided she had been wrong about Jerry being likable.

The funny part was that Gary was already there, he had just hopped in his car and beaten the ambulance. Of course he had lived in Las Vegas for a long time and knew every possible shortcut. Gary would even cut through parking garages if he was in a hurry, he knew most of the attendants, so they let him. Anyway, he was there, having an argument with a hospital security guard because he had parked in the emergency driveway that was supposed to be just for ambulances. He was looking frantic, which didn't impress the security guard, Gary finally had to move his car. The fact that he had beaten the ambulance upset him a good deal. He was trying to convince the guard the ambulance had had a wreck or something when they finally drove up, at which point Jerry sort of calmed down and helped get Jessie out.

Harmony was hoping they had seen the last of him but it wasn't true. He caught her by the pay phone in the hospital hall and asked her if she'd like to go out but Harmony definitely wasn't interested, she just told him she was married, which was actually true but not the real reason. Jerry was impressing her more and more as being a sicko. He tried to be a good sport though and offered to loan her an issue of the magazine about artificial limbs, he seemed to think that might be good for her morale but she just said no thank you, I've got to make a call, and he finally left.

Then she couldn't get Monroe, the muffler shop was closed and he was nowhere to be found. Gary was of the opinion that Monroe might have another girlfriend—he whispered the suspicion while Jessie was being X-rayed.

"I don't know, Gary, it's a surprise to me he could even get one," Harmony said. She meant it, Monroe was no great looker. It seemed to her he had only got Jessie because she happened to be on the rebound from a man named Rupert who had stolen practically every piece of jewelry she owned to get more money to lose at blackjack. Rupert had a bad blackjack habit and he had never been that kind to Jessie, even before he started stealing. He was one of the reasons Jessie had been understanding about Denny stealing the insurance check. She knew how it was to love a man who didn't hesitate just to take things when he needed money.

Finally while they were sitting in some chairs in the hospital hall wondering what the story was with Monroe the doctor came out and delivered the worst possible news: Jessie's ankle had been shattered, he used the word three or four times. It immediately made Harmony cry to think of Jessie's ankle shattering—shattering was like what happened when you broke a glass. It was really upsetting. Gary cried a little too and looked like he might be about to get sick to his stomach.

He said well, what do we do now, and the doctor said there was not much to be done until morning. They were going to give Jessie a sedative so she could sleep and then in the morning they'd operate and try and put her ankle back together. That was as far ahead as he could predict it except it was definite Jessie would have to stay in the hospital for a while, maybe she'd be in traction or maybe not but she was definitely going to have to keep still until the ankle got a chance to heal.

Of course it was terrible news, Jessie would just lie there and cry the whole time, she'd probably drown herself crying if they didn't watch her.

114

"She doesn't respond to adversity very well," Gary said, putting it mildly in Harmony's opinion.

Fortunately though Jessie had already had her sedative and was a little groggy, she sort of dozed off while they were getting her room ready. The best they could do was semiprivate but it was not too bad, the other patient was an old woman who had had her vocal cords removed, at least that was what the nurse said, the old woman herself was sound asleep. Once in a while Jessie woke up but she was too groggy to cry. Her main concern was Francois who was picky about what he ate, not that Harmony didn't know that already, she had to promise several times to stop by the all-night Safeway and buy him some dog food with a liver flavor. Jessie had not planned on shattering her ankle and there was nothing in the house but dry dog food which Francois probably wouldn't eat even if it meant starving.

"As soon as you get out you're moving into my house, you can help Myrtle with her garage sales," Harmony said. "Maybe if she had some company she wouldn't drink all day."

Jessie seemed pleased to have that to look forward to, she seemed to have forgotten Monroe. Her only comment was that she didn't know if Francois could get along with Maude or the peacocks. He was not used to rivals, if they didn't like him he would be at a disadvantage because he was so small. Harmony kept telling her not to worry, though she was getting worried herself that Gary was never going to come back, he had gone down to the business office to make financial arrangements, naturally Jessie didn't have any insurance.

When Gary finally did come back Jessie was asleep. The hospital had given him a bad time because of Jessie's lack of insurance. It was hard to know what to do about Jessie, neither of them wanted her to wake up alone and be scared, but on the other hand they didn't want to sit around the hospital all night, either. The nurse said oh, go on, she'll probably sleep, so they did. It was not that far to Debbie's and Marty's and they both felt they could use a drink so they went and had a few. Harmony had five or six vodka tonics but they weren't having much effect, she was wound too tight or something, plus Gary sort of made her nervous by running off to the pay phone every five minutes to call Monroe. He was becoming obsessed with Monroe, every time he didn't get him he looked a little more strung out.

"Gary, it doesn't matter, I'll stay at the hospital," Harmony said. "I'm not sleepy anyway."

"No, I better do that," Gary said. "You go get the dog food, you make her nervous anyway."

Harmony thought that was an unnecessary remark, though it was true she and Jessie sometimes had little spats, mainly it was due to the fact that Jessie was such an indecisive dresser. She would change clothes five or six times before going out on the simplest date, even to eat pizza she would change a time or two and Harmony sometimes got impatient and made a comment, she didn't see the point in spending hours watching Jessie change clothes. Over the years Jessie had gotten defensive about it and if she was getting her period or something she might get angry and make a comment back, but it wasn't serious, it was just a spat once in awhile it didn't mean Jessie wouldn't want her to stay at the hospital.

Of course Gary soon realized he shouldn't have said it. He apologized nicely and said the truth was he hated Francois and didn't trust himself to feed the little idiot, he might lose control and strangle him which would disturb Jessie worse than breaking her ankle.

Harmony could understand that, she said okay and dropped Gary off at the hospital and then went to the

116

Safeway and got the dog food with the liver flavor, which Francois proceeded to ignore, he was annoyed that it was Harmony rather than Jessie and wouldn't even get off the bed.

Harmony gathered up a few things that Jessie had requested, just some gowns and her bathrobe and some paperbacks. Jessie was a big reader of teen romances, she had admitted to Harmony several times that she fantasized being a teen again and having a wonderful teen romance like those described in the books. She also admitted that nothing very wonderful had happened when she had been a teen. She had kind of got off to a low-grade start, her hometown of Chico, California, had not been exactly full of wonderful guys. Jessie seemed to feel that if she could have got off to a better start she wouldn't have ended up such a worrier, but Harmony was doubtful, Jessie just basically had a worried outlook.

She herself had not had such overwhelming teen romances, either. In fact her first serious boyfriend, a banker's son named Teddy, had tried three nights in a row to make her not a virgin, with no success. He finally suggested she ought to see a doctor, he couldn't face any more failures and had read in some sex book that doctors sometimes had to help out a little. She refused of course but it didn't constitute such a great start where romance was concerned. Still, it hadn't made her a worrier, like Jessie.

While she was packing the gown and the books the long-lost Monroe walked in, so greasy that he looked like he must have fallen in a hole full of oil. The sight of him explained why Jessie's bathroom was full of heavy-duty soap.

"Oh, Monroe, where have you been, Jessie's disc broke and she shattered her ankle," Harmony said. Normally she would have hugged him at such a time but she had an aversion to grease and didn't quite get around to the hug.

117

Francois didn't help matters, evidently he hated Monroe, he came running in from the bedroom snarling, which was ridiculous, one kick and he would have been dead.

It turned out Monroe hadn't been lost, he had just been under a truck that had broken down on the freeway. He seemed tired and kept yawning, despite being upset that Jessie was hurt. He sat down on the couch and looked like he was either going to cry or go right to sleep. The most off-putting thing about him from Harmony's point of view was that he had so much oil and grease packed under his fingernails that they looked like they could never be cleaned, and they never *were* cleaned. Even when Monroe showered with the heavy-duty soap and made himself presentable his fingernails were still totally black underneath. Probably they had been that way for so long he had forgotten they were supposed to be cleaned once in a while. Sometimes on Sunday Monroe made an effort and took Jessie to a nice restaurant, often Harmony went along and she always found the fact that Monroe hadn't managed to clean his fingernails very noticeable, though Jessie didn't seem to notice it, which was odd, after all Jessie could easily spend a whole afternoon just changing clothes and redoing her makeup.

"That woman's accident-prone," Monroe said, after a yawn. He wouldn't have been so terrible-looking, except that his nose was totally flat. Gary once said it looked like someone had dropped a car on it, which could have happened, Monroe spent a lot of time under cars. Also he had a purple birthmark on one side of his neck, it always seemed to be the side Harmony was looking at him from. She knew looks weren't everything, she had had some strange-looking guys herself, she guessed, guys with plenty of defects but usually a little more appealing than Monroe. The fingernails were a real downer in her book.

"She was worried we couldn't find you," Harmony said.

"Well, I'll marry her, I been trying to anyway," Monroe said, as if that were the only possible solution now that Jessie had shattered her ankle. Harmony didn't know about that, it seemed to her Jessie ought to come and recuperate at her house and keep her options open a little longer, anyway Myrtle would enjoy the company.

When she got back to the hospital Gary said Jessie hadn't even blinked. He was exhausted from worrying so much and said maybe they should go to his house and get a little sleep. That was fine with her, she often slept in Gary's guest room if there was a party or something. But when they got to his house she didn't feel sleepy. Gary said fine, you can borrow the car if you want to go home and change or something, but one of them definitely had to get back to the hospital before Jessie went in for her operation.

She thought maybe she'd go home, but once she got in the car she didn't feel like it, she was in sort of an unusual mood, she felt like a little company and it was still too early even for Myrtle to be up so if she went home she wouldn't get any and she didn't feel like just putting on her sleep goggles and lying there. If she did that she would just start thinking about Denny. It was the most in love she had been for a long time, it was just too bad he didn't love her too. He had seemed to at first but maybe she had been imagining things. Myrtle said she ought to train herself. When he first took off she thought about him nearly every minute of the day or for maybe the first week.

She started to go back to Debbie's and Marty's but then if nobody was there to talk to she'd just stuff herself with peanuts or drink too much. What she did instead was drive back to the Stardust. She started feeling very lonely and wanted to stop the feeling, it was a feeling of suddenly not having one single person available who cared that much about her. Of course Gary did but he had just gone to sleep and wasn't available.

119

It was late, there were very few people walking on the Strip, which didn't help her lonely feeling. She thought of stopping at the Amoco station and having a chat with Wendell but Gary's car was full of gas and that ruled that out. At least the casino was still buzzing, the town wasn't as deserted as it looked from outside.

It occurred to her that there wasn't much point in keeping Dave on hold too much longer, Denny was not going to suddenly show up and be nice, she might as well go on and give up, it was sort of unfair to keep Dave waiting. At least he didn't strike her as the kind of man who would steal somebody's insurance check. Luckily Dave was still there, he was off in about twenty minutes, he sort of looked slightly taken aback when she showed up and asked him if he wanted to go eat breakfast or something, obviously he had not expected to get taken off hold so quickly but once he got used to the idea he was willing. He said he'd meet her at the keno bar, so Harmony went and sat at the bar right by the cash register and had a word or two with Leon, the main bartender. She also had another vodka tonic or two, hoping they would have an effect on her lonely feeling but they didn't, they just went down like water.

"How come you never flirt with me, Harmony, you flirt with everybody else?" Leon wanted to know. It was true she had known him for ten years and never flirted with him, he was a short guy and pudgy, though that wasn't the reason, a lot of guys were short, including several she had developed attachments too, Ross for example and Gary too for that matter.

"Oh, Leon, I'm just saving you," she said, giving him a smile. Leon didn't really care. He had just been making conversation, maybe even trying to cheer her up a little.

"That's awful about Jessie," he said. "Some people are accident-prone. I remember once she twisted her ankle just getting off a barstool."

120

That was true, if there was any way to pick up an injury Jessie would find it. Dave was taking a while, it seemed to her twenty minutes was up and he wasn't there. She was beginning to wish she had just decided to flirt with Leon for a while, after all he was an old friend whereas Dave was sort of an unknown quantity. Good-looking, she liked the streak of gray in his hair, it sort of made him look dignified, but still an unknown quantity.

Then just when she was trying to decide if maybe she should just vanish and pretend she had got an emergency phone call from the hospital or something, the last person in the world she wanted to see, namely Bonventre, wandered out of the casino and sat down by her. She felt like Pac-Man had made it through the maze and selected her as the next person to eat, as usual Bonventre looked full of energy though it was nearly dawn.

"Harmony, don't you ever go home?" he said, making it sound like she owed him rent for the barstool or something.

"Jessie's ankle was shattered, I'm just having a few drinks to calm down," she said, she was hoping he wouldn't mention Pepper but of course it was the next thing he mentioned.

"Fine, hang around another couple of hours and I'll have someone drive you down to the sheriff's office so you can sign the work consent form," Bonventre said. "We don't want to neglect that little piece of business. I want Pepper to get started learning the routines."

"Jackie, can't you just forget it, Pepper needs to finish high school," she said.

Bonventre just snorted and took the Scotch and soda Leon handed him, at which point Harmony noticed Dave. He had been on his way but had sort of stalled at the sight of Bonventre, he was hanging back pretending to be interested in the keno.

"Harmony, you know better than to argue with me," Bonventre said, stirring his drink with his finger. Then he licked the finger. It was one of his habits, she had seen him do it a million times.

Harmony suddenly felt pretty depressed at the thought that she didn't have anyone strong to stand up for her. There was no use pretending she herself was strong. A million people had pointed it out to her that she wasn't and they were right, she spent large amounts of time doing what someone wanted her to do, such as twenty years doing what Bonventre had wanted her to do on stage. If he wanted Pepper for the understudy he would get her probably. Besides, if Pepper *wanted* to understudy she would do it no matter what anybody said, even Gary's opinion probably wouldn't stop her, so what was the point of the argument?

Pepper and Bonventre were both sort of like bulldozers when it came to going where they wanted to go, the difference being that Bonventre sort of looked like a bulldozer whereas Pepper looked like a beautiful young girl. Pepper just happened to have a will of iron, whereas she herself had a will of Cream of Wheat, as Gary put it when he was in one of his witty moods. It was hard to be a good mother if you happened to have a child with a will of iron, maybe Jessie was lucky just to have a pet. Definitely motherhood had been more fun when Pepper was younger and would sit on her lap and let her do her hair, that was before she developed a mind of her own about clothes and hairstyles and stuff.

"Oh Jackie, why do you want her?" she said. She felt sort of a sinking and wished Dave hadn't stopped to watch keno, at least he could have sat down by her.

"I want her because she's got star quality and besides she can dance," Bonventre said. "Thirty percent empty seats last night, I hate figures like that. Every conventioneer in America has seen Monique by now, it's time she started a cooking school or something.

Well, you could get rid of Murdo, he *is* the worst ventriloquist in Las Vegas, Harmony thought but she didn't bother saying it, why make life difficult for Murdo? She finished her drink and paid Leon, there was no point in staying and getting more depressed. As she was picking up her change Bonventre tapped her on the wrist.

"Harmony, don't get stubborn," he said. "Pepper doesn't need high school and if I don't hire her somebody else will. You should be proud to have such a talented daughter."

Harmony couldn't think of any words to say, Bonventre was probably right, actually she *was* proud of it, it was just a shock to think that she and Pepper would be on the same stage.

Bonventre didn't bother to say anything else, he knew perfectly well he'd get his way and was not interested in a lengthy discussion. Harmony thought maybe he'd have something to say about Jessie, after all she'd worked for him quite a few years too, but Bonventre wasn't thinking about Jessie, he was thinking thoughts of his own and stirring his second Scotch and soda.

Dave had gotten kind of nervous from being taken off hold so quickly, he didn't have a lot to say, also he was not quite as reassuring as he had seemed when she and Cherri were at the craps table. Harmony felt hungry, it had been quite a while since her taco between shows. She asked Dave if he felt like hitting the Waffle House but he seemed to think that was kind of extravagant, he said they could have breakfast in his apartment.

Harmony was agreeable, she loved getting a look at a guy's apartment. Seeing what kind of decorations they had could be interesting, only in the case of Dave's apartment interesting was not quite the right word, horrible would have been more like it. As Dave himself explained, he got his apartment for practically no rent in return for managing the other five apartments in a little green apartment building on Charleston Avenue. He candidly admitted that cheap rent was the one good thing about it. Harmony definitely agreed it would have to be that if anything, it was at the back of the building next to a garbage collection center. There was no garbage there but the trucks that hauled it were parked right next to Dave's kitchen window and smelled about as bad as if they were garbage themselves.

Dave said he hoped the smell didn't bother her, he couldn't lower the window because he didn't have air conditioning, he didn't believe in it, his theory was that it sort of weakened you and his years in the Marines had convinced him it didn't do to get weak. One of his kitchen walls was covered with pictures of mercenaries holding machine guns of various kinds or hand grenades or something. Evidently Dave's reading consisted mostly of magazines for mercenaries because his kitchen table was covered with them.

Harmony definitely began to get the sense that she hadn't made the best choice in the world. The fact that Dave had been nice enough to show up at the craps table every night just when she had her break could have been a misleading fact. Still, he was sort of trying to be sweet and hadn't put any rush on her or anything, probably she could just be a good sport and have breakfast. Dave seemed pretty nervous—probably some bacon and eggs would make them both feel better.

But when she opened the icebox there was nothing there but beer, at which point Davd said, "I hope you like K rations." It turned out that his cabinet had no normal food in it at all, just shelf after shelf of K rations, it was sort of an amazing sight. Dave explained that because of his Marine background he had grown to like K rations and had just sort of stopped eating normal food or anything else, after all they were cheap and there was quite a variety.

Her philosophy of being a good sport was soon put to the test since to be gallant Dave opened three different kinds of K rations. For him it was a big deal, sort of like taking her to a fancy restaurant or something, usually he just restricted himself to one kind at a time. The sun was just beginning to come up, which made Harmony wish she had just gone on home and put on her sleep goggles, at least she would have been able to feed the peacocks and make Pepper breakfast. Why was she sitting around smelling garbage trucks when she could have been smelling the desert and feeding her own beautiful child and beautiful birds? Plus she had to eat at least a few bites of the K rations, variety or no variety they were not exactly what a normal person would choose for breakfast.

Dave didn't have any liquids available except beer so she drank quite a bit in order to wash down the K rations. The smell of the K rations made her a little nauseous. She thought this is a disaster I've walked into, what am I doing in this kitchen? This is something Jessie would get herself into, how come it's me this time? To make matters worse Dave began to get his feelings hurt when he noticed she was just sort of picking at the K rations, he had obviously made a special effort by opening three different kinds. He started making remarks like waste not want not, trying to make out like it was joke although it was definitely no joke, nothing about the occasion was what she would call a joke. She felt she was probably going to vomit every time she put a bite in her mouth, her only hope was to immediately wash it down with a lot of beer, but the beer didn't mix too well at all with the vodka tonics. They might not have had an effect but they were there. She got the feeling she was going to be very lucky not to get sick, although she could usually eat anything, it had just been quite a while since she had given her stomach that much of a test.

She told herself she was never going near that particular

craps table again, Gene could pine all he wanted to, it wasn't worth it. While she was wondering what she'd do on her breaks from then on Dave sprang a surprise. He had just been sitting there reproachfully, watching that she didn't somehow manage to sneak the rest of the K rations down the Disposall or something, then suddenly he forgot about the K rations and jumped at her, his hand went right between her legs before she could even drop her fork. Maybe it wasn't a total surprise, she had sort of guessed he was thinking about it, she would just have expected a little more subtlety though, an invitation to inspect the bedroom or something, although there wasn't really a bedroom, just a little living room with a turquoise rug and a daybed. It was just about the time Dave made his move that the vodka tonics plus the beer finally had an effect.

She felt sort of disconnected while the big event was happening, not that she tried to stop it, anything was better than eating K rations and anyway, after all, she had been the one who had taken him off hold. Besides, it was a short event, Dave was disappointed in himself and said he was out of practice, it had been quite a while, which made her feel a little sorry for him, so what if he liked K rations? it was just his Marine background. She held him close for a while, after all he had needed her a lot and she did like the gray streak. It was too bad he had such a horrible apartment, Pepper would have some awful things to say if she ever saw that turquoise rug. Dave seemed sort of helpless lying there beside her. She couldn't help feeling a little love, although she did plan to avoid the two-dollar craps table for a while.

Then when Dave slept she got dressed and found that besides the K rations there was no phone. She had to use a pay phone across the street at a laundromat to call Pepper and tell her she would have to cook her own breakfast, Jessie's operation would probably be taking place anytime.

126

Pepper was kind of uncommunicative but that was nothing new. "I guess you spent the night at the Waldorf-Astoria, is that right Mother?" she inquired. Harmony just let it pass, why go into it? At least Pepper promised to tell Myrtle about Jessie's accident. Myrtle and Wendell worried about Jessie constantly, maybe they would want to send some nice flowers.

IV

No SOONER had her mother hung up than the phone rang again and it was Bonventre, he said he hoped he hadn't awakened her, obviously he was making a big effort to be super-polite. Nope, I'm up, she said, and waited—she wasn't going to build his ego by giving him any chatter, chatter was her mother's department.

"The reason I'm calling is about the audition," he said. "We were wondering if you could come this afternoon at about three?"

"How long will it take?" she asked. For all she knew she could be getting married that afternoon.

"Oh, about an hour, we just want you to try out a few routines," he said.

"How about two-thirty then?" Pepper asked. "My lesson starts at three-thirty and Madonna doesn't like it if I'm late."

"Fine," Bonventre said. "And if you're late and she gives you any trouble I'll just send someone to strangle her."

That was the kind of remark he was famous for—Pepper just let it pass.

"If you like we'll send a car to get you at school," he said, he was definitely coming on like Mr. Smooth.

"It's okay, I got a car," she said. "I'll just show up. Why did you say Madonna had an ass like a prune?"

She just thought she'd hit him with that, why not? He was surprised, too—there was total silence on the line for quite a few seconds. Then he finally managed a chuckle.

"Pepper, it was just a lovers' quarrel, don't take it seriously," he said.

Bullshit, she thought, you're not Madonna's lover, but she didn't say it. He sort of chuckled again, he seemed to find her attitude pretty amusing.

"How did one like Harmony ever have one like you?" he said. "See you at two-thirty."

The stupid peacocks were pecking at the screen door, they were pissed that their momma hadn't come home to scatter them some corn. Their momma had sounded pretty drunk, in fact, no doubt she had met some criminal on the order of Denny and had popped right in bed with him, that was totally par for the course. Pepper threw a few handfuls of bird feed out in the yard, at least it would keep them from pecking a hole in the screen. She got a bowl of cereal and some orange juice and went to see if Myrtle had survived the night or if Wendell had got the Buick fixed or what.

Myrtle was already outside in her bathing suit. Once in a while when the garage sale scene had gone totally dead she got on a sunbathing kick and would sit around in her bathing suit rubbing oil on herself. It was grotesque since she was a total mass of freckles anyway. The tow truck and the Buick were there, only the Buick hadn't been disconnected from the tow truck, probably Wendell had been too tired when he got home.

Myrtle had already oiled herself good, which annoyed Maude—she didn't like the smell. Maude was the world's most spoiled goat, all right. She immediately came over and began to butt Pepper's shins a little, she was hoping for some of the cereal.

"Get away from her, you little bitch!" Myrtle said. She was hung over and not in a fantastic mood. Maude totally ignored her, she sort of acted like she was starving so Pepper let her clean out the cereal bowl once she had eaten all she wanted.

"Hey, can I use the Buick if you're going to sunbathe?" Pepper asked, why let it go to waste?

"I thought you had a Jap driver now," Myrtle said.

Actually, why go to school? Pepper was thinking, maybe she'd just wake up Woods and they'd skip it and hit the arcades, maybe it was time to reveal that she was going to be his godmother-in-law. Or they could drive out to the lake or something, it didn't seem like a day for classes.

"Where's Harmony, them peacocks have been having a fit," Myrtle said.

"I don't know, except she's drunk, she just called," Pepper said. "Jessie's stupid disc broke and she shattered her ankle. I think they're operating on it this morning,"

"Oh lord, Wendell will die," Myrtle said. "He thinks that Jessie hung the moon."

"So is he ever going to take the Buick off the tow truck or what?" Pepper asked. So far as she could see the one unusual thing about Jessie was that she was the only one in town who consistently got worse boyfriends than her mother. Of course her intentions were good. She had given Pepper a stuffed animal for every single birthday and Christmas that she could remember. Pepper had the feeling that when she was sixty-five or so she would still be getting two stuffed animals a year from Jessie. Quite a few of them had got practically eaten by Maude, who liked stuffed animals even better than Cheerios. Jessie was always checking on them on her visits and looking real distressed if they happened to have a couple of limbs chewed off or something.

"Jessie's never been strong," Myrtle said, she was more upset than she wanted to admit. The next thing she did was kick over her bottle of suntan oil, so that pretty soon a little stream of suntan oil had trickled all the way down the driveway to the road.

"She's not going to die, she just broke her ankle," Pepper pointed out. About that time Wendell came out of the door barefooted, in his pants and undershirt, and stopped and looked sort of puzzled when Myrtle told him the bad news. "My goodness," he said. That was about all he ever said, but he did go down and unhook the Buick from the tow truck. When Pepper saw that she cut back in the house and got dressed, meaning to get out of there before Myrtle thought of a garage sale she wanted to recheck, in which case she would take the car.

She wanted to call Woods but decided that might arouse suspicion, she just got the Buick and took off and intercepted him just as he got off the school bus. His parents insisted that he ride the bus because they didn't want him spoiled by money. Woods was one of the few kids around who didn't have his own car. His mother was a paranoid about car wrecks and just wouldn't allow it.

Woods was sort of proper in some ways, he wasn't wild about missing school but on the other hand he was hers to command and when she said it's hooky day, let's hit the arcades, he just got in and pretended to vomit at the sight of all the goat hair. "We ought to sell this car to a mohair company, we'd make a fortune," he said. Still, he considered himself an eccentric and sort of enjoyed riding in the car of a true eccentric like Myrtle.

He had a little dope which they proceeded to smoke and Wood said he needed food so they got him a couple of chili dogs at a place near the Circus Circus. He was in sort of gross condition, seemed to have gained maybe twenty pounds overnight, but it didn't slow him down at the arcade. Before long he had a little crowd watching, it was obvious just from the way the machine sounded that the king had come. Woods gave it his total concentration. She got a little bored and went out and sat on the fender of the car, thinking more about the audition than about Mel.

The main thing she was wondering was whether she'd have to do the top drop, usually you did at auditions according to reports. It meant a lot of creeps like Bonventre got a free look at your tits, of course they would get that anyway if she became the lead dancer. Woods finally came out looking a little annoyed, he had been on the verge of breaking his own record at Space Invaders but someone in the crowd had had an epileptic seizure, fell right over backwards according to Woods, naturally it had broken his concentration. Woods was kind of nervous, not because of the guy falling over backwards but because he was afraid someone would spot him and tell his mother. Woods sort of lived in terror of his mother, which was understandable, she definitely wasn't afraid to punish her kids. No doubt she would ban Woods from the arcades for several months if she knew he was playing hooky.

"I don't know why I take all these risks, I guess you bring out the masochist in me," Woods said. He was sort of scrunched down in the seat and was ready to go even lower if they happened to pull up beside his mother at a stoplight. Pepper liked it, it was sort of amusing to keep Woods on the edge of trouble. Buddy would never defy his parents for her or anyone else, he was a total chickenshit in that regard. All Buddy had going for him was his looks.

Woods suggested they go out to the lake, he was more comfortable in an area his mother didn't frequent, so while they were driving out she sort of told him the big secret, she was going to be his godmother-in-law. Woods had to admit that was kind of the ultimate in weird. He said Mel often came to their house for dinner, he and his parents were very old friends. It was going to be pretty strange having Pepper come to dinner as Mel's wife. Woods knew all about the lingerie though, that was how Mel knew his mother—when he had been a fashion photographer she had been a lingerie model, hosiery particularly. That was interesting, just from seeing Woods's mother around the pool it had always struck her that she had great legs.

Woods was definitely glad she was getting rid of Buddy though, he liked to describe Buddy as a local yokel. They sat around the lake for a while, smoking the last of Woods's dope, then they drove back and she dropped Woods off a block from school, he was going to try and sneak in and do his science lab, hoping no one would notice that he had just arrived.

Pepper went to the studio and got her stuff but it was a long time until the audition so she decided to hit Gary's just on the off chance that he was up. He had a weird little house not far from downtown, the walls all covered with photographs of guys he thought were fantastic-looking, plus a few of her and one or two of her mother and Jessie in their younger days. Gary was sitting on his little midget patio in just some shorts. In shorts he didn't look so great, his legs were scrawny and he had a pot belly, plus he was pretty white, he made very little effort to keep a tan.

"Pepper, that's a stunning blouse, you wear black better than anyone I know," he said. He looked dulled out from being up all night, but dulled out or not Gary always responded to a good outfit.

"So what's the deal about Jessie's ankle?" she asked.

Gary sort of smiled. His basic attitude was that life was mostly funny, only once in a while bad events started happening, when quite a few of them happened at once he called it the Crud Flood. He definitely seemed to be in his Crud Flood mode, dulled out and probably stoned, as he often was when he wasn't working.

"Well Jessie's flat on her back for a couple of weeks," he said. "Your mother was talking about letting her live at your house so Myrtle can keep her company when she gets out of the hospital."

Then they had a laugh. Pepper thought of something funny, which was what if Maude mistook Francois for a stuffed animal sometime when he was asleep and ate a couple of his legs off? In Gary's state that possibility struck him as hilarious, he laughed himself silly and went to get a beer. Then he informed her that her mother was asleep in his guest room, she had gotten very sick at her stomach because some nut she had breakfast with had fed her K rations. Pepper had only vaguely heard of them but Gary explained they were stuff soldiers had to eat during wars. Where her mother had found someone who actually ate them regularly was beyond him.

"Why do you look so keyed up?" Gary said, he picked up right away that she was a little nervous. The thing that sort of was nagging in her mind was that after all Mel had taken quite a few pictures of naked guys, Fritz and Buddy for two. It was a little strange, maybe he was slightly gay or something and if anyone would know Gary would, there was nobody gay in Las Vegas that he didn't know.

In fact Gary was so surprised when she told him there was a rich guy who proposed to her that he stopped being dulled out. Then she mentioned the audition with Bonventre and it turned out he knew about it, in fact the reason he wasn't asleep was because he was supposed to be there in case they wanted to see how she looked in a few costumes. He had kind of been feeling guilty because he hadn't told her mother about it, he was kind of in a conflict of loyalties situation, plus he wasn't sure what he thought about her working at the Stardust anyway, he had been trying to think about it but Jessie's accident had thrown him off schedule.

"Jesus, what else is going to happen today?" he said, the marriage bit took him aback. It turned out for once there was somebody in Las Vegas he didn't know. He had heard of him a few times vaguely but that was it. Mel didn't hit the discos or the Strip or the bars so Gary was no help, although so far as he knew Mel wasn't gay, he didn't know any guys who had been his lovers.

137

She told him about the modeling bit, the old underwear, and Gary got fascinated. "I'd probably be doing it myself if I had the money," he said, "I do understand the turn-on. Of course if the guy's that visual he would want to marry you, he's not gonna find better looks."

Then she told him Mel had already given her on the order of five thousand dollars, which naturally made Gary whistle, he himself seldom had a dime.

"So how come you're botherin' with Bonventre?" he wanted to know. "You're sixteen years old, Pepper, I know you're a fine dancer but you don't know everything. Maybe the guy would take you to New York. Good as Madonna is she's not as good as teachers you could get in New York."

The point was Gary thought she ought to think the Stardust move over very carefully. Obviously Bonventre wanted to get rid of Monique but that didn't mean Pepper needed the job, particularly now that Mel had entered the picture. However Gary admitted it was all getting sort of super-complicated and would take some thinking through. He frankly wasn't up to it, thanks to no sleep. "I don't suppose there's any hope you'll discuss this with your mother?" he said.

"No way," Pepper said.

"Pepper, I just wish you had a little more sympathy," he said. "It's a puzzle to me how you got so much control, people twice your age don't have your level of control."

Then he sort of sighed. "Your poor mother doesn't have six ounces of that particular commodity," he said. "That's why she ends up eating K rations for breakfast now and then, I guess."

Pepper had never noticed that her mother had even one ounce, all the more reason it was time to get away from home and not have to deal with the consequences, such as boyfriends like Denny or the one before him, an Italian named Roberto who had thought he was some kind of great cook only he never washed a dish and used so much garlic in everything that the whole kitchen had begun to smell like garlic.

Pepper got the sense that Gary was sort of intrigued by Mel, he confessed he had always been fascinated by rich people. At least he didn't bother telling her that marriage was a serious affair or she was too young or anything, he had lived in Las Vegas long enough to notice it didn't always have to be that serious. Plus he thought a guy who got turned on by making movies of her in old underwear was bound to have some interesting quirks and quirks were one of Gary's main interests. He was keeping notes on quirks he had observed during his years as a wardrobe manager and was going to type the notes up someday and maybe have them published, just quirks, like a showgirl who put bottle caps over her nipples when she was in the dressing room—things like that.

They took the Buick to the Stardust, Gary said her mother would need his car to go visit Jessie. Then he made her stop at a drugstore, he wanted to refill a pill prescription, it was going to take a pill or two to get him through another night.

While he was in waiting for the pill prescription to be filled she heard a click click. She looked and who would it be but Denny, she had had the bad luck to park about ten feet from him. He was leaning on a car shooting pictures of her, there was not much she could do except show total scorn.

"Hi, do you give blow jobs?" he said, walking over to the Buick. He was obviously proud of how crude he was.

"No, but you can probably get some in jail," she said.

"Your momma wouldn't put me in jail," he said. "I left her too many beautiful memories."

Pepper rolled the window up and ignored him, only just then Gary came out and saw him. Denny looked slightly

139

taken aback, he hadn't expected Gary to be around. Gary definitely wasn't afraid of him either, he ran right out and said "Get away from that child, we're having you arrested, you'll be lucky to get out in ten years."

Denny told him to fuck himself or something, but Gary just said let's go. They drove off and left Denny standing there pretending to be super-cool.

"Why don't we call the cops? I'll tell them he tried to get me to give him a blow job," Pepper said, but Gary vetoed the idea, unless her mother was willing to go through with a prosecution it was hopeless.

"Then it's hopeless," Pepper agreed, the more she thought about it the more furious it made her that he would walk up and say something like that to her.

They went on to the Stardust, where Bonventre was waiting with a couple of choreographers. She was expecting the top drop bit and was sort of in the mood to tell them to go suck their own dicks if it came up. After all she didn't need them, there was no doubt that Mel would give her plenty of money if she asked him. The way Bonventre and the two guys watched her just brought on more scorn. The choreographers showed her a few routines and she just did them without saying a word. Once or twice she goofed but she just did it again, most of it was simple. The audition didn't last but about twenty minutes and she was angry the whole time, the guys were sort of standing there like judges but they didn't say much, it was obvious Bonventre made the decisions. Gary was just wasting his time being there, they didn't use the costumes and they didn't ask to see her tits either, it was just a little dance audition. Bonventre was wearing his black suit and sort of smiling like he knew some great secret. Finally he said, "Pepper, I know you need to get back to school, thank you very much for coming, do you need a ride?"

That was all he said, then both the choreographers told

140

her she moved beautifully, everyone was extremely polite. She said thanks, she had stopped being quite so angry. Gary walked her out, he had decided to go back to his place and soak in a bath to see if it would wake him up a little.

"So what's the deal, did Bonventre like it?" she asked, she didn't know what to think.

Gary just grinned and held her hand for a little. It turned out he had been extremely impressed with the audition.

"Denny did you a favor, I don't think you're aware of how totally haughty you are when you're angry," he said. "Those choreographers had their minds boggled. They expected some little teen queen who would be about ready to faint with reverence and in walks Miss Hauteur, boy did you give them a surprise. Do you know you get a little red spot on each cheekbone when you're angry like that? It's better than makeup."

It was true the choreographers had been impressed, but they were peons, actually, Bonventre was the boss and he was harder to judge.

"Oh, forget it," Gary said. "The audition was just a formality. He wanted to see you on stage is all, he definitely intends to hire you."

Gary was yawning a lot, he was super-tired. "Pepper, I don't know what to think of you having all these possibilities," he said. "It seems like just the other day I went to your first birthday party." But he admitted she had seemed grown up since she was twelve, the fact that she was taller than most girls and wore clothes so well may have helped.

They made a date for Sunday, Gary loved being her adviser and said what they should do is sit down and discuss her options intelligently. He loved sort of analyzing people's options.

Pepper said fine and dropped him off. Gary was sweet but she didn't exactly feel in the mood to wait for Sunday, after all he had been analyzing her mother's options ever since she could remember and it hadn't changed a thing, her mother still just went around getting in love time after time, mainly with idiots or pricks of various kinds.

Actually she was more in the mood to take Woods's advice, which was simple, Woods just said the way to live was to do everything. Although he sort of toed the line where his mother was concerned he liked to describe himself as a total hedonist. His attitude was you should dance all the dances, take all the drugs, play all the video games, do all the sex acts, and get as much money as possible without risking criminal prosecution—he always stuck that one in, he wasn't eager to risk criminal prosecution even though his father was a lawyer.

Woods was a student of doomsday, he knew a good deal about nuclear arsenals and stuff and said the Big Poof was likely to happen any time. His view was that Idi Amin or somebody equally weird would steal a few H-bombs and start things off and then there'd be the Big Poof, so why make elaborate plans? He himself was not even keen on going to college, he was more interested in being a total hedonist until some nut got loose in the arsenals and blew up the world.

Pepper didn't know about doomsday but she definitely felt in the mood to just do it all, not the one thing Woods really wanted her to do which was sex acts with him, but basically anything else she was ready to go for, like marrying Mel and having a lot of Jap servants to wait on her and also dancing the lead at the Stardust and being a star for a while. She was thinking maybe a year or two, then if she got bored she would see about New York and the great teachers. Although from what she could see of New York on the news it looked sort of horrible, lots of clouds and junk. There were definitely some good aspects to life in Nevada.

142

She went on and had her lesson and didn't say a word about the audition. Madonna was not in a great mood, she looked like she might have a migraine or something so Pepper just didn't bother updating the news. Madonna looked sad enough as it was. It was sort of odd that she didn't have boyfriends, she was about a hundred times more beautiful than Myrtle and Myrtle had two boyfriends. Madonna just had cats, six of them in all, but no sign of a boyfriend or a girlfriend either.

When she got through Buddy was sitting on the fender of the Buick looking totally freaked out. He definitely couldn't bear the thought of losing her and apologized quite a few more times for not letting her borrow the Mustang to go to Mel's. He seemed to think that was the main reason she was giving him so much trouble, he also said he had some very good dope, he was counting on that doing the trick if the apologies didn't. It showed the level his mind operated on, obviously Mel had access to all the dope she could possibly want.

She started just to get in the Buick and drive off but Buddy actually grabbed her, he was so freaked out at the thought of losing her that he wasn't going to let her leave. It was very embarrassing, because of course Madonna was watching it from the studio window.

"Get your fuckin' hands off me, Madonna's watching!" Pepper said, which was enough to make him let go.

"Okay, but when can I see you?" he asked. He was red in the face and definitely not behaving like the cool guy he was supposed to be.

"Listen, go suck your own dick!" she said, Buddy turned out to be the one who caught the remark. She had no intention of explaining anything to him, let him read about it in the papers. She just drove off, thinking that after all Madonna wasn't dumb, she had had Buddy pegged as an idiot all along, which was probably why she hadn't dropped any compliment on his looks, unlike her mother, who practically couldn't stop talking about how great-looking Buddy was.

She expected him to come tearing past, with a few cops chasing him, but he didn't and she just drove on to Mel's house. Mel must have been watching from some vantage point because he came out in the driveway grinning at the sight of the Buick, which was probably the ugliest car that had ever been anywhere near his house. "Love your car," he said and leaned in and gave her one of the little kisses at the corner of her mouth. Then he sniffed a little and asked if she had goats for pets, so she told him about Myrtle and Maude.

Mel was in quite a good humor. She expected him to be revolted by the appearance of the Buick but Mel didn't care at all.

"Why there's no reason why the most beautiful girl in the world shouldn't drive the ugliest car," he said. "I like the beauty and the beast effect." The car had so much goat hair in it it did sort resemble a beast.

"It looks like a gorilla died in it at some point," Mel said. "What's your mood today, Pepper?"

It was kind of impressive, the way he looked at things. He pointed out that he hadn't always been a rich man, he had endured a few scuzzy cars himself along the road to riches. He said he definitely wanted to meet Myrtle at some point, she sounded like a character.

They had a swim and then Pepper told him about the whole day. He got a great kick out of the fact that she had made Woods play hooky, he thought Woods was superbright okay and was very close friends with his parents. Mel liked to listen and had smart things to say about whatever she told him. She got the impression he was quite a bit smarter than Gary, who was definitely a great listener but sort of had so many theories about things that whenever she told him something usually it would remind him of a theory. Unless they were just talking about fashion Gary could never keep his mind on whatever the subject was.

The thing with Mel might seem a little unreal when she wasn't with him but once she got back in his house and sort of told him a few things it started feeling real again and she felt she could trust him, she didn't think he was gonna spring any tricks. Also she didn't feel she had to hide anything, if she had an anxiety she could just mention it. She tried that out while they were resting from the swim. She said, "I want to know why you want to *marry* me. I'd live with you, you know."

"Nope, that's too low risk," Mel said. "I'd rather marry you and see if I can keep you. A lot more's at stake that way."

"Such as what?"

"Such as a lot of my money. Not to mention my ego. If I don't manage to keep you my ego's going to take a beating."

"Were you ever gay?" she asked, she thought now's the time to hit him with some of the big questions.

Mel laughed, he liked it. "Now I'll ask you one," he said. "What had you rather: that I'm gay or that I'd rather drag your mother out of the supermarket some morning and fuck her."

"That you're gay," she said, that was no choice, the thought of her mother getting him was revolting.

"I think we'll get along great," Mel said. "I'd much rather have you than your mother."

"You didn't say if you were gay," she reminded him, it was just as well not to forget that issue.

"I'm a voyeur," he said. "A real one. I'm very visual. I've had my gay interludes but I've never found anyone I like to photograph as much as I like to photograph you."

145

She could believe that. He asked her if she was in the mood for a little posing, she thought why not? He shot her topless in some old panties that came up to her navel, plus he had a couple of very lovely nightgowns he wanted her to try on. For the first time he stopped using the movie camera and took still photographs. He had set up some lighting equipment just for that purpose, but it wasn't a long session or boring. He was very sensitive about when she had maybe had enough. When they finished he took her into his bedroom for the first time. It was very stark, the TV was built into the wall, there was a big white bed and one glass wall with a great view of the desert and the mountains. On the other wall was a huge blow-up of a shot of her in the blue bra, taken from one of the movies. It was sort of flattering, it was the only picture or decoration in the room. She was used to pretty messy bedrooms—Buddy's looked like a battle had been fought in it, he had never closed a drawer in his life.

"Do you think it's too austere?" Mel asked, he could tell she was kind of startled.

Pepper shook her head. It wasn't depressing or anything, it was just that she had never seen a bedroom so cleaned out. She was just beginning to understand that Mel's house was the one place where you didn't have to look at anything ugly. Everything in it was well designed, it had never been a big deal to her but then she had never had an opportunity to see that much well-designed stuff. Mel's couches were certainly a far cry from the one Myrtle had, for example—Myrtle's had been a bright blue until Maude had started eating the foam rubber out of the cushions. Now it was so covered with little crumbs of foam rubber that Wendell had to brush himself off every time he sat on it.

"I like it," Pepper said. It was just a little scary, such a big room and sort of empty. She was still wearing the silly panties and one of the old nightgowns and Mel asked her if he could just get one more shot, he wanted her to sit

right in the middle of the bed. She said sure and he shot
for about a minute, getting her from several angles. Then
he slid back a wall and disappeared for a second into a giant
closet. He came out with a white fur in his arms—she
thought he must have bought her a fur coat, which would
have been weird, but the fur was like a bedspread, it was
very thin. He made her lay down and got on the bed with
her and pulled the fur over them—it was nice because she
had been a little chilly from the air conditioning. Mel lay
beside her and caressed her for a while and while that was
going on she got sleepy and dozed off, it was very comfortable under the fur. It was just a little nap, then she woke
up with the yawns, which Mel didn't mind at all.

She asked him about the Stardust again, if they were
going to marry maybe he wouldn't want her working till all
hours.

"Take the job," he said.

"Yeah, but what's the reasoning?" she asked. "Why do
you want me to?"

"Oh, maybe to see what a little stardom does to you,"
he said, he had a nice grin. "We'll find out how ambitious
you are and that'll be interesting. I don't think you're all
that ambitious but I could be wrong. Maybe you're going
to want to be world famous."

"What if I do?" she asked, she had never thought about
it much.

"Well, it will depend on how good you are," he said.
"You won't get world famous here in Vegas. You'd have to
go to New York or L.A. if you turn out to have that in
mind."

Better L.A., more sunshine she thought, but it wasn't
the major question.

"Would you come?" she asked.

"Nope," he said. "I've done my time in those places.
I'm staying here."

It was nothing she planned to worry about, she hadn't

even started work yet. Mel was caressing her again but he seemed sort of friendly, not too turned on, she kept yawning and once in a while when she yawned he would kiss her, he liked slipping into a yawn which was okay. Her basic feeling was he was a little too weird to figure out, but nice, very nice, he wasn't going to start dragging whips and chains out of the closet or anything. He did like playing tongues a little when she yawned.

"Hey, what's the schedule, are we getting married any time soon?" she asked.

"What about three or four weeks?" Mel said. "My parents can't come this month, my Dad has the spring swim meets to get through."

That was a surprise, she had just thought they'd go down on the Strip to one of the little motel chapels and do it, she hadn't been thinking about parents.

Mel noticed how surprised she was—it would have been hard to miss.

"I love it when you look startled," he said.

"Why would they need to come?" she asked, she felt a little nervous about that.

"I know we had an unusual beginning, but I want to marry you like I would any girl I fell in love with," Mel said. "I want my parents to come and my sister, and I'd like to meet your mother. Maybe we can have your mother over to dinner on Sunday sometime and Myrtle and your father too, for that matter. You've never mentioned him, I don't know if he's around."

"He lives in Reno," Pepper said, she had no memory of him at all. Meanwhile she was freaking at the thought of her mother and Myrtle having dinner at Mel's house. It had never dawned on her he would go in for scenes like that, getting a lot of parents together and stuff. She was so freaked she was ready to forget the whole idea, her mother in Mel's house would just never work. It was hard to imagine—after all they were lying on his giant bed under a fur that probably cost more than her mother made in ten years, plus Mel was giving her a little feel through some panties that were about forty years old, it was definitely all out of the ordinary, and now he just wanted to bring in the parents, including her mother. She didn't know what to make of it but she was freaking which turned out to be a big turn-on for Mel.

"God you're beautiful when you're startled," he said, he soon had the panties off and they had to kick the fur away, it got much too hot. It was a surprise that he got so passionate suddenly, it was a day for surprises. She didn't really get into it, which Mel noticed, he was perfectly aware that she didn't come but at least he didn't want to discuss it, which Buddy would always do. Buddy felt it must mean she was mentally deranged or something but Mel was very sweet, he kissed her a lot and then suggested they go in the Jacuzzi. He hugged her for a long time. Obviously he could tell she was upset about the parents but he didn't freak out like Buddy did when she was upset, he just held her and sort of waited for it to pass.

When they were in the Jacuzzi it finally did pass, maybe it wouldn't be such a big deal if his parents came and his sister. He pointed out that it couldn't be just them and the servants all the time, there were other people in the world and sometimes they would show up. Besides, he said his parents would adore her, they had no prejudice against his marrying a younger woman or anything.

"Do you think I'm smart or is it just the way I look that interests you?" she asked, she had been wondering if it was just the looks and nothing else that did it. Despite wondering she felt very safe with him, she could doze right in his arms and not worry about a thing, it was just that when she woke her mind started jumping around and she felt a lot of anxiety, mainly the anxiety of realizing she couldn't figure Mel out—he was mysterious. Everything he said sounded okay, but he was still mysterious, it wasn't like she was dealing with Buddy, whose whole personality could be understood in about ten seconds.

"Oh, you're smart," Mel said. "Why do you keep trying to figure out the key to my attraction? Why wouldn't I be attracted to you? I have been from the moment you walked in, you know. I totally ignored those good-looking guys."

That was for sure, Fritz had never forgiven her, either. She saw him at discos once in a while and he wouldn't so much as say hello, his vanity would be about a decade recovering from that one.

"You don't need to figure out why I'm attracted," Mel said. "There are a lot of elements in it. For one thing I'm not that interested in maturity."

That was odd, he seemed a lot more mature than anyone she knew.

"I like it that you have terrific looks and a good brain and almost no experience," he said. "I mean I know you've had boyfriends but it's been basically a sort of crude experience you've been offered so far. You don't even know anything about sex, although you depend totally on sex appeal and get worried if nothing happens when you think it's supposed to. Your instincts sort of operate at the speed of light, and yet they have no experience guiding them, they're just pure instincts. I find all that very exciting."

It was no thrill to be told she didn't know anything about sex, although probably it was true none of her boyfriends had been such great lovers, mainly getting high had helped with most of them.

Then he began to kiss her, she liked that, really liked to kiss him, she would sort of stop thinking for a while when he kissed her.

"You want to talk about the big point?" he asked, when they were out and wrapped up in the giant towels.

150

"What big point?"

"The big point is that you're afraid I'm going to be attracted to your mother," Mel said, he made it sound like a perfectly normal worry.

"I don't even think you want me to have her over here for dinner," he said. It didn't take a genius to notice she had reacted badly to that one, but it was good he mentioned it.

"She has horrible taste," Pepper said. "You've seen her in those outfits, why do you have to have her over here?"

"Because she's your mother," he said. "Just because she wears loud blouses doesn't mean you have to disown her."

Pepper could feel some anger coming, she really didn't like it that he was taking up for her mother, every male in the world seemed to think they had to do that.

"Yeah, but you don't have to live with her," she said. "She has horrible boyfriends, one's a criminal. He asked me today if I gave blow jobs."

Mel didn't seem surprised, he was hard to surprise.

"That's her misfortune," he said. "I guess she has bad taste in men and clothes both. But not everyone has wonderful taste like us, Pepper. My father dresses just as badly as your mother. He wears white shoes and every coat he owns has checks in it. But he's a decent man and I respect him. It's too bad you don't respect your mother."

"I don't want her to come here!" Pepper said. "I won't marry you if she comes here." She felt too angry, she was ready to blow it over that point. No doubt her mother had flirted with him at the supermarket, that made her madder, just thinking about it.

Mel smiled, he didn't seem to take the threat seriously, but he was wrong, she was ready to head out.

"I want this to be private!" she said, what he didn't know was that the duplex was like a bus station half the time, plus it was messy, her mother never really had the

151

energy to clean, she mainly sat around in the afternoon. Pepper liked it that she had a place to come to that was totally private.

"Well, privacy may be a novelty in your life right now but it will soon get old," Mel said. "I can stay here six months and never see anyone but the servants and be perfectly happy, but not everyone is that way."

"So maybe I'm that way too, what do you know?" she said.

"I doubt it," Mel said. "You're a girl who's very mad at her mother. You can't make her stop existing, you know. When you tell her you're getting married she's gonna want to meet the guy you're marrying, which is her right."

"I don't have to tell her!" Pepper said. "I don't have to tell her anything! I'll just tell her I've got a new boyfriend and I'm moving in with him."

"You certainly must have some grudges," he said, then he kissed her again. She remembered how he had shaky legs at first, she had thought he was weird, there were the Chiclets, but they weren't a bad idea, he had sweet breath. It was starting to seem like he was the only one who *wasn't* weird, he definitely had his life worked out the way he wanted it.

"Can I move in?" she asked. "I don't want to wait three weeks."

The thought of being home was kind of revolting, his house was so much more tasteful, plus he could give her a little support, which at home was hard to come by unless Myrtle just happened to be sober or it was Sunday and Gary could come out.

Still, it made her nervous to ask, Mel had his own ideas, maybe he wouldn't want it.

"You certainly can," he said, she was so relieved she would have done anything for him, she really was ready to get away from home.

He took her and showed her the room which was going to be hers. That was a surprise, she'd assumed they'd sleep together.

"Nope, you've got to be careful about intimacy," Mel said. "Too much of it can kill you right off."

Her room was a beautiful room, right next to his bedroom. At one point he had tried to be a painter and the room had been a studio. He said very matter-of-factly he had given up painting, no talent he said. There was no sign of any of his paintings, just an empty room, with another glass wall and another beautiful view.

"Now Pepper, I want you to furnish it," he said. "After all it's your room, I think it should reflect your taste." He had a lot of amazing furniture catalogues, some from Italy and L.A. and various places. He said to look at them and see what attracted her, so she took them out to the pool while he made some phone calls. There was so much furniture available that it was confusing, she sort of let it drop and just sat and watched the night come on. Mel had a little office in the pool house, she could hear him on the phone, then he came out, grinning, and said, well, the rich get richer.

She loved it that he could just talk on the phone for a while and make a lot of money. Woods's father was rich but he had to spend about twenty hours a day at his office.

Pepper was hoping maybe she could spend the night but Mel said no, I don't care how mad you are at your mother you owe her a little consideration, you tell her what's happening and then if you want to move in tomorrow that's fine.

She felt some anger again that it always had to be her mother that came up. She was ready to tell him forget it, marry my mother if you're so interested in her, for a second she was ready to flash out of there. But then if she did that would probably be that, Mel looked like he could be pretty firm if the mood suited him, why blow it? She could tell her mother and if she freaked too bad. Anyway if Jessie was going to move in for a while it would be easier if her room was empty.

Mel was interested in her ideas about the furniture, but she was impatient, it was just one room, she didn't see the point of calling Italy or anything, there was some pretty expensive stuff in Las Vegas, she said she had rather go to a store and look. He said fine, maybe he'd come with her, which was a surprise. She didn't think he ever left the house except for the occasional weird-out at the Safeway.

The one thing she still felt uncertain about was the Stardust but Mel pointed out that she had been dancing since she was five and that she might as well find out how she liked doing it on stage.

Then the servants came out with a great Japanese meal, it was just delicious. She hadn't really eaten all day and was basically starving. Mel didn't mention her mother again and she got in a better mood and took the Buick on home, only to find Myrtle in her best dress drinking vodka and walking up and down the driveway, she only walked up and down the driveway if she was really upset. It turned out she and Wendell had gone to see Jessie in the hospital and then Wendell had brought her home and gone off to the Amoco station, only he forgot something and came back and caught her on the phone with Bobby. She didn't know how much he had overheard but she was definitely freaked, she wasn't even paying any attention to Maude, who was bleating up a storm.

"I don't know why I done it, all that damn Bobby wants is to get in my pants," Myrtle said.

"So did Mother call?" Pepper asked.

"No, we seen her at the hospital, she said tell you she'd come home and fix your breakfast in the morning," Myrtle said. "The pore thing, she's exhausted, she's got dark circles under her eyes. Jessie's real low, she can't even move her foot for two weeks, I'd go crazy if that happened to me."

Crazier, Pepper thought, you're already crazy. The dress was one Myrtle had bought in Hawaii, it was only about twenty-five years out of style, but who cared, not too many visitors were likely to hit the driveway that night.

"That guy Bonventre called, he said tell you you got the job and please call him, I think they want you to start in a couple of days," Myrtle said.

Okay, that was quick, Pepper thought, but the immediate problem was how to get Myrtle calmed down, she was very hyper. Meanwhile the peacocks were screeching—nobody had fed them.

"Well, I'm glad you got hired," Myrtle said. "If Wendell moves out you may have to support me for a while, this recession has killed the garage sales business, I hear it's that way all over America, too."

Pepper said fine, but it had no effect, finally she had to take Myrtle to Wendy's. She ate herself into a stupor and went to sleep on the way home. Nobody could wake Myrtle when she konked out after a binge so Pepper went in and got a couple of blankets to cover her with and put Maude in the car to keep her company and let her sleep, it definitely wasn't the first time it had happened.

V

1.

"I'M GLAD Jesus loves me, I'm just not so sure about Monroe," Jessie said. Harmony was holding her hand and trying to get her not to cry. When she cried she got her pillow wet and the nurse was annoyed, but trying to get Jessie not to cry when she was upset was like trying to get the rain to stop raining once it started or something, all Harmony could really do was keep handing her Kleenex.

Monroe had come while Harmony was asleep at Gary's, and evidently it hadn't been such a great visit. Jessie had got upset because Monroe said Francois wouldn't eat his dog food. It was her fault, really, she had got the wrong brand. It was liver-flavored, but it was still the wrong brand and according to Jessie Francois would just go on a total hunger strike until he got the brand of his choice. She was convinced he would starve himself to death in protest, sort of like an Irish freedom fighter. Jessie had been very upset by those hunger strikers.

Apparently Monroe wasn't that crazy about Francois, didn't like Francois snarling at him every time he came in covered with grease. Anyway, he had not wanted to go get a lot more dog food, he said any dog will eat when he gets hungry but Jessie said he just didn't understand Francois, who would certainly prefer to starve rather than eat a brand of dog food he didn't approve of.

Harmony promised to go get some more dog food herself, she could run over to the Safeway between shows, which would be a long time before Francois reached the starvation point. Her promising didn't solve the problem though—the problem was Jessie was losing confidence in Monroe.

"Maybe he was just tired and grumpy, he had to work under a truck all night," Harmony pointed out. "I know he loves you Jessie. He said this very morning that he'd like to marry you."

"I know, but how can I marry him if he doesn't get along with Francois?" Jessie said. She was definitely devoted to her poodle.

Harmony had a headache, she had only got to sleep about four hours, which was less than half of what she needed, nine was her preferred number of hours. Besides, though she had gotten real sick to her stomach she still felt queasy as a result of the K rations. The breakfast had really been a severe setback. She didn't have the strength to take up for Monroe, anyway she had never thought he was much of a boyfriend. But at least he *was* a boyfriend and when Jessie didn't have one she could be difficult to get along with and would be even more so now that her career was probably over.

It was lucky that Myrtle and Wendell showed up at that point. Myrtle was wearing her Hawaiian dress and had actually made an effort to fix her hair. Wendell was wearing his green sports coat, Harmony thought they looked like a very happy couple. Myrtle immediately invited Jessie to get well and come out and help her with garage sales, although Harmony knew she was just being nice, a garage sale that only took in 75 cents a day didn't need two people to run it.

Wendell seemed nervous. The old woman who was the other patient in the room woke up and began to wheeze, she made a very unpleasant sound, which Wendell said

160

reminded him of a pump sucking air. He leaned over to whisper it to Harmony, which was a mistake because Myrtle was so jealous that anything like that made her mad at Wendell. Harmony was always forgetting how jealous she was—things that were completely innocent, such as a whisper, didn't strike Myrtle as innocent.

I guess I better get out of here before I get Wendell in worse trouble, Harmony thought. She told Jessie not to worry, she was definitely going to get Francois the right brand of dog food, maybe she could even do it before she went to work, though in fact what she did was go back to Gary's and hold ice packs under her eyes, she got puffiness and dark circles when she didn't get enough sleep.

The ice pack took care of some of the puffiness but the dark circles were definitely there. She had expected Gary to be asleep but instead of sleeping he had taken a bunch of pills and was irritable and hyper. She was really glad to get to work because she felt she and Gary were probably on the verge of a major fight. He started needling her about a belt she had bought, he said it looked like it was made of tinfoil, like it was a belt of chewing gum wrappers or something. She knew it wasn't real silver but it definitely wasn't made of tinfoil. Gary only picked on her clothes when pills or something upset his metabolism, but she wasn't at her best due to lack of sleep and they barely got to the Stardust without the major fight breaking out. There was a thing or two about him that she wouldn't mind criticizing if he wasn't going to let her alone.

They ran into Cherri in the parking lot. She was in a great mood because Bonventre had decided he wanted her sister Patti to come and try out for the show. In fact she was arriving the next day.

"Oh good, now you'll have your sister for company," Harmony said. It might be Cherri's lucky day but it definitely wasn't hers because the first person she ran into on the way to the dressing room was Bonventre. He took one look at the dark circles and frowned.

"Harmony, you look awful, will you come see me in my office before you put your makeup on?" he said.

"Jackie, it's just because of Jessie's accident, I didn't get any sleep," Harmony said, but he wasn't listening. If you had dark circles under your eyes it didn't matter to him if it was World War III that caused them, he hated dark circles.

She decided just to go on to his office, if she was going to get lectured it might as well be soon. His office was kind of a pigpen. Bonventre was too paranoid to let his secretary clean it out except once a year, he was afraid she'd stumble on information he didn't want anyone to have.

He seemed surprised to see her quite so soon, actually she had just stopped at the craps table to tell Gene not to look for her during her break, she thought it might be better to avoid Dave for a while. That perked Gene up quite a bit, his jealousy of Dave had been about to get out of hand.

"Harmony, your daughter had a beautiful audition this afternoon, I guess you heard," Bonventre said.

"No, I didn't hear," she said.

"Well, Gary was there, I assumed he told you," Bonventre said. It made her wish there had been the major fight, maybe she would have killed him, what did he mean not telling her he had been at Pepper's audition?

"Well, be that as it may the audition was beautiful, the choreographers were extremely impressed, and we would like her to start as the understudy next week if that's all right with you. Here's the form you have to sign."

He handed her a piece of paper—the form the parent had to sign if a child that was still a minor wanted to work in one of the shows. Quite a few did, she knew of instances

162

where girls who were only fourteen got their parents' consent and went right to work.

It wasn't that she was absolutely against it, it was just that she hadn't had a chance to think about it or talk it over with Pepper. Maybe it was something Ross should be consulted about, after all he was still her father even if he wasn't around. But Bonventre was standing there looking impatient, he wanted her just to sign it instantly, he hated not getting his way if it had anything to do with the show.

Harmony tried to sort of think about it quickly but she was too tired. Besides, it hurt her feelings that Gary hadn't told her about the audition, sometimes he and Pepper sort of teamed up against her. It was mostly just over clothes and she didn't take it too seriously, but now she got the feeling that everybody was teaming against her, Pepper and Gary and Bonventre and probably Myrtle— Myrtle must have known about the audition but she hadn't let out a peep. It was really the wrong time for people to team up against her, she had two shows to do and was so tired she needed all her energy just for the shows.

"Was it topless?" she asked, meaning the audition—it was something she kept thinking about.

"No, Harmony, it wasn't topless, it was just a dance audition, will you quit stalling?" Bonventre said. "Pepper's going to be wonderful. She's going to be a very big star. I wouldn't think you'd want to stand in her way."

"I don't want to. I just want to think," Harmony said. Bonventre grinned like he was about to say something about her brainpower, but he didn't. She was getting her feelings more and more hurt that nobody had told her about the audition. She felt she was about to cry, despite the fact that it was only thirty minutes till show time and would not help her face, which was not at its best anyway.

163

"Jackie, I'll give it to you at my break, I just have to discuss it with her father," she said, feeling she had to get out of the office at all costs.

"Oh fuck, Harmony, you don't even know where her father is!" Bonventre said. He was on the verge of being in a rage.

"Yes I do," she said, which was a lie. She thought Reno but it could have been Tahoe, Ross tended to go back and forth. Anyway, she could always find him because she knew his best friend, a guy named Martin who was a cashier in Reno.

"I'll give it to you at my break, I have to do my makeup now," she said. She got up and hit it out of there before Bonventre could stop her.

"Cover up those dark circles!" he yelled, as she was leaving. She happened to notice that Murdo's dressing room was empty, which was unusual, he was usually there playing low-grade blackjack with Lucy, the girl who was the magician's assistant—she and Murdo were from the same hometown, some place near Chicago. Harmony popped into his dressing room, where she would have a little privacy—she tried to choke off the tears but she couldn't, all she did was choke them off enough that it felt like she was crying through her nose. Fortunately Murdo didn't come in, he was always getting a sore throat just before his act and having to rush to the emergency clinic for a last minute spray job, maybe that explained his absence.

Harmony couldn't stop the tears, she just felt for a minute that she didn't have one single person on her side, even Gary her closest friend hadn't told her about the audition. It wasn't that she wanted to stand in Pepper's way if she wanted to be a star, it was just kind of sudden not to have a child anymore. It wasn't that long ago that Pepper had still played with her dollhouse and had been a little girl—

maybe only about five years. Pepper had got quite grown when she was twelve. It just seemed suddenly that she didn't have a child—people were making decisions and she wasn't even being told.

But despite her hurt feelings time was running out, she was usually out there waiting for the feathers to come down on the hoist by this time. About all she could do was rush into the restroom and splash water on her eyes. It wasn't going to be the best night of her career but she couldn't help it. Most of the girls were in the last stages of getting their makeup on when she finally got to the dressing room. Fortunately she was very efficient about that process and just ignored the chatter and fixed herself as best she could. Instead of being first on stage she was last, Gary was about ready to have a fit. He was looking really nervous, probably part of it was the pills.

"Harmony, don't do this to me, we're barely going to make the curtain," he said. She just held out her arms and didn't say a word, it was not time to go into the business of why he was teaming up against her. Gary could tell she was not at her friendliest though.

"Did you hear about Murdo?" he said.

"Did he get a sore throat?" Harmony asked—it was unusual for Murdo not to be in the dressing room.

"No, he got arrested for writing a hot check," Gary said. "Bonventre won't make his bail so I guess we're without a ventriloquist for the first show."

That was too bad—people loved Murdo even if Genevieve did say she could see his lips move. The check part reminded her of Denny and she had to press her lips tightly together as she was getting on her disc. She didn't want to cry again. They had put Cherri on Jessie's disc, she looked a little nervous about being up high. Harmony wanted to wave at her not to worry, but before she could the show started.

2.

GARY WAS waiting for her when the finale was over. It was not just that he wanted to take care of her costume either.

"Harmony, I'm sorry, please forgive me," he said. "I don't know why I didn't tell you about the audition. I guess I just didn't want to upset you anymore right now. I know it was a wrong decision, I just wasn't thinking too clearly. Do you want to go get something to eat?"

They drove up to the Waffle House because Gary said his body clock was all screwed up, his body clock felt like it was time for bacon and eggs. The Waffle House was full of old couples who were all dressed up and eating waffles. Probably they had decided that rather than spring for a dinner show they would just eat waffles and save a little money.

Harmony ordered a waffle herself, but when it came she was too tired to eat. Mainly she drank coffee, hoping she would somehow be able to stay awake through the second show. It was a relief that Gary had apologized, she could understand that he hadn't wanted to upset her. He told her about Denny making Pepper mad and how beautiful she looked and how all the choreographers thought she danced so well. Hearing him describe it she got over the bad feeling and just decided to go on and sign the work consent form. Why shouldn't Pepper be a star?

"Do you think Ross would care?" she asked Gary. He had known Ross quite well.

"Ross would love it," Gary assured her, probably he was right.

Then she went to the ladies room and sort of went to

sleep sitting down. Probably it was only a nap of about a minute, but what woke her up was a dream about Francois having starved to death, his corpse was lying right there on Jessie's bed.

It was a big relief to realize she was still in the ladies room and it hadn't happened yet, although maybe it had. Francois was so tiny and so annoyed if he didn't get his way, maybe he had starved to death in record time just to make them all feel horrible.

"We gotta hit the Safeway," she told Gary. They still had plenty of time before the second show so they hit it. Gary definitely wanted to be able to tell Jessie Francois was fit as a fiddle. Harmony was nervous until they got to Jessie's apartment and saw that she had just had a bad dream while sitting in the john. Francois was very much alive and not that grateful, they had to wash all the wrong brand dog food down the Disposall before he would touch a bite.

"You know my theory," Gary said. "Only people who have unhappy sex lives keep animals this small. It makes me wonder about Jessie and Monroe."

"Gary, I've told you ninety times I wasn't big on Monroe," Harmony said.

"Well, he's a kind man," Gary said.

"Okay, but that doesn't mean a sex life," she said. They sort of had a little argument about what Jessie ought to do as they drove back to the Stardust. It was wonderful that Gary had thought to apologize so they could be friends again and have a serious talk about Jessie. After all, Jessie was the one with the serious problems. Harmony didn't think the mere fact that Jessie loved Francois meant she had an unhappy sex life, but once Gary developed a theory he sort of clung to it. He seemed to think the fact that Francois was a miniature was very significant, but it was a part of the theory that Harmony couldn't follow, she was just too tired.

Just as they got to the Stardust Gary said, "Harmony, there's something else I've been concealing because I didn't want to upset you."

"Gary, I don't know why you don't just tell me things," she said. "Is it about Pepper getting married?"

"That's right, hold onto your hat," Gary said. "She's not engaged to Buddy. She's been going out with an older guy who's very rich. She says he's very nice and he's crazy about her and wants to marry her."

Harmony took that in stride. The only point that bothered her was that if it had been going on for a while then Pepper was a little too good at keeping secrets.

"How old is he?" she asked.

"I get the impression maybe forty-five or so," Gary said.

"Gary, Didier was about sixty when I fell in love with him and I was seventeen," she reminded him. "That was one of the best things that happened to me in my life, maybe Pepper will be as lucky as I was."

The second show went better than the first. The fact that Gary had apologized helped her be less tense, she sort of got a second wind and got through it all without falling asleep on stage or anything. Cherri was so excited about her sister coming that it sort of gave everyone a lift. Cherri was very bouncy when she was happy and was getting up a group to hit the discos, but Harmony had to pass, what she needed was sleep. Gary had given her his car, he was going to catch a ride home with the disco crowd. His body clock was still screwed up, he thought he might even dance a little while the pills wore off.

Before she left the dressing room she signed the work consent form. Gary had convinced her it was okay, he said how many sixteen-year-olds get a chance to dance the lead? Besides he had talked to Monique and Monique was giving serious thought to moving to Reno. She wanted to live a life that didn't involve Bonventre, which sort of ruled out the Stardust.

She took the form in and handed it to Bonventre, who was on the phone. He glanced at it and put his hand over the receiver. "Thanks, would you wait a minute?" he said, and went back to his call while Harmony leaned against the door. She felt so tired she was afraid she might go to sleep and dream another terrible dream about Francois being a starved corpse. But Bonventre didn't talk long. He asked her if she would like to sit down.

"I'm so tired I'd have to make an effort to get back up," she said. "I'd rather just lean. So when will Pepper start?"

"Next week," he said. "It's not what I want to talk to you about, though. I want to talk about you."

Harmony thought maybe he had heard about Dave and wanted to warn her or something. He didn't have to bother —one breakfast of K rations was all the warning she needed.

"What have I done now?" she asked.

"Nothing, when's your birthday?" Bonventre asked. He seemed sort of tired himself.

"Next month, the fourth," she said. It was a surprise question. What was he going to do, give her a birthday party for the first time since he'd known her?

"You'll be thirty-nine, right?" Bonventre said. "You know what I think? I think that might be the ideal time for you to retire from this profession. Quit while you're ahead."

That was a jolt, he had never mentioned quitting to her before, though it was one of his well-known habits. He was always telling girls they ought to quit, then if they didn't he fired them anyway. But he had never said one word about her quitting. Maybe the dark circles had brought it on, though he should know a little sleep was all she needed to correct that.

"Jackie, I don't know why you think I'm ahead," she said. "I have plenty of bills. I even lost my Visa, I can't afford to quit."

"This is not the only job in the world, you know," he said. "There are even some that pay better. You don't have to work at the Stardust forever just because you lost your Visa."

She didn't feel like arguing, she had never even thought of having any other kind of job. Except for the three weeks as a waitress when she had first come to Las Vegas she had been a showgirl the whole time. What did he think she was going to do, become a secretary?

"Is it just the dark circles?" she asked. "I told you I didn't get any sleep. Jessie doesn't break her ankle every day."

Bonventre sort of sighed, as if every word she said was exactly the words he didn't want to hear. At least he was not going into a rage, though. Maybe he was too tired for a rage.

"Harmony, you've got eyes," he said. "You know every girl in this show. How many of them are thirty-nine years old?"

Actually none, the next was Linda and she was just thirty-seven.

"I know, but I haven't gained," Harmony said. "I haven't even gained a pound."

Bonventre looked more tired. "You might never gain a pound," he said. "I would be the first to admit that you take excellent care of yourself. You might not gain a pound in the next twenty years but that doesn't mean you can go on being a showgirl until you're sixty."

Harmony began to get a bad feeling. Bonventre wasn't in a rage, but she was getting the bad feeling anyway. One thing she didn't want was beating around the bush.

"I just came in to give you the form," she said. "Are you firing me, Jackie?"

"Harmony, I'm firing you," he said. "As of your birthday."

170

Harmony didn't say a word, she was trying to think if there were any new shows about to start along the Strip, maybe there was still time to audition. Gary would know. Meanwhile she didn't have the energy to work up a big rage, neither did Bonventre evidently, he was almost friendly for once, now that he was firing her. Of course she had known hundreds of girls Bonventre had fired, some had screamed at him, some had cried their eyes out, some had just got their stuff and split. Anyway there was no appeal if Bonventre fired you, you were definitely fired.

"Jackie, what's the real reason?" Harmony asked. She was so tired she felt like she had taken some kind of drug, a downer of some kind. She didn't even feel like crying or screaming, she just wanted to know the real reason. One night of dark circles couldn't be it.

"We need a new lead dancer," Bonventre said. "It's going to be your daughter. I don't want to put a mother and a daughter on the same stage, it could mean some tricky publicity. You could be a grandmother soon, you know. Topless grandmothers just aren't what the public wants to see, I don't care if you haven't gained a pound."

Harmony just leaned against the door, wondering where the disco gang went, she definitely needed to see Gary.

"I thought I still looked okay," she said. Most girls got fired because their breasts began to sag too much, or they gained weight or got pregnant—not because they had a daughter who had just been hired.

Bonventre gave a little shrug and stood up. "It's comparative," he said. "Ten years ago you were the most beautiful woman in Las Vegas. Can you remember yourself?"

Not when I'm so tired, Harmony thought. Once in a while looking at her pictures she'd see a shot of herself with some celebrity, Elvis maybe, or Mr. Sinatra or Jerry Lewis, she had had her picture taken with all the greats, once in a while when she looked the pictures she would

171

think hey, that was me—but that was about it, just a moment once in a while, she wasn't one to always be thinking about the past. She had known plenty of girls who practically spent their whole life being insecure about getting old. Dressing rooms were good places to hear about those worries, but she just tuned it out, she had things going on she'd rather think about, guys maybe, or Pepper's birthday parties or heading to the lake on the weekend, there was always something coming up.

She tried to think about ten years ago, but it was sort of hard to pinpoint a year like that, they hadn't been that different from one another. Basically she couldn't remember herself, maybe she had looked a little better then, but not *that* much.

"Let's get out of here," Bonventre said. "You look like you're about to fall over. You want me to get one of the guards to drive you home?"

That was a new one, he had never shown the slightest concern. Maybe he thought she was really tired of being a showgirl—maybe it wasn't that final. She could go home and get some sleep and talk to him about it tomorrow.

"I got Gary's car, I'm not going to have a car accident," she said. "Thanks anyway."

"Well, I hope Cherri's sister really has tits identical to hers," Bonventre said, as they were walking into the casino. "If that's the case our problems are solved, we'll just put the two little sisters from Texas up on the discs."

It was like he was thinking out loud, he had just figured out who ought to go on the discs, his mind never stopped working on problems like that. The way he said it caused Harmony to feel a bad sinking. He wasn't thinking about her anymore, he was just thinking about the show, it *was* final. He didn't want her or Jessie anymore, he wanted beautiful young girls with breasts that stuck straight out. He wasn't even being mean to her, why bother? She didn't really work for him anymore. Bonventre didn't even notice when she stopped walking with him, he just went on into the keno bar to get a nightcap or two.

Meanwhile people were playing the slot machines all around her, or else keno, or watching basketball scores come in on the big board. The casino was going full speed ahead but Harmony felt she'd be lucky to make it to Gary's car she was so tired.

It just made her realize Bonventre was right. There had been plenty of years when she could have skipped a night's sleep and still hit the discos with Gary and the gang and thought nothing of it. Now she was barely making it down a row of slot machines, too tired even to get mad at Bonventre. He had just slipped her daughter in and kicked her out without a by-your-leave, she should have given him some wrath, but she didn't even feel any wrath, she just mainly wanted to get on home. That Bonventre, he was a genius of some sort, he had picked the one time to fire her when she wouldn't have stabbed him with a letter-opener or something. All she could do was yawn.

She finally made it to the car. Then she started feeling lonely. It was strange that she was too tired to feel mad but not too tired to feel lonely. It was driving away from the Stardust that brought the loneliness on, after all she loved it and didn't even mind its disadvantages, such as that the elephant had been farting more and more. Plus she had a lot of friends there, she knew half the people who worked in the casino. You got to know people when you worked in a place twelve years. Of course she could still go in and say hi, they wouldn't ban her from the casino or anything.

Then she remembered Howie. For about ten years Howie was the main security guard. He was a big guy and he took his job very seriously, he was always patrolling the casino looking for troublemakers. Howie had got to be her friend. There was never anything else between them because Howie was a happily married man, but they were really friends, his eyes sort of lit up when he saw her hit the casino. He liked to refer to her as the queen of the Stardust. If he happened to be talking to some tourists and she walked by sometimes he would show her off a little, he would say let me introduce you to the queen of the Stardust. Then his wife had died of cancer and he had begun to drink a little too much and lost his job. Howie had plenty of friends in the casino too, he was a very popular security guard, and they all told him be sure and come back and see us. Howie said he would, but he never did. Once or twice Harmony saw him on the street and he said he'd probably be dropping in at the casino in a few days, but he never did. Gary's theory was that once you've sort of been a boss it's a big blow to just suddenly be a peon.

Well, she definitely wasn't the queen of the Stardust anymore. She was going to go check the discos and find Gary and tell him the bad news, but then she felt guilty about it, after all Gary had been kind enough to loan her his car, why load him down with any more bad news when his body clock was all screwed up anyway? Gary deserved at least one night when he didn't have to be bothered with anyone's problems. She and Jessie between them had sort of overdone it with the problems in the last few days.

But she didn't want to go home, either, she had to talk to somebody, after all she had been fired. She decided it would have to be Wendell and whipped into the Amoco station even though the gas tank was still three-quarters full.

"Oh Wendell, I got fired!" she said, before he could even ask her if she wanted unleaded or what, he was not used to seeing her in Gary's car.

"My goodness," Wendell said, then while he was getting the windshield Harmony started to cry. She didn't even try not to, just sat in the front seat and cried while Wendell got the windshield.

174

"Well, I guess it's been one of them days," Wendell said. He always put on a clean uniform every night, even though he wasn't manager. It was one of the things Harmony liked about him, it showed he still had some self-respect even if there had been tragedy in his life.

She was too tired for much of a cry, it had been too long a day. Then to her surprise Wendell said it was about time for his break, could he buy her a cup of coffee?

"Sure, but Myrtle got mad because we whispered, what's she gonna think if we have coffee?" she asked.

"I heard her talking to another man, I guess I'll take my chances," Wendell said. Harmony was so shocked she forgot even to reach over and unlock the other door for him when it was time to go, he had to knock on the window. It was definitely the first she'd heard that Myrtle was talking to another man.

"She called him Bobby, I was hoping you knew what was going on," Wendell said. Gary just had a Datsun and Wendell was big, he sort of filled the car. He must have shaved before he came to work, Harmony could smell his after-shave. One thing she liked was that his sideburns were silver, she thought that was appealing. He was definitely too big for the Datsun, though—she kept bumping his leg with the gearshift when she shifted, which seemed to embarrass him a little.

They just went to the McDonald's, it was handy. As for this Bobby, Harmony didn't have a clue, she had supposed Myrtle and Wendell were a happy couple, although it was her opinion Myrtle didn't treat him very well.

Wendell was not what you'd call a big talker. He mainly held his coffee cup in his hands and stared into space. Harmony suggested maybe Bobby was just a man who ran a garage sale or something, but it didn't seem to be much consolation. Definitely Wendell had sad eyes. The hair on his wrists and arms was silver too, like his sideburns. He had a blood blister under one fingernail. When she asked about it he said a jack had slipped, really that was about the extent of the conversation.

Driving back to the Amoco Harmony wondered if maybe Wendell was sorry he had taken the risk of having coffee with her, he knew what a jealous nature Myrtle had. The more she thought about it the more she thought it might be understandable that Myrtle was talking to another man. If she wanted to talk to a man at all it would probably have to be another man. Wendell didn't say a word on the way back. Still, he was sweet though, he had probably suggested the coffee because he knew she was sad about being fired. She really wanted to hug him for the kind thought but was afraid to, she still had her makeup on and if she left traces on his clean uniform Myrtle would find them and go through the roof.

"Don't tell her I asked about Bobby," Wendell said, after he had managed to get out of the Datsun. "She don't like nobody to pry."

"I won't, thank you for the coffee," Harmony said. He looked so sad in his clean uniform that she had a longing to do something kind for him, but then a car came up behind her before she could think. She just blew Wendell a kiss and drove on home.

Once she got on her own road, bumpy as it was, she felt a little better. It was always a happy surprise to be reminded that there was a place that wasn't the Strip. Once you were on the Strip it sort of took you over, you could easily forget that there were other places and other ways to live. The night air smelled wonderful and the stars were very bright. She saw a little winking red light on an airplane flying over the mountains, it was hard to imagine why an airplane was flying around at that time of night.

When she drove into the driveway she saw that Myrtle and Maude were spending the night in the Buick. Maude woke up and bleated a time or two when Harmony parked but Myrtle was sound asleep. Pepper had covered her with some blankets.

She checked in Pepper's room and sure enough Pepper was there asleep, with her radio on. Harmony took off her shoes and tiptoed in and turned it off. Pepper rolled over in her sleep but didn't wake up.

Harmony was thinking the things people say are true, your children grow up before you know it. In another month her little girl sleeping there, with one leg dangling off the bed, would be the lead dancer at the Stardust. Maybe she would be the greatest star in the history of Las Vegas. Maybe she would go on to New York or Hollywood or Paris. Maybe the rich man who loved her would be a kind husband and always take care of her, or maybe she would get tired of dancing and just be rich and have children, making *her* a grandmother, like Bonventre said.

The one thing she knew was that Pepper had grown up and wouldn't just be her little girl anymore, although over in the corner there were still some dolls and quite a few of the stuffed animals that had been presents from Jessie, many of them mangled from times Maude got in the house.

Poor Ross, she thought, as she was taking off her makeup. He missed all those years. Harmony had a scrapbook of all Pepper's birthday parties and dance recitals. She thought it would be nice for Ross to see the pictures, if he ever came back, it would make up for his having missed Pepper at various ages.

She was so tired she didn't know if she'd even need the sleep goggles, but she put them on anyway and for once didn't think of Denny, maybe it was finally going away or maybe it was just that she was so tired.

3.

THE PEACOCKS woke her. She took off the sleep goggles and raised the shades and looked at them. They were calling, walking around the yard spreading their beautiful feathers, but the poor goats that Myrtle didn't love weren't paying any attention. Harmony decided she'd get up and feed them and feed Pepper, then she could go back to bed and sleep till it was time to visit Jessie. She put on her robe and went out. She hadn't slept long, but just being in the yard in the early morning with the peacocks was almost as good as sleep. She sat on the steps and let them eat corn out of her hand. When one got a little corn it would walk away a few steps to be proper, then after a bit would come back for a little more.

While Harmony was feeding them, her robe tucked around her, she heard the shower running. She went in and started breakfast and pretty soon Pepper came in, rubbing her hair with a towel and looking disgusted.

"Pepper, why are you making that face? it's a beautiful day," Harmony said.

"Because I got up and I didn't need to—I'm not going to school anymore," Pepper said. "I didn't remember until I'd already washed my hair."

"I don't really like you quitting school. Maybe you can take a correspondence course," Harmony said. "Your father always said a high school diploma was important."

"Well, it isn't, I've already got a job," Pepper said, and went back to get her blow-dryer. She brought it and plugged it in by the refrigerator and sat at the table drying her hair while Harmony scrambled some eggs.

In the midst of scrambling the eggs, Harmony suddenly

remembered that she was fired. It didn't seem very real. It occurred to her that maybe it had been a dream, like the one she had had about Francois being a starved corpse. Maybe she had gone to sleep leaning against Bonventre's doorway and had a dream that he had fired her. In fact the whole day after getting sick from the K rations had seemed like a dream, maybe she had been out on her feet and imagining things.

She watched Pepper while she was scrambling the eggs. Pepper was looking totally beautiful—it was not hard to believe a rich man wanted to marry her.

"Pepper, stop making that face, it's no big deal that you woke up early," Harmony said, but Pepper was blow-drying, she didn't pay any attention.

The thing was, Harmony didn't believe it had been a dream, that explanation was looking on the bright side, which was important but just not always true. Sometimes the truth lay on the other side from the bright side, which was where it lay in this case. She was really fired.

She gave Pepper her eggs and juice and sat down at the table, she wasn't going to mention the bad news and spoil Pepper's breakfast. The lucky thing was it was a very bright day, the kitchen was filled with sunlight, which always sort of gave her hope. It would have been horrible to have to know you were fired if it had been a cloudy day.

Harmony just had some coffee and kept quiet, hoping that Pepper might have something to say about the marriage or the audition or whatever was going on in her life. It made her feel like a good mother when Pepper told her things. Until she was about fourteen Pepper had told her everything, but lately she took the opposite tack and told her nothing. It was hard to feel like a good mother if everybody knew more about your daughter than you did, often she had a left-out feeling, but it did no good to gripe at Pepper about it, Pepper didn't respond to gripes.

"Pepper, do you know anything about a Bobby?" she asked, she wanted to get that point cleared up. Maybe she could reassure Wendell.

"Yeah, he's Myrtle's other boyfriend," Pepper said. "He fixes air conditioners or something."

"Oh, poor Wendell," Harmony said. "Now why would Myrtle do that? Wendell's so sweet."

"Yeah but he's boring," Pepper said. "He never talks."

Pepper was still hungry. Fortunately there was about half a pint of ice cream in the fridge, she got a spoon and went about finishing it off.

Harmony couldn't argue that Wendell was a talker, they both knew better than that.

"Pepper, I heard you had a beautiful audition," she said. There was no point in pretending she didn't know.

"It was okay," Pepper said, she was eating the ice cream. "Denny took my picture and asked if I gave blow jobs."

Harmony sort of flushed at that, it made her feel ashamed that she had had a boyfriend who would say such a horrible thing to her daughter. Although Pepper wasn't upset, she was just eating the ice cream.

Thinking about it made Harmony feel so awful that even the sunlight didn't help. She had meant to ask Pepper about the marriage but she couldn't, she was too ashamed. She went out and sat under the umbrella, not crying, just feeling ashamed and hurt, remembering stuff it didn't do any good to remember, then feeling flashes of anger, maybe she would kill him if she ran into him, not for stealing the check, just for what he said to Pepper. Then she could just go to prison, she didn't have a job anyway. She stroked the peacocks a little bit, they liked for her to sort of tickle their heads, she did that for a while and went back in to see what Pepper was doing.

Pepper was just lying on her bed listening to tapes, she didn't seem very excited that she was about to be a star.

"It's hard to get used to you not going to school," Harmony said. "What are your teachers going to think?"

"Maybe they'll think I became a hooker," Pepper said.

"I don't know why you say things like that," Harmony said. "Nobody thinks you could be a hooker. I guess I ought to tell you what happened to me."

It annoyed Pepper a little that her mother had come into her room. After all it was her room and nobody had been invited in. She couldn't enjoy the music with her mother standing there looking sad. In fact she looked terrible, she had big dark circles under her eyes, plus the lines around her mouth were showing. People wouldn't think she was such a great beauty if they had to see her in the morning, without her makeup.

"It's funny how things work out," Harmony said. "You got hired and I got fired."

That was news, Pepper hadn't been expecting that.

"No kidding?" she said. "Bonventre fired you?"

"Yep, he's a genius, he fired me last night when I was too tired even to be mad," Harmony said. At least Pepper was taking an interest in something she was saying for a change.

"So what's the reason?" Pepper asked.

"Oh well, Pepper, I'm nearly thirty-nine," she said. "Jackie told me I could work until my birthday."

Pepper scooted back a little so her mother could sit down on her bed. She wanted to hear all about it.

"So is it a law you can only work until you're thirty-nine?" she asked.

"Not a law, it's just that they like younger women," Harmony said. "There's two girls from Texas who have very good bosoms, I think he wants to put them on the discs. I'm sure that means Jessie's fired too, I just haven't told her yet."

"I thought Jessie was younger," Pepper said.

"She is but she looks the same as me," Harmony said.

"I think it's because she worries so much, it makes lines you know." But then she looked at Pepper, whose face was perfect. How would she know about lines, or even about worry?

"I didn't have to do the top drop," Pepper said. "I only danced about twenty minutes. They sure make up their minds quick."

"Jackie always does," Harmony said. "He said it wouldn't be too good to have a mother and a daughter on the same stage. I guess I can see his point."

She could, too, looking at Pepper—it was just a point she had been tuning out for quite a few years. It had only got through to her a little at the Taco Belle, when she noticed where the guys' eyes were going. All through the years she was used to looking up from a meal and if there were guys around they would usually be watching her, eating or just walking through the casino she was used to picking up the looks. Maybe it was because the looks had kept coming that she had just tuned out the age question. She wasn't prideful about it, she just assumed she was as good-looking as anybody around. Ever since Didier had fallen in love with her, over twenty years ago, she had felt that way. Besides, she had always been gifted with energy, she kept active and didn't sit around brooding about her age, like some women did.

But the bad night and the K rations and getting so sick at her stomach had taken her energy for the time being. Now that she was slowed down from her usual pace she could see what Bonventre and Gary and probably a lot of others had seen, which was that Pepper was the truly beautiful one now. Pepper was so fresh, she was like a perfect flower that had just bloomed in the desert—obviously if you put them on the same stage Pepper was going to be the one who would get the looks. Gary had said several times that Pepper's face was flawless, he loved to use that word and he was right, sitting on the bed with her hair all rough from the blow-dryer she looked wonderful.

"What will you do, Momma, go to dealer school or what?" Pepper asked.

"Pepper, you know I can't count, how would I ever get through dealer school?" Harmony said.

She hadn't given it a thought, really, after all she'd only been fired a few hours. Maybe she could go back to the Trop, just because Bonventre didn't want her didn't mean she had to absolutely quit.

"Did Gary tell you I'm getting married?" Pepper asked. She was getting the impression Gary had been a fink, but she wasn't mad, it was just as well he was the one who spread the news.

"He said you knew a guy, only he didn't know much about him," Harmony said.

Pepper didn't say anything, and she didn't either—the basic information had been exchanged and Pepper wasn't ready to supply a lot of details. Harmony felt unhappy that her life and Pepper's life wasn't a shared life anymore, the little talk on the bed was the most they had shared in maybe a year or two. She had just been pretending to herself that Pepper was still a little girl.

It made her want to go get all her scrapbooks, the ones with the pictures of all the birthday parties, she knew Pepper wouldn't want to look at them but she had a great urge to go get them anyway, not just to see the shots of the birthday parties but also some of the scrapbooks had shots of her on stage when she was younger. She wanted to see the shots Didier had taken of her when she first came to Las Vegas, when she was Pepper's age. It was like jealousy suddenly, she just wanted to see if she had ever looked as good as Pepper looked. All through the years people had told her she was the most beautiful woman in Las Vegas, it sort of pepped her up, sort of made up for the times that weren't so great in some respects, she always was the one with the best looks—only now her own daughter had slipped past her, Pepper was the one with the best looks.

Feeling jealous was horrible, that was certainly no way to be a good mother, it was upsetting that she had such an urge to get the scrapbooks, there was no way to explain it, Pepper would think she was crazy if she started dragging out scrapbooks.

In an effort to make herself stop feeling so horrible she took a shower and washed her hair. It was not very reassuring though, she had never looked her best with wet hair, when she looked in the bathroom mirror she decided it was sort of amazing Bonventre hadn't fired her sooner, luckily he never saw her with wet hair.

Then her blow-dryer wouldn't work, it started blowing cold air at her which was really annoying, who needed a blow-dryer that worked like an air conditioner? She said as much to Pepper when she went in to borrow her blow-dryer and Pepper sort of giggled and said maybe Myrtle could get Bobby to fix it.

"Oh, Myrtle shouldn't cheat on Wendell, he just adores her," Harmony said. It just made things seem more out of kilter that Myrtle had another boyfriend. Actually things couldn't be much more out of kilter, after all Jessie was hospitalized, Pepper was getting married and she was fired, life was definitely changing.

"I hope you won't do anything like that when you're married, Pepper," Harmony said. "Can't you even tell me his name, maybe I know him?"

"His name is Mel and you don't know him," Pepper said in her snippy voice, as if it would be some terrible crime if she knew her own daughter's fiancé.

But it was true, the only Mel she could think of was a doorman at Caesar's and he had died of a heart attack a few years back, it couldn't be him.

"So when's the wedding? Maybe your father would like to come," Harmony said.

"Why? he doesn't even know me," Pepper said.

"He doesn't have much confidence, I think he was afraid he'd do something wrong," Harmony said, that was her reading on Ross. Besides liking to change lives he didn't want to take a chance on making a big mistake. He would hardly even change a diaper he was so afraid he'd stick the pin in Pepper.

Harmony waited to blow-dry her hair, she was hoping Pepper might be feeling friendly and might tell her a few things about Mel, after all she hadn't expressed any hostility to the marriage plans or anything. Why wouldn't Pepper just describe the house or what he did for a living, just the normal things a mother would want to know?

But Pepper was not interested, she was just lying on her bed thinking her own thoughts and listening to tapes, so finally Harmony went to her own room and did the blow-drying. In the process she started feeling horrible again, it was beginning to sink in that she was fired. She could only do the show for two more weeks. Maybe she could get on with another show but it would just be luck probably, they would just think she was too old. But she had quite a few bills, she was going to have to get some kind of work, Denny had certainly picked the worst possible time to steal the check.

Then she remembered the scrapbooks, they were up on the top shelf in her closet, she went and got one or two while she was blow-drying and sat on the bed looking through them. She just picked at random and one of the ones was only a couple of years old. It was mostly snaps made when Roberto was her boyfriend, in just about every picture he seemed to have his hand on her leg. If Pepper was in the picture she looked sullen, unlike Roberto, who was always smiling, showing off his big white teeth. At such a late date it was hard to remember what she had seen in Roberto other than the big white teeth. Pepper had had a lot of friends then and it was embarrassing if she invited a lot of kids on a picnic and Roberto spent half his time trying to get a hand under her clothes.

The other scrapbook was earlier, it wasn't the Didier one, it was mostly pictures when she had first come to the Stardust and was definitely the lead showgirl. There was one of her getting crowned Miss Las Vegas Showgirl, Maurice Chevalier was putting on her crown, and there were a few with Dan Duryea and several with Hugh O'Brian. She thought he was one of the handsomest men she had ever seen, they took a nice picture together, he was just the right height. For a week or two she had hoped maybe they would have a romance, she would have gone for it in a second, but they didn't, Hugh O'Brian had a tight schedule.

Looking at the scrapbooks was a mistake. She had lost interest in comparing herself with Pepper, why do that? it was just a mood. But the scrapbooks reminded her of how much fun she had had. She was just about always laughing in the pictures. If she had on her sunglasses she might look a little mysterious but she was never downcast, that had not been a way she felt much.

Harmony hated it when she lost her optimism, she liked to be thinking about good things, it was just that being fired hadn't really happened to her before. Then when she was looking at the scrapbooks and wondering when there would be some more fun Pepper happened to walk by and see her, Pepper gave her a sarcastic look that was just too much, why would her own daughter give her such a cruel look?

"Oh, Pepper, I don't know why you hate me," she said, crying. "I tried to be a good mother, I gave you birthday parties every year!" It was all she could think of to say in her own defense, it wasn't that easy giving birthday parties if you were a single parent. Fortunately Jessie and Myrtle had helped, Jessie enjoyed birthday parties almost more than the kids.

"Who hates you? Just don't burn out my blow-dryer," Pepper said.

Maybe Pepper just didn't realize how depressing it was to have your own child give you sarcastic looks when you were in a low mood anyway. Harmony knew she probably didn't, after all Pepper was a teenager, not a mother. It wasn't hate, it was just that Pepper had been a loving little girl but she wasn't a loving teenager, she treated her as if she were some tacky person who had barely had the right to even be in her life. She was getting married and she hadn't said two words about the groom.

It turned out Pepper had just been going to get a Coke, she stopped in the door for a second on her way back and Harmony thought she might as well ask a question or two, it was better than just being ignored.

"Why can't I know a little bit about your fiancé?" she asked. "I know he's older but I don't care. I think it's usually good if you have an older person if you're getting married young."

"He's not like any of your men, Mother," Pepper said. "He's very intellectual and he has extremely good taste. He doesn't go around asking people if they give blow jobs, that's for sure."

Harmony just gave up, it was not a day when there was any use trying, Pepper was just going to hold it against her that she had made a big mistake falling for Denny. Giving up was about all she could do, she had definitely made the mistake, she just got up and shut her door and put the scrapbooks back in the closet, then she put on the sleep goggles and tried to sleep. If only he hadn't made that terrible remark, the truth was he was very brash. At first it had been part of his charm, but it definitely wasn't charming if he did it to your daughter. She kept clenching her fists as she was trying to sleep, thinking that if he ever said one more word to Pepper she would kill him.

4.

WHEN SHE woke up Pepper was gone. Harmony snooped a little in her dresser drawer, not disturbing the clothes. Pepper kept her clothes laid out very neatly, she just snooped a little hoping to find a picture of Mel. She was curious to know if he was grayheaded or good-looking or what, if Pepper wasn't going to tell she felt it was her prerogative to snoop a little, but it was a waste of time, there were no pictures of Mel, although stuck in one of Pepper's dance magazines was a Polaroid of Pepper and Buddy and some kids at the lake. They were all skinny-dipping, maybe that wasn't really so bad but it was still a shock to see Pepper with several naked boys. Pepper was in the water so it was hard to say if she was really totally naked but she was definitely topless.

While she was having her yogurt she decided to put in a call to Martin, Ross's friend. She didn't mention that she was fired, she just asked him to have Ross call, there were big changes going on down in Las Vegas. Then Harmony went out to discover that Myrtle had just sold the three brown goats to a man with a little tiny pickup. It was a Datsun like Gary's car, only a pickup, and the three goats just fit perfectly in the back end, the man was just driving away with them when she came out.

"Is he a goat trainer?" she asked, remembering that the goats had been going to have a career.

Myrtle had already forgotten the three goats, actually

had forgotten them long ago. She asked Harmony if she was feeling rich.

"Myrtle, are you kidding?" Harmony said. "First Denny stole the check, then I got fired last night, why would I be feeling rich?"

"Because you're about to have a rich son-in-law," Myrtle said.

"Maybe so, but I haven't met him. Have you?" she asked.

"No, but he's got a Jap chauffeur, he must be pretty stinking rich," Myrtle said. "I thought we'd go in together and put in a swimming pool if you was already feeling rich."

Harmony just got her sun hat and walked down to get the mail. There was no way she would ever be rich enough to go in on a swimming pool. The walk was mainly for nothing, the mailbox just had a couple more circulars for the tire sale. Harmony had been hoping somehow magically the insurance company would have sent a new check but that was only wishful thinking.

When she got back Myrtle was hosing down the driveway so Maude would have a cool place to lie for a little while, that was actually about as close to a swimming pool as they were going to get, in Harmony's opinion.

Still, she was feeling better. She had expected to have bad dreams but she hadn't, she'd just sort of had dull dreams about spending a lot of time in the Safeway looking for Francois' brand of liver-flavored dogfood. Monroe was in the dream for a few seconds, maybe it meant he was going to try to be a little more positive about Francois. Anyway, a good sleep always improved her mood no matter how bad her mood had been. The sun was still shining and the world hadn't ended yet, so she decided to go find Gary and see if he knew of any auditions. What she really wanted to do was turn the tables on Bonventre by getting a new job in one day. Maybe a showgirl would have just quit at one of the other shows and she would be lucky.

"So how's Wendell?" Harmony asked, she was sort of curious if there had been new developments.

"I guess he's fine, all he has to do is look at tits all day," Myrtle said.

That was hardly fair, one of Wendell's problems was that he only got three hours sleep in the late afternoon and another three in the early morning. Only getting to sleep between jobs might have been one of the reasons he didn't talk more, Harmony thought. Maybe he was just too tired.

Then Harmony heard the phone ringing and dashed in to get it, she thought it might be a producer who had heard she was fired and wanted to put her right to work. She was afraid it would stop ringing before she got there, her heart was beating fast, but she got it and it was Ross, he was so loyal he called the minute Martin told him things were going on.

"Oh, Ross, how are you? I had to run to get the phone, just let me catch my breath," Harmony said.

"You sound like you ran a mile," he said. "Where were you, down at the highway?"

One of the things she and Ross had in common was that he was from Wichita, Kansas, which was not that far from Tulsa. He had a soft voice, like the people she had known when she was growing up, it was very reassuring to her for some reason. His voice always sounded a little sad, mainly because Ross usually *was* a little sad. He was one of those men who never felt their lives were working out, though he was a perfectly good light man and could find work anywhere. Except for when he got his worst depressions he was always working—then he might quit for a while and go fishing in Idaho.

Once or twice they had discussed what they might do if they were still together when they got old and it was Ross's idea to go to Idaho and run a little motel. Harmony thought that might be boring but Ross didn't. He said there would be new people coming by every night, at least in the summer season—how could it be boring?

"Ross, I got fired," Harmony said, she made a quick decision not to say anything about the insurance check. In all the years they had been separated she had never mentioned boyfriends. After all, he was still her husband, maybe he even still had a crush on her despite leaving and not coming back. She didn't want to hurt his feelings and take the chance that he would stop sounding loyal. Besides, he had never mentioned girlfriends either, if he had them he was discreet about it.

"Uh-oh," Ross said.

"It just happened last night, you won't believe all the things that have happened just in the last two days," she said.

"Try me," Ross said, so she tried him, she told him about Jessie breaking her ankle and about Myrtle supposedly having a new boyfriend, which didn't interest him too much, after all he had never even met Wendell. But what interested him was the news about Pepper, he always took quite an interest in his little girl. Once in a while when Pepper applied herself and got a good report card Harmony would Xerox it and send Ross a copy. Once she even Xeroxed a theme Pepper had written called "My Ambition," that was the topic they had been assigned and Pepper wrote that it was her ambition to be a great ballerina. She even named several roles she hoped to dance. Ross had been glad to get the theme and had written Pepper a note saying that her old Dad wished her a lot of success.

So when Ross found out that Pepper was going to understudy for the lead at the Stardust he was quite amazed. "Is that so?" he said, several times. Then Harmony got up her nerve and told him Pepper was also planning to marry, which amazed him so that there was total silence on the line.

Harmony was nervous about having to admit she didn't know much about the groom. She was afraid Ross would think she hadn't been a good mother if she had let things go that far without checking on the groom. But Ross was too amazed to criticize, he had almost never criticized anyway except once when she had been inexperienced and had put the water on hot at a laundromat, causing his socks to run all over his shirts. That upset him enough that they had a little fight, Harmony felt the laundromat should have printed better instructions. Ross kept saying his mother would never have done it until Harmony got a little annoyed, so what if she wasn't the most experienced person in a laundromat?

Ross was calling from a pay phone. Harmony kept trying to get him just to make the operator reverse the charges so he wouldn't have to keep putting in $1.65 every three minutes, but Ross wouldn't hear of it. He pointed out that she might have trouble making ends meet unless she got another job right away. Fortunately he had lots of change and just kept putting in the $1.65.

"Pepper wants you to come to the wedding," Harmony said, she felt her heart beating fast again when she said it because it was a big gamble, there was no guarantee Pepper would want either one of them at the wedding.

It definitely made Ross nervous too, Harmony could tell he regarded it as a demand on his time. The truth was it made her nervous also, they were both silent for awhile, during which time Ross had to feed the phone $1.65. Harmony felt dishonest, the truth was she wanted him to come for her sake, not because of the wedding. She was very curious if he was any more bald, she knew she didn't have any right to make a demand but she didn't have anyone else to turn to, either. She thought she would just try and see if Ross had enough of a crush to do it.

Then Ross surprised her. He said maybe to the wedding, the thought made him pretty nervous, but to Harmony's total surprise he said, "I don't guess you'd want to try and get on with a show up here?"

"Do you think I could?" Harmony asked, it had never crossed her mind for one minute that she would ever leave Las Vegas, much less that Ross would ever want her to come to the same town he was in. She had only been to Reno once, that was when she did a little tour as Miss Las Vegas Showgirl and then Ross had been in Idaho fishing.

"I don't know, I could ask the producer, he might get you on," Ross said, sounding a little nervous. He was probably not totally sure about the suggestion but at least he had been loyal enough to make it. Harmony was touched.

"I bet you're still as beautiful as ever," Ross said, it was sweet the way he said it.

"I don't think I'm too ugly if I get my sleep," Harmony said, being modest. "If I don't get my sleep I definitely get dark circles."

There was some more silence, not $1.65 worth but some. Harmony didn't know if she was imagining things but she had an inkling maybe Ross was beginning to want to try and get back together, after all they had never got divorced. As for her she would try it in a minute—she didn't know if she should be bold and say something or not. She wished Ross would have reversed the charges so they wouldn't always have to be expecting the operator to break in.

Finally she couldn't stand it, she just wanted to say what her heart felt. "Oh, Ross," she said, "I want to see you, don't you think it's been too long?"

Ross didn't seem scared off, he said it had been too long all right. He said he would look around and see if any of the producers he knew in Reno had an opening for a showgirl. He said he would have to think about the wedding, it might be hard for him to get off. He could hardly

193

believe their little girl was getting married, he thought of her as a child. It was lucky he hadn't seen the Polaroid with the naked boys in that case, Harmony thought.

The call cheered her up a lot. When things looked blackest there was nothing better than having someone loyal who might want to get back together—at least it was something to take her mind off the fact of being fired.

Then she saw what time it was, Jessie was going to think she was a terrible friend. She freshened up in about two minutes and headed on to the hospital, wondering what Jessie would think about the news that she and Ross might be going to give it another try. On the way she stopped and bought some mums, in case Monroe or Gary hadn't thought of flowers.

It was a good thing she hurried, too. Jessie was there alone looking scared, she was trying to read a teen romance but said she couldn't concentrate on it. Monroe had had a crisis, one of his mechanics quit, then Gary had come but the pills had worn off and he was totally exhausted so Jessie took pity on him and made him go on home.

"I didn't know you had to have so many shots just for a broken limb," Jessie said, she was a coward about shots.

"It isn't a limb, it's your ankle," Harmony pointed out, although she didn't know why that would mean shots.

There was actually a wonderful flower arrangement already there, all the people in the cast had taken up a collection. Jessie was very proud of it. The card from the cast said "Get well and hurry back!" It made Harmony feel a little confused, maybe Jessie wasn't fired.

But it turned out Jessie already knew about Cherri's sister coming, plus she knew Harmony had been fired. Gary had picked up both items on the grapevine before he came to the hospital.

"Maybe Bonventre means to put you on the line when you get well," Harmony said, but Jessie was too pessimistic to believe anything like that, she was of the opinion they were two fired showgirls.

Jessie said Monroe wanted her to take an accounting course so she could keep books for the muffler shop. He had promised to try and be more patient with Francois, maybe it was time just to give up and marry him.

When Harmony mentioned that Ross had called and that he might be able to get her a job in Reno Jessie got quite excited. She thought if Ross and Harmony actually got back together it would be almost as wonderful as a teen romance, though neither of them were teens.

Then Harmony thought of the peacocks, she couldn't take them to Reno. It was a saddening thought, but then after all maybe there'd be no openings, maybe she wouldn't go, maybe Ross would decide he wasn't up to getting back together. She began to lose a little of her optimism—being in a hospital was not cheerful. She held Jessie's hand while she got a shot and then she cut over to Gary's and made coffee for him. He was in a very groggy state, too groggy to immediately focus his mind on the question of which show might need a thirty-nine-year-old showgirl.

Harmony drove them to work. Gary said he didn't feel like being responsible for his actions for a while, just getting the wardrobe ready was going to be strain enough. Then Billy, the sweet young security cop, came up and hugged her practically with tears in his eyes, he had heard she was fired, word had spread, he said they were all sure going to miss her around the casino. It upset her because it reminded her it was really true, she was really fired. It was all she could do to keep from crying again but she managed not to, she didn't want to look horrible two nights in a row.

VI

IT WAS interesting that Mel actually wanted to go shopping for the furniture. Pepper had got used to thinking of him as a creature of his house, she thought he might get a little freaked being on the outside, but that was not the case at all.

"Once in a while I enjoy an outing," he said, offering her some Chiclets. He had put on a tan suit for the occasion, he looked very trim and nice. Another appealing thing about him was that though it was a hot climate he was almost always cool. He just had his life arranged so he didn't have to be uncomfortable very much. That was in contrast to Buddy, who had a fair complexion and couldn't be out in the sun two minutes without sweating and turning red.

A saleswoman was waiting for them when they got to Neiman's, it was like she had been assigned to them. Her name was Meg and it was obvious she had been assigned to Mel at some point before, they called one another by their first names. Meg had a voice Pepper immediately didn't like, too educated, plus she was good-looking and not that old, maybe thirty. Pepper immediately wondered if Mel had arranged to have Meg wait on them. She was very well dressed, could have been in *Vogue* Pepper decided.

She took them up to a showroom and showed them a lot of expensive furniture, very modern, Meg talked like she knew every designer in the world. The stuff interested Mel more than it interested her, after all they were just talking about a couch and a bed. The couch she chose was pure white and about the size of her room at home, it cost four thousand dollars. Pepper was thinking it would freak Gary out if he knew she was buying a four-thousand-dollar couch for her room, but she just acted like so what? She didn't want Meg to think she was wildly impressed. Mel and Meg were chatting like old friends, maybe he had bought all his furniture from her, who knew? Pepper thought it was boring, she had no big interest in furniture although it was definitely nice to just spend thousands fixing up a room. She chose a bed that was also as large as her whole room at home, it cost two thousand six hundred dollars.

Then Pepper thought that's that, but Mel kept thinking of things. It was a big room, he said. Before they were through she had picked out a couple of chairs and two chrome tables and several lamps.

Mel was definitely enjoying his outing, chatting with Meg and pointing out pieces of furniture he thought Pepper might want to consider. Pepper decided she was dumb to have ever thought he might be gay—Meg was obviously a girlfriend. The sound of them talking about various designers was making her mad. Meg's voice alone was enough to make you want to vomit, although it wasn't making Mel want to vomit, he was perfectly cheerful. After all she wasn't around the house much, he could be fucking Meg right along for all she knew.

Then Mel said, "How about clothes, Pepper?" She thought fine, maybe this is where we ditch Meg, but it didn't happen, Meg came right along to the fashion boutique. That was boring but the clothes weren't. Mel didn't seem to be setting any price limits so she bought some very expensive outfits, a Valentino and a couple of Missonis, it served him right if he was fucking Meg.

"Oh, Pepper, you chose beautifully," Meg said, she was being super-polite but Pepper just ignored it, she felt almost as angry as she had when Denny asked her about the blow job. On the way out they stopped by the cosmetics and Pepper bought three hundred dollars' worth of shampoos and stuff. She was really angry but it didn't stop Meg, she hung in there until they got back to the car.

"Bye, Pepper, call me anytime you want to come down," she said. Mel gave her a kiss on the cheek before he got in and shut the door.

"Well, that was a nasty little performance," he said. "Why were you so rude to Meg?"

Pepper didn't answer. She was remembering that he had said he expected her to have boyfriends. No doubt he meant to have girlfriends too.

"You're certainly beautiful when you're sullen," he said. He just sounded friendly and offered her some more Chiclets but she hit the box and knocked them out of his hand. Mel whistled and looked amused.

"Pepper, I'm getting the impression you're jealous of Meg," Mel said.

"Sure, did you fuck her?" Pepper asked.

"Why no," Mel said. "I knew her slightly when she was trying to be a model in New York. Unfortunately she wasn't beautiful enough, or at least the camera didn't think so. The camera didn't love her. She's bright enough, and has wonderful taste. I helped her get this job."

"I want to stop at the record store," Pepper said. She didn't believe for a minute he wasn't fucking Meg.

Mel didn't seem nervous, he was acting like it was no big deal that she was ready to kill him. When they got to the record store she told him she didn't want him to come in. All she wanted to do was buy a poster of a punk group called The Ten Skunks, she didn't need millions to buy a poster, plus she was in the mood to let him wait.

"Well, I guess it's good you're not armed," Mel said, when she got back in the car. "I think if you were armed there's a good chance you'd have done me serious injury by now."

"So did you call and ask for her to wait on us?" she asked.

"Sure," Mel said. "It's her job to wait on important clients. Mostly it's a boring job but we happen to be important clients with superior taste. I thought it might be a nice change for Meg. I didn't know you were going to treat her like she had herpes."

"I hope she does," Pepper said, she didn't like it that he was so cool about her being mad.

"Did you know you get a little spot of color right over your cheekbones when you're angry?" Mel said.

"Right, every asshole I meet points that out to me," Pepper said, she was trying to remember who else had mentioned it.

Mel laughed out loud, he thought it was all funny. She hit at him for laughing but he caught the blow on his arm. There was no point hitting him in the car, there wasn't room.

Pepper decided to forget the wedding, she didn't trust him. He was so rich and such a good planner, she would never know what he was doing, plus she definitely didn't believe he hadn't fucked Meg.

"I don't believe you, she's too good-looking," she said.

"Actually, she's not great-looking, she just dresses well," Mel said. "Just because she's good-looking doesn't mean I'm attracted to her. Are you attracted to every single good-looking man you see, or are there some who are pretty good-looking but leave you cold."

"Fritz, but he's gay," she said. Anyway, it wasn't the looks, it was the way the two of them had talked, Meg and Mel—as if they had been talking over all the designers

202

for years. It bugged her, who cared about the stupid designers?

"Well, *I* care about them," Mel said, when she mentioned that factor.

"I don't, I'd rather just buy junk than listen to that voice of hers," she said.

Mel shrugged. "Be as jealous as you want," he said. "I get turned on by photographing people who photograph well. Meg didn't, or I suppose we would have got involved. When we get home I'll show you what I mean."

In a room behind his office he had a lot of big flat file drawers full of the photographs he had taken when he was doing fashion photography. There were thousands of photographs, many of them blowups. The clothes were not exactly the latest fashions—he hadn't done it in several years. But the pictures were all organized. It only took him a minute to find the photographs he had taken of Meg and Pepper had to agree that she looked terrible in the pictures.

"So where's the pictures of the good ones?" she asked. "I want to see the ones you were involved with."

Mel just grinned and showed her some of the still shots he had done of her the day before, he had already printed a few of them.

"These are the pictures of the one I'm involved with. Don't you think she photographs beautifully?" he said. There was no doubt she looked about ten times better than Meg. She was beginning to be not so mad.

"We didn't eat," she said. "I'm hungry."

"I was going to take you to the Riviera," Mel said, "but you were so mad I was afraid you might destroy the restaurant. I like the restaurant and I wasn't taking any chances."

"Get someone else the next time we go shopping," Pepper said. "I hate her voice."

"There's nothing wrong with her voice, she just happens to be from the East," he said.

She decided she wanted to go to lunch anyway, and Mel was agreeable so the Jap took them to the Riviera. The waiters treated Mel like he was President or something, it was a little disgusting.

The thing that was bothering her was that she couldn't keep calm about him whereas he could keep very calm about her. One minute she would be thinking he was great and good-looking and not tight with his money and the next minute she would be hating him because of someone like Meg or because he was just sort of amused that she was so angry. She would decide she was ready to split, forget the marriage, he was just a weirdo, and then the next she'd think how nice it was just to buy three hundred dollars' worth of shampoos and stuff in about ten seconds, plus the outfits were great and she could be wrong about the girls, maybe he wasn't interested in anyone but her.

It was just that she couldn't be sure, he was too far ahead of her in terms of knowing stuff, he wasn't like Buddy or Woods who would always back down if she got really mad. Mel just waited for her to cool off. She didn't know if she could live with that or not, she enjoyed blowing Buddy out of the water whenever she felt like it, it might be something she was going to miss.

The waiters made a big production number out of the lunch. All she ate was a trout, but Mel had something that had to be flamed at the table, plus a bottle of wine, and while that was going on who should spot them but Woods's mother. She was just leaving, with a guy Pepper had never seen.

Woods's mother was named Gail. She came over looking cheerful and said "Hi, Pepper." Mel got up and gave her a kiss. Gail seemed to think it was perfectly natural that she and Mel would be having lunch at the Riviera. She didn't bat an eyelash. The guy she was with was tall and gray-headed. Pepper caught him giving her a look or two, but she didn't say anything. She could hardly wait to drop this piece of news on Woods, no doubt Gail was fucking the grayheaded guy.

"So did you tell her about us?" Pepper asked, when they were gone.

"No, we haven't talked lately," Mel said. "Gail has perfect legs, you know. She could probably still model if she wanted to."

"So were you involved?" she asked. She was curious about how many times he had been involved.

"Yep, for about a week," Mel said. "We couldn't put up with one another. Gail needs more attention than I can supply."

"I guess she gets it from that guy," Pepper said.

"No, he's just a lawyer for an environmental group she's active in," Mel said. "You seem to think all life is romance, Pepper."

"I gotta go to my lesson," Pepper said. It was the one thing that hadn't changed completely in the last few days.

She had worn one of her new outfits to lunch—Madonna was quite surprised when she came in wearing it, it was definitely not the kind of outfit most people wore to dance lessons.

Then Madonna got on her case, she was dancing okay but everything she did Madonna made her do over about twenty times. She stood there looking critical and making her repeat things until Madonna finally got enough.

"Why do I have to do it over?" she asked. "I did it perfectly."

"Do it over!" Madonna said, she got angry if you questioned her. "You are going to be a lead dancer, you have to work much harder. Bonventre will fire you if you dance like this for him."

After the lesson she got Woods on the phone and told him about his mother not batting an eye. Woods wasn't surprised. He said his mother never allowed anyone to be more sophisticated than she was, she was actually super-sophisticated. He also said he had just bought a record by the most revolting punk group of all, The Bed-Pans, he said they were a total gross-out. Pepper wanted to hear it. Of course the Jap was waiting. She was feeling a little rebellious, Mel was a little too cool, so she told Woods to come and get her and sent the Jap on home.

She laid around Woods's bedroom for a while, smoking dope and listening to The Bed-Pans. They were the worst group in history all right, none of them could even play their instruments. Woods had every punk and New Wave record ever made, his room was totally full of records and stereo equipment, though his big campaign at the moment was to get his parents to buy him a couple of video games so he could practice at home and break his own world record.

Meanwhile the fact that she was lying around his room getting high was causing Woods to fall more and more in love with her, although he was well aware it was hopeless, he brought it up about every five minutes. Pepper felt almost rebellious enough to let him, the fact that Meg and Mel and Gail had all been so cool was definitely annoying. The thing about Woods that was kind of sweet was that there was no way he could be cool when she was around, he was too much in love. But he wasn't a maniac like Buddy and he had more interesting taste, Buddy just had records by the Beach Boys and groups like that, Buddy was way behind when it came to music.

The good thing about Woods was that she could always drive him out of his mind. She didn't even have to fuck him to accomplish it, he was totally in her power. Mel was crazy about the way she looked but he still wasn't totally in her power.

Before she could make up her mind to fuck Woods and

drive him even more out of his mind Gail showed up. She knocked on the door and looked in.

"Well, Pepper, you play the field, don't you?" she said. Woods got very nervous at that point and lost his chance of getting balled any time soon, he was too afraid of his mother.

She made him take her home—Mel had said she could spend the night at his house and she wanted to get a few things. Woods was depressed, he decided he had blown his big chance. Pepper said, "Hey, don't commit suicide or anything just because Gail showed up," but Woods went off deeply depressed, he had very low moods.

She got Mel on the phone, she was curious to see if he was mad but he wasn't, he had just been making his business calls. She said maybe he should send the Jap in about an hour and he said fine.

The place was deserted. Myrtle's TV was on but there was no sign of her or the Buick. It didn't last, though, the last person she wanted to see showed up, namely Buddy. He had figured out from the fact that the phone was busy that she was home and had rushed out to tell her he was leaving town.

"Come on," she said. "Why would you leave town?"

It turned out he had taken PCP and freaked out all night, and when he came off it a little discovered he had done the most horrible thing imaginable, which was to smash Victor's Mercedes. All he could remember was sitting in it, he couldn't even remember driving it, but the rear fender was smashed, he must have backed into something during the night.

Victor happened to be in New York and Buddy's mother was in San Francisco, so nobody knew about the accident yet. But Victor was due home any day. Buddy had been to every Mercedes dealer in town and offered them any price if they would somehow fix the car immediately, like in a few hours. He definitely didn't want Victor to come home and see that his beloved car had a smashed fender. But of course the Mercedes dealers had other problems, they couldn't just fix it in a few hours. So Buddy was going around feeling that he was definitely doomed, Victor was a maniac about the condition of his Mercedes.

"Why'd you sit in it, you asshole?" Pepper said. If he was going to freak out he could have just done it in the Cadillac as far as she was concerned. Buddy said he meant to get in the Cadillac, he was just so high he couldn't tell one from another, he didn't remember a thing. When he found out her line was busy he rushed right out, she had such a good brain she might be able to think of some way out of the predicament. He had the notion maybe he could pretend it was stolen, that some criminal had smashed the fender, he thought Victor might believe that.

Pepper blew that theory, she reminded him that Victor was totally paranoid about thefts anyway and had such a good security system that no criminal could possibly steal his Mercedes. You could barely even get orange juice out of the refrigerator at Buddy's house without setting off the security system, Victor would never believe a criminal had stolen that car.

Then of course Buddy wanted to fuck. He said the only reason he had taken the PCP was because he was going crazy because they had broken up, he decided he might as well be totally crazed if he couldn't have her anymore. But finding her alone had given him hope. He was convinced she thought he was fabulously sexy, which she sort of had at one time, but the spell was broken, she wasn't interested. He kept trying to hold hands or put his arm around her, then he sort of made a big pass, he grabbed her and she had to fight to shake loose.

"Listen, I'm engaged, you asshole!" she said. "I'm getting married, you can forget it."

208

That was news, it freaked him even more, he stomped around the house saying shit and fuck and acting like he was ready to kill himself or something. He couldn't believe she was leaving him for an older guy like Mel, he said Mel was gay anyway.

"Up yours, he is not!" Pepper said. Then she said she hoped Victor had him sent to prison for smashing the fender, he deserved to live among criminals.

Then Buddy started taking PCP again, he said he saw no reason to be in his right mind any longer, he said he was going to run away from home, anything was better than facing the maniac.

Pepper was a little scared, she didn't want to be around Buddy when he was really freaking out. Usually she could handle him but not if he was totally out of his head, he might decide to kidnap her or something. While he was in the bathroom she got on the phone and told Mel to send the Jap right out.

Mel figured out that she was scared, he asked if anything was wrong but she said no, just send the Jap, Buddy probably wouldn't have time to kidnap her. Buddy heard the last part of the call and became insanely jealous, he couldn't stand having her prefer anyone to him. He called her a cunt and said he would get even when she was least expecting it. Then he got a bottle of vodka out of the cabinet and began to drink it straight, between the drugs and the liquor he was quickly getting messed up, he could barely walk he was so bombed. He went out in the yard and sat under the umbrella, crying and drinking the vodka. He was still doing it when the Jap arrived. Pepper didn't try to pack anything, she could always come back when Buddy was gone.

Just being in the Mercedes was a relief, she was back in Mel's world and it was very soothing, it had been a little scary there for a few minutes with Buddy.

She immediately told Mel about the freak-out. Since Mel knew Victor he could appreciate the situation with the car. He was of the opinion it would be good for Buddy to get out of town anyway, he was too old to be living at home.

Then he sprang a surprise, he took her to her room and it had all the stuff in it she had picked out that day at Neiman's. Mel had just persuaded them to let him have the floor models, he didn't think she'd want to wait several weeks for the stuff to come. That was great, the three hundred dollars' worth of shampoo was already in her personal bathroom, all she had to do was stick the poster of The Ten Skunks on the wall over her bed. Mel didn't bat an eye, he said it was her room, she could do what she wanted with it.

They weren't too hungry thanks to the late lunch at the Riviera so Mel sat on her bed and watched her try on the clothes she had bought. He loved to watch her dress and undress. He said Gail had called, she was sort of curious about the situation, first she was at lunch with you, then she's in Woods's bedroom smoking dope Gail had said. Pepper decided Gail was a fink, what made it any of her business?

"Woods is in love with me," she said, she thought she'd mention it to see if it mattered.

"I'm sure he is," Mel said.

"So would you push him off a cliff?" she asked, she was curious.

"Of course not, he's a very bright boy," Mel said. "Why would I push my godchild off a cliff just because of something natural like that?"

"You said you'd push Buddy," she reminded him.

Mel laughed. Buddy would be a modest loss to humanity, he said.

She sort of wished she'd fucked Woods just to see—

maybe it would have disturbed Mel or something, there had to be *something* that disturbed him.

When she got through trying on the new clothes he brought out a few old nightgowns, then set up the lights and took some pictures of her taking off the nightgowns. He loved to get her just as she was pulling the gowns over her head—she would be naked but the gowns would be hiding her face, weird, she thought, but the minute she got tired he clicked off the lights and they lay in her new bed. She felt very comfortable with him and soon went to sleep.

When she awoke it was deep in the night and he wasn't with her, probably he had gone back to his own room. The sky outside was white with moonlight. Pepper felt a little frightened, the bed was so huge and so was the room. It was definitely strange to be living in a new place—almost every night of her life had been spent in the duplex. Except for slumber parties and camping trips she had always slept in her own room, but probably she never would again, she wouldn't have to listen to Myrtle's TV going all night, or the peacocks screeching in the morning. Plus Mel was definitely kind, it was just confusing about him not wanting too much intimacy. She felt lonely in the big bed.

Once or twice she thought it's too weird, what if he stops liking the way I photograph? It was a bad thought. Also she remembered Madonna said she was dancing sloppy, what if Bonventre fired her? She began to feel not confident, didn't like being alone in the big bed, she thought about going into Mel's room to see what was going on but she lost confidence, she wasn't sure what the rules were about going in his room. She sort of wished she'd brought a few stuffed animals, chewed or not at least they were familiar. She was beginning to feel bad, leaving home wasn't working out, she didn't like feeling so lonely. Then just when she thought it totally wasn't going to work she saw Mel in the door. It was as if he had figured out she needed him. As he got in the bed he said, "What's the matter, Pepper?" She didn't answer, she was just glad he had come. He said he had been talking to England, it was the middle of the day there and the best time to talk. He said, "It's nearly morning," but Pepper didn't care, she held him and went back to sleep.

VII

1.

ALL DURING the day that was her last day at the Stardust Harmony tried to keep her mind off the fact, but it was hard to do because everyone kept reminding her, mainly by trying to be kind about it, they all seemed to think she'd commit suicide the minute the last show was over and she got her makeup off. Since it was her birthday, too, Gary and Jessie were giving her a big birthday party afterwards, at Debbie's and Marty's—they were taking no chances.

Jessie was out of the hospital and living in Pepper's room. She could hobble around on crutches a little but not enough to be much help with the arrangements for a birthday party. Gary did most of the arrangements. He was determined to make a big deal out of it in hopes it would keep Harmony cheered up for at least a few days.

Then the day got off to the worst possible start. Jessie was trying to take a sponge bath and got her cast wet. Jessie had been very high-strung since the accident and getting the cast a little wet upset her a lot, it was strictly against her doctor's orders and she was afraid that her leg would rot off or something. She was so upset she woke Harmony before she got her sleep out.

Harmony got up and drank some coffee but Jessie had made the coffee and she made terrible coffee, Harmony just poured it all out and made some of her own. It was so good by comparison that she drank four or five cups, although she knew that was too much caffeine to be taking into her system, but at least it got her awake.

"Jessie, your leg's not going to rot just because you got the cast a little wet," she said. It seemed to her Jessie was becoming a worse hypochondriac every day.

Then Myrtle made matters worse, she came wandering in with Maude to drink a little coffee, since nothing was happening in the driveway. Myrtle thought Jessie was a crybaby, she liked to tease her so she promptly told Jessie she'd get gangrene at least. It was just a joke but Jessie didn't know how to take Myrtle, even after all these years she still believed every bad thing Myrtle could think of to say.

Harmony's nerves were on edge, she lost her temper and told Myrtle to go home and take her goat if all she could do was make Jessie worse. Actually Harmony had been put out with Myrtle anyway, because of the terrible way she had been terrorizing Wendell. Lately she bawled him out so often that the poor man was afraid to breathe. Harmony sort of got the sense that maybe Bobby had proved undependable or had got a new girlfriend and Myrtle was taking it all out on Wendell. She had watched about enough of it and was getting ready to lower the boom on Myrtle anyway. Somebody had to take up for Wendell, he just wouldn't take up for himself.

When Harmony lost her temper Myrtle got upset, she said it was just a joke, anybody would know you didn't get gangrene from a sponge bath.

"Calm down, calm down," Jessie said, she hated to be the cause of a fight.

"Let me tell you something else, Myrtle," Harmony said. "Wendell's too good for you. I don't know why he doesn't leave you high and dry and get a girlfriend who appreciates him."

"Yeah, don't think I don't know you want him yourself,"

216

Myrtle said. She slammed out in a fury and went back to the driveway to get drunk, only she didn't push the screen door shut and Francois ran out in the yard.

"Oh, get him," Jessie said. The peacocks happened to hate Francois and tried to peck him every time he got in the yard. Francois immediately realized his danger and began to run around the yard at top speed, yipping as if he was about to be eaten. The peacocks tried to head him off but Francois was too fast for them. Jessie was afraid one of them would somehow paralyze him with one peck or something so finally Harmony had to put on her sandals and go catch him. Then when she came back in she noticed Myrtle had forgotten Maude and Maude was standing in the kitchen nonchalantly eating the bottom out of one of the kitchen chairs, with Jessie sitting two feet away engrossed in being a hypochondriac.

It was not much of a way to start her last day at the Stardust, but that's how it started. She pitched Francois in on Jessie's bed, then she shoved Maude out the door and went outside again to feed the peacocks. Since Pepper had left they were about her only source of comfort. It was soothing to sit and tickle their heads, or watch them spread their beautiful feathers. Otherwise everything felt crazy. She was basically living with two madwomen and her own daughter had suddenly grown up and slipped away.

Every afternoon Pepper was rehearsing at the Stardust. Harmony had watched part of one rehearsal from the wings, she didn't think Pepper would want her intruding. Gary could hardly talk about anything but Pepper. In less than a month Monique was moving to Tahoe and Pepper would be the lead dancer. It seemed Pepper's life was going great. She looked totally beautiful and hadn't even been particularly catty the last few times Harmony had managed to talk to her. So far as she could tell Mel was working out fine. Just last week when she was wondering if she'd ever get to meet him, he called in the afternoon and said he was Pepper's fiancé, he hoped she didn't mind. They had had to postpone the wedding because Mel's father had had a mild heart attack, it might be a month or two before he felt well enough to travel.

Harmony said "Oh sure, whatever you and Pepper want," and Mel said, "Well, one thing I want is to meet you, after all I'm going to be your son-in-law."

Harmony couldn't get used to the idea of having a son-in-law, but she said fine, when do we meet?

He said how about tomorrow afternoon, which was fine. She dressed very carefully, she remembered that Pepper had commented on his taste so she took pains and Mel sent a chauffeur over with a car. From the first moment she liked Mel, he had a friendly smile and made eye contact, he wasn't just being polite in having her over, he actually wanted to get to know her a little. The house was a little intimidating it was so clean and spacious, but Mel took her out by the pool and gave her a drink. The pool was Olympic. Mel explained that was because his father was a swim coach—he was no Olympic swimmer himself.

"Harmony, I wish Pepper wasn't so jealous of you," Mel said. "However, she is and I don't think there's too much either of us can do about it. I think she'll just have to outgrow it."

It was sort of startling, it had never quite occurred to her that that was the explanation of why Pepper was always so catty, but maybe that was it.

"Why would she be jealous of me, I'm her mother?" she asked. Mel was so friendly, she felt she could just be frank.

"Probably because all these years she's been hearing you were the most beautiful woman in Las Vegas—now she's a beautiful woman herself and she wants to be the most beautiful. She feels she's been overlooked in favor of you."

Mel sort of seemed to feel sorry that he had had to be

the one to point that out. He seemed to think jealousy of her explained a great many of Pepper's attitudes—maybe it did, but with her last day at the Stardust starting off so badly Harmony had a hard time understanding what there was to be jealous of. After all, she was fired, and not one single show had expressed an interest in hiring her. She went to the Trop and the Dunes and the MGM before she got discouraged. Everyone was extremely polite, they hadn't wanted to hurt her feelings, but even so it was obvious she had no chance of getting hired.

So unless Ross came up with something in Reno it was definitely her last day as a showgirl. And as far as beauty went there was probably not a person left who thought she was the most beautiful woman in Las Vegas, and if Jessie and Myrtle didn't start behaving better she was going to look even worse than she did. Practically every day since Jessie moved in she lost her temper, Jessie was hard to live with. At the last minute she had backed out of marrying Monroe, she was just too afraid Monroe didn't mean it about being nice to Francois.

That was no tragedy, Jessie couldn't count either and probably would have made a mess of the bills and stuff at the muffler shop if she had actually tried to keep the books. It just meant that Jessie wasn't going back to her apartment, she couldn't face it, she was probably just going to live in Pepper's room for a few years. After all she was Harmony's oldest friend and there was no sense in the room going to waste. Anyway Jessie couldn't afford the rent on her apartment now that she was fired.

The more Harmony thought about it the more it seemed she was the one who ought to be jealous, not Pepper. After all, Pepper was going to be dancing the lead, plus she had a fiancé who was kind, not to mention rich and smart, with a beautiful house and an Olympic-sized pool. She herself didn't even have a boyfriend at the moment, or even a

219

prospect of one, unless Ross decided he wanted to get back together and Harmony was doubtful of that, he hadn't called.

In the mornings, when she went to bed, she always longed for a boyfriend, just someone to hold her, but there was no one showing that much interest except Gene, and she wasn't letting herself encourage Gene, he was definitely too young. Also it might be true that Wendell cared for her, he still gave her special attention when she hit the Amoco station, but she couldn't do anything as bad as stealing Myrtle's boyfriend, she wasn't that treacherous, all she meant to do was make Myrtle behave a little better.

That reminded her that she had hurt Myrtle's feelings, she got up to go apologize. It was a little sad that Pepper wasn't home anymore, Harmony missed cooking breakfast for her. Even if it was just ten minutes and Pepper was catty there was something nice about it, she got to see her daughter. It felt odd to get home from work and have Jessie be there instead of Pepper. Of course Pepper was full of herself and a little spoiled, probably just from being talented from such an early age, anyway Harmony missed her at breakfast, it had always been the time they had together, all those years.

Myrtle was sitting in the lawn chair wiping away tears. She acted tough as nails but if you lost your temper at her she turned out not to be so tough. Harmony felt a little ashamed, it was just that her nerves had been on edge.

"Myrtle, I'm sorry, I just lost my temper," Harmony said.

"No, you was right, I treat that man like dog shit," Myrtle said.

Harmony had even more regrets, once Myrtle got down on herself getting her back up was a long process, but she was too tired to start the process. She sat on the fender of the Buick for a minute, enjoying the sunlight. Myrtle had stopped crying and was watching an "I Love Lucy" rerun, some days she did nothing but watch reruns.

"So what about Ross, he's about your only hope," Myrtle said. She had been worrying a good deal about the economic situation.

"Well, he hasn't called," Harmony said.

"Why wait? Call him," Myrtle said.

She had been meaning to, it was just that she hoped Ross would call first, she didn't want to put pressure on him.

"You just want to get rid of me so I won't steal Wendell," Harmony said. She gave Myrtle a hug so Myrtle would know she hadn't meant it.

Jessie was at the kitchen table polishing her nails, she devoted more time to them than anything. While she was recuperating she also spent a lot of her time reading want ads, trying to decide if she could do any of the jobs that were available.

"What about computers?" Jessie said. "There's a lot of computer jobs. Do you think I could run one?"

"Maybe a little one," Harmony said, she knew very little about them really.

Then she called Martin to ask him to have Ross call and Martin sounded a little grumpy, maybe he had just got up.

"You *can* call him yourself, he has a phone now," Martin said. That was a surprise, Ross had always just used the pay phones in the casino.

"Hey, Ross has a phone now," she told Jessie and then she called it and got the shock of her life, a woman answered. Harmony just hung up, she thought she dialed wrong. Then she tried again and the same woman answered, she sounded quite young.

"Is Ross there?" she asked, feeling nervous.

"Yeah, but he hasn't got up yet, may I ask who's calling?" the woman said.

221

Harmony just hung up, she didn't want to say who was calling. Then it occurred to her she should have said something, hanging up might get Ross in trouble if he was living with the woman. But it was too late, she definitely wasn't going to call again.

Jessie could tell she was shocked. "What's the matter?" she asked.

"I got a woman," Harmony said.

She was feeling there goes my last chance, it was a big shock, it had just never occurred to her that Ross might be living with a woman.

"Oh my goodness, that would be bigamy," Jessie said, she was one of the few people who knew that Harmony had never got the divorce.

"Not if he's just living with her," Harmony said, but she really didn't want to discuss it, it was too big a shock. She decided it would be better if she got out of the house to sort of think things over. Neither Myrtle nor Jessie were the most helpful people in the world when a shock occurred. She got her sun hat and walked down to the mailbox although it was an hour too early for the mail.

Of course it was her fault—there was no reason to think Ross wouldn't have somebody, after all she had had quite a few people over the years. It was just the way he had said she must be as beautiful as ever in such a sweet way, it had given her the notion that maybe he wanted to get back together. In her mind she had just never thought of him with someone, it wasn't that she wanted him to be lonely or anything.

There was no mail yet of course. She thought of walking down to Gino's and having a Coke but it was half a mile and the day was hot so she just went back and told Myrtle.

"Well, forget Reno," Myrtle said. "Where was it you was from?"

"Tulsa," Harmony said.

222

"Might be a good place to settle down," Myrtle commented.

"Myrtle, will you quit trying to get rid of me, it's my birthday," Harmony said. "I didn't mean it about Wendell, you know that."

"It ain't you I'm worrit about, it's Jessie," Myrtle said.

"Oh, my goodness," Harmony said, that was a farfetched thought in her opinion.

"Well, she's always been insecure and Wendell's got a big heart," Myrtle said, she was definitely paranoid where Wendell was concerned.

"Forget it, Jessie's not the least bit interested," Harmony said—the second she said it she wished she had thought of another way to put it, Myrtle immediately took it wrong.

"Why not, does she think she's too good for him?" Myrtle asked. It was one of those days when it was just about impossible to get along with Myrtle. Harmony turned her back on the problem and went in just as Jessie was hanging up the phone.

"Oh no," Jessie said. "It's Ross, he wanted to explain."

Harmony grabbed the phone but it was too late, Ross had already hung up.

"Jessie, what did he say?" she asked, it was a great relief to know there was an explanation.

"I don't know, he didn't explain, he just said he wanted to," Jessie said. "I think I'm getting a migraine from all this tension."

"Well, I can't stop breathing just because you get migraines," Harmony said. "Did he say call him back or what?"

"No, he said he'd call you. He called from a pay phone, hoping to catch you."

Harmony felt horrible, if only she hadn't gone for the stupid walk she'd know what the deal was about the woman. There could be any number of explanations, maybe Ross had a younger sister she didn't know about.

But then she sat by the phone for three hours, hoping Ross would call back and explain, and the phone never rang. Jessie was in the bedroom with a cold rag on her forehead, nursing her migraine.

Finally she decided this is no way to spend my birthday, she borrowed the Buick and headed for Debbie's and Marty's, thinking Gary might be there. "If Ross calls again just make him explain," she told Jessie and Jessie promised. She had had two dates with Ross herself before Harmony had been introduced to him, she always liked to hear how Ross was doing.

2.

GARY WAS at Debbie's and Marty's all right. He had decided her party had to have balloons so he had bought quite a few balloons and rented a little pump to blow them up with. His problem was he was a little shaky. Harmony suspected he was hitting the pills again, he had recently fallen in love with a young cop and it was driving him to pills. The young cop was very good-looking but didn't have a very good awareness, also he was not the least bit in love with Gary, it was another unrequited passion.

The fact that Gary had the shakes made it difficult for him to tie off the balloons, so Harmony offered to do it, after all it was her party. She had a couple of vodka tonics while she was doing it—it was her last night, if she got drunk and fell off her disc, so be it.

Giorgio fixed her the vodka tonics himself. He stood behind the bar and smiled at her constantly, maybe the time had finally come when he was going to get up his nerve. Blowing up the balloons had a peculiar effect, it reminded her of Didier, who loved balloons and magic acts and acrobats and ventriloquists. Didier liked to think of himself as a man of the circus, one of his big disappointments was that he could never get the Trop to let him have horses on stage, he also loved equestriennes. In all her years in Las Vegas she had never met a man who knew as much as Didier—he knew about everything, wine and flowers, music and dance, he talked to her of the world in a way no one else ever had. In a lot of ways her first love had been her best, which didn't fit in with an optimistic view of things. It made her wonder if Pepper was repeating —she had read an article somewhere that said children sometimes repeated their parents' lives. Now Pepper had a wonderful smart man who was kind like Didier and who knew the world. It was great that Pepper had Mel, so far he seemed like the perfect son-in-law, but even so the thought of things repeating made her sad. She kept thinking about things repeating and thought how sad it would be if Mel died, like Didier, and Pepper had to drop to someone like Dave, not that Dave was so terrible just because he liked K rations, he hadn't been that terrible but still he wasn't on the level of Didier. Of course when she knew Didier she had been young, just starting out, her breasts had been perfect and she had the best legs in Las Vegas—probably it was just easier to be happy when you had youth going for you, which Pepper had.

Gary noticed her looking sad, he said "You don't look much like a birthday girl."

"It's my birthday, only I'm not a girl, that's the problem," Harmony said.

"Come on, look on the bright side," Gary said. "It's one of your most wonderful skills, after all."

"What is?" Harmony asked, she was still thinking about Didier.

"The ability to see the bright side," Gary said. "I love that about you, it takes courage, you know."

I guess, Harmony thought, she didn't know, she was just hoping Pepper wouldn't repeat and have her best love first, not unless it could last for a lot of years.

"Does it surprise you that Ross has someone living with him?" she asked Gary.

Gary shrugged. It hadn't been the question she wanted to ask, anyway.

"Do you think it's possible he'd want me back, it's been fourteen years. Don't lie," she said, she wanted a frank opinion.

"If he doesn't he's a dope," Gary said.

3.

IT WAS between shows that she finally got the explanation of the woman answering the phone. She had been about to go down to the bar and have a drink or two, the last show was coming up, and then Bonventre came out of his office and said she had a phone call. He even let her use the office to take the call, which was a first, usually if a call came she had to call back from one of the pay phones in the casino.

"Hi, Ross, I'm sorry I missed you," she said, trying to sound friendly, after all it might have been a younger sister and even if it wasn't it wasn't all that much of her business.

Since she sounded so friendly Ross instantly poured out his heart, which was quite a surprise. Even when they were living together he had never poured out his heart to such an extent. The woman who answered the phone hadn't been his sister, of course it was a girl he was living with, her name was Linda, she was only twenty years old and the tricky part was that she was pregnant, she was going to have a baby in about four months.

"Oh Ross," Harmony said. "You should have told me about this sooner, I guess I'm going to have to give you a divorce, after all these years."

"No, that's not what I want," Ross said. The real news he had to pour out of his heart was that he still loved her and wanted her to move to Reno so they could maybe get back together.

"But what about Linda, she's pregnant!" Harmony said, she couldn't believe Ross was the kind of man who wouldn't care about a helpless baby.

Ross assured her she didn't understand. Of course he cared about Linda and the baby, the thing was Linda was a lot younger and had different attitudes, she had friends who had a commune and she was going to take the baby to the commune to raise it. She didn't want to marry him or anything, she just wanted a baby, she was very motherly. He said she would let him come to the commune anytime and see the child.

He made it sound like Linda and the child wouldn't be any problem at all, Linda had different attitudes, if Harmony wanted to move to Reno that would be fine with her.

Then Ross sprang another surprise, he thought he might even be able to get her a job.

"In a show?" Harmony said. It was a wonderful thought, it meant the show she was about to do wouldn't be her last show after all. She got all her hopes back in about a tenth of a second, so fast it made Ross a little nervous. He wasn't sure about a show, the producers were hard to pin down, but if it didn't happen to work out with a show she could definitely get a job at the casino where he worked.

"Doing what?" Harmony asked, thinking Ross might have forgotten she couldn't count.

"You could be a hospitality hostess," Ross said. Then

he explained that a lot of junkets came to Reno and the casino needed someone with poise who could greet the junketeers when they arrived and give them a little tour of the casino, just sort of be their hostess while they were there.

"As beautiful as you are, you'd be the best hospitality hostess in Reno," Ross said, he was very excited about the idea.

Harmony wasn't totally negative, it was just that she would much rather get in a show, which Ross said was quite likely. As soon as the producers saw her they would probably want her on stage.

Then Bonventre came back in and began to look annoyed, he hadn't meant she could keep his office for the whole break. About all Harmony could do was tell Ross it was definitely a possibility that she'd come. She was touched that he wanted her, although she couldn't say so with Bonventre standing there frowning.

"Hey, did you get my card?" Ross asked. "Happy birthday."

He had been saving that for last and it gave her an even bigger boost, although she had forgotten to look in the mailbox when she left, no doubt the card was there, Ross was very loyal when it came to birthdays.

"Jackie, don't you know a show I could get in, I don't wanta quit," she said, when she hung up. She realized how true it was, too—she loved it out there with the feathers and the music. It had been her life since she was seventeen.

Bonventre looked annoyed, he acted like he had important business to do in the office, he knew how to make you feel you were taking up his time.

"Harmony, quit!" he said. "My god, you've stood out there with feathers on for thousands of nights. Find something else to do with your evenings."

"Well, I don't want to!" Harmony said, but she was wasting her time, even if he knew of fifty shows that needed showgirls he probably wouldn't tell her.

She still had an hour to kill. Ross had been at a pay phone, as usual, and hadn't had to put in too much change, despite all the explanations. It was a little bit funny that he stuck to the pay phones even though he had a phone at home, maybe Linda didn't have such different attitudes after all.

4.

IN THE keno bar she was just having a vodka tonic and wishing she could work up to a flirt with Leon, a flirt with practically anybody would have been a welcome change, after all it was her birthday. But Leon was in a depression and was trying to work out of it by polishing glasses, seeing the glasses all perfectly polished was the one thing that cheered him up.

There was always the two-dollar craps table. The thought had at least crossed her mind that Dave could probably be broken of the K rations habit, the fact that he was a little out of practice was nothing to hold against him. But she didn't get up and wheel over to the craps table, it was just a thought that passed through once in a while.

While she was sitting wondering if Gary was off buying her a cake or what a short man in a cowboy hat walked up to the bar. He had white hair coming out from under the hat, plus a string tie with a turquoise clasp and very elaborate cowboy boots.

"Pardon me, are you Harmony?" he asked, he sort of had a gruff voice. She decided to be polite—maybe he had just seen the show.

"Hi," she said. The man looked like he was probably from Arizona.

"I'm Dub," he said. "Dub Dooley. Is it true you got laid off?"

That was unexpected, but then everyone in the casino knew she was fired, it was no big secret. Still, Dub didn't look that nice, he wore a big diamond ring and she had never liked diamonds on men. Dub just wasn't very likable, why would he mention that she was fired when she was just sitting there trying to relax?

"Hey, didn't mean to be rude," he said. "The thing is, I run a show. I just can't figure why Jackie Bonventre would let a sexy hunk of woman like you go. I thought maybe you might wanta come and be in my show—here's my card."

Dub was wearing a Levi's suit. He reached in his pocket and took out a little lizardskin case full of credit cards. He seemed to have a few dozen credit cards, but the card he handed her had nothing to do with credit, it read DUB'S TOTAL NUDE, HOUSTON TEXAS.

"I got postcards too," he said, handing her one. It showed a big honky-tonk with a giant nude woman painted on the wall. The door that let you in was right between the woman's legs, and there was a big sign out front saying DUB'S TOTAL NUDE.

"Oh, are you from Texas?" Harmony said. She didn't want the card, it was horrible that the door was right between the woman's legs.

"Houston," Dub said. "I can tell you one thing, we don't put it out to pasture near as quick down in Big H as they do out here in Vegas."

Harmony decided he was a scuzzball, he looked like one and his manners weren't that nice.

"I seen the show two nights," he said, "and you're the best-built woman on the fuckin' stage. I don't care what the calendar says, I'm offering you a job right now."

230

"I'm sorry, I don't do nude," Harmony said. "It's nice of you to ask."

She was just trying to be decent, she had never been one of those women who could just say things like fuck you, though she had heard a lot of that kind of talk over the years. Denny said it even if she just asked him to wash out the lavatory after he shaved, fuck you was practically his favorite expression. But even if Dub was a total scuzzbag she couldn't just say stick it up your ass or something, after all he was offering her a job.

Dub acted as if he hadn't even heard her say no thanks, he was still holding up the postcard with the giant nude on it. The nipples seemed to be neon but the rest of the nude was just painted on the wall.

"Well, I know you're a high-class lady, but we all got to live," Dub said. She could see he was just a horrible version of Bonventre, even Bonventre wouldn't have asked her to do total nude.

"How does two thousand a week sound?" Dub said, grinning. He had three gold teeth right in front.

"I don't do total nude," Harmony repeated.

"You drive a hard bargain," Dub said. "I'll make it two thousand plus expenses. There's some real nice apartments across from the club, you could have one of those."

"No thank you," Harmony said. Dub was sitting a little too close. Of course Leon was right there, but he had his back to them, polishing glasses, so depressed he probably wasn't even eavesdropping.

"Why not?" Dub asked. He was grinning but it wasn't a nice grin.

"Because I don't do total nude," Harmony said, wondering why he didn't listen, she had said it three times in plain English.

Dub shrugged. "You oughta try it," he said. "It ain't much different from these tits-and-feathers shows, it's just a G-string of difference and total pays a lot more money."

"Well, I've got a job in Reno, my husband lives there," she said. She put some money on the bar for Leon and got up to go but Dub said "Wait a minute" and scribbled a phone number on the postcard and insisted that she take it. He said it was his private line, she might change her mind.

"We got a real friendly club and you wouldn't have to do very long sets," he said. "It's just a matter of showing the customers what they really wanta see."

Harmony didn't say another word. The thought of walking around in front of customers without her G-string was an awful thought. The more she thought about it the more horrible it felt that someone would ask her to do that. Just because she did topless didn't mean she'd ever do bottomless, after all topless was beautiful, as Gary had pointed out, but bottomless was just bottomless, there was nothing so beautiful about it. The thought of being out on stage that way was very upsetting, it made her want to cry, but it was nearly show time, she had to control it. She just went into the restroom and tore Dub's postcard into several pieces, that was one phone number she definitely didn't need.

5.

THE BIRTHDAY party was a big success, practically everybody from the show came, all the showgirls and most of the dancers, plus Murdo, who was out on bail finally. There were balloons everywhere, and a cake with thirty-nine candles, she blew them all out but two on the first blow, and when they sang Happy Birthday it nearly raised the roof of Debbie's and Marty's. Jessie was there on crutches and Myrtle was all dolled up, even Wendell came

232

over a few minutes on his break, and to her surprise Pepper showed up, she was already friends with several of the dancers. The party was Gary's triumph. Despite being shaky and in the midst of unrequited love he had done a fabulous job. It was strange though, the only person in the whole place who looked sad was Gary, she kept catching glimpses of him looking at her and he seemed sad, he kept saying, "Darling, are you all right?" He seemed to think she was in danger of going off the deep end from the fact that she was through at the Stardust.

"I'm fine," she said, and she danced quite a lot. She would have liked a private moment with Gary to tell him about the horrible man who asked her to do total nude, but there was no way to get a private moment, the place was absolutely packed.

Inside, she wasn't quite as fine as she pretended to be for Gary's sake. It was sort of a complicated birthday, getting off to the bad start and then finding out that Ross was living with Linda, then doing the last two shows, which had gone fine. When she stopped dancing she felt mixed up, from the complications. Any other night she could have had a long talk with Gary and he could have made her feel better, with his understanding, but he couldn't do it amid hundreds of people.

She began to drink quite a few vodka tonics, she wanted to feel gay. She had always been a person who had a reputation as the life of the party, but this time the gay feeling wouldn't quite come. After a few drinks she kept noticing Giorgio still smiling. She decided I'm gonna make him like me, this has gone on long enough, I'll just make him like me.

So she proceeded to make Giorgio dance with her, he didn't dance quite as well as he smiled, didn't have a whole lot of rhythm but that was a small failing and the fact that she had encouraged him to dance definitely did have the result of making him like her. It looked like all he had been waiting on was a little encouragement. During the last few hours of the party Giorgio practically never got an inch away from her—he even began to act a little jealous when other people asked her to dance.

Gary looked a little disturbed. Once when Giorgio had to go to the bathroom he looked at her askance.

"What'd I do now?" she asked.

"You shouldn't have switched him on," Gary said. "I mean he's a nice guy basically but I don't think you should have thrown the switch."

It was just more pessimism, Harmony decided. At the slightest sign of a boyfriend everybody she knew immediately began to discourage her. It was a little annoying, after all it was her birthday, why couldn't she be optimistic about Giorgio? At least for an hour or two, it might make the gay feeling come back.

The party wound down about sunup. By that time Harmony had had quite a few too many vodka tonics and wasn't too clear about anything except that a lot of people hugged her and quite a few cried, they were all sort of sorry she was fired. Not as sorry as I am, she thought. Giorgio became nervous, Gary was kind of right about a switch, she had definitely hit his jealousy switch. A few dances wouldn't normally make a man that jealous, but it did Giorgio, he was glad when the party ended and he could take her home.

He stopped and wanted to kiss her in the hall of the apartment building before they even got to his apartment. Riding over Harmony had sort of felt a lift, she was pretty drunk but it was still a lift that she had finally got Giorgio to like her, plus the sun was up and the day looked beautiful.

I guess I'm starting another year, she thought, riding home with Giorgio seemed a good way to start it. He was

234

wearing a beautiful silk shirt and was actually quite good-looking. But pouncing on her in the hall wasn't a great success, just as he did it two little girls came out of an apartment all dressed up nicely to go to school and it embarrassed them—as soon as Harmony noticed them it embarrassed her too.

She made Giorgio quit but still it embarrassed her and broke the mood. He had been trying to unbutton her blouse, she wished he could have waited, she kept remembering how shocked the little girls looked and it affected her mood. Didn't affect Giorgio, though—he had the blouse unbuttoned the minute they got in the door. Harmony wanted to get things in a slightly slower gear, she was a little woozy and slower would have been better, but Giorgio couldn't slow down, apparently he had really been wanting her all those years when he stood behind the bar smiling. He had the urge to make up for lost time so they didn't even make it to the bedroom, they just made it to the couch, though just for starters. By the time they got to the bedroom Giorgio was ready to make up for more lost time. The fact that she was so sleepy she couldn't keep her eyes open didn't matter to him.

Well, I sure made him like me she thought while he was making up for the lost time.

6.

HARMONY DECIDED she and Wendell had the most in common, if only because he suffered as much from Myrtle's jealousy as she did from Giorgio's. All of her men had been capable of jealousy, even Ross, though Ross wasn't capable of much, but she had never seen a man as jealous as Giorgio. In no time at all she knew why Gary had been of the opinion that she shouldn't have thrown the switch. The bad part was that he was even jealous of Gary, though he knew perfectly well Gary was gay. But gayness didn't matter, Giorgio was even a little jealous of Jessie, didn't like it that Jessie was living in her house. He had known showgirls who were girlfriends, he said. Harmony couldn't argue, she just pointed out that Jessie definitely wasn't her girlfriend, in that sense.

Basically Giorgio didn't want her breathing in the vicinity of another human being. He wanted total possession. When she was younger she might have taken it as a sign of real love and been glad but this time she just took it as a sign of real jealousy and in no time she lost her optimism. The main problem was that for her love hadn't really hit. The truth of the matter was that it had been her last night at the Stardust and a lot of vodka tonics had hit. After about a week she admitted love wasn't likely to hit, either, despite the fact that Giorgio was good-looking and a nice dresser, she just didn't love him.

That made the jealousy hard to handle, because of course she had had to stop going to work and didn't have a whole lot to do. Giorgio wanted her to sit around the bar all day so he could be sure she wasn't breathing in the vicinity of another human being, but a couple of days at the bar were enough. When it became the time of day when she would normally have gone to work she couldn't of course and got depressed. She was beginning to hit the vodka tonics a little too hard, she would have daydreams of being in the dressing room putting on her makeup, things like that. If she sat around the bar she daydreamed and got drunk, and she had never been big on drinking, but if she tried to go over to Gary's for a little understanding Giorgio threw a fit. And if she went home to feed the peacocks and see how Jessie and Myrtle were doing he threw another fit. He was even jealous of the peacocks.

236

The main thing was that she needed the understanding talk, she needed Myrtle and Jessie and Gary, particularly Gary, she didn't want to make do with vodka tonics. She just had to face the fact that Giorgio wasn't going to work out. Since love hadn't hit and the sex wasn't exactly the best she'd ever had it wasn't that terrible a thing to face. Terrible was the fit Giorgio would throw when she told him.

One morning Giorgio had to leave early to go see his beer distributor and as soon as he left Harmony just packed the few things she had with her and called a cab and went home. It was a little discouraging. Giorgio had only lasted six days and she didn't have another prospect in sight, except maybe Ross. Besides, there would be the fit to get through when Giorgio found out she was calling it off.

Moneywise she was down to two hundred and fifty dollars, and she hadn't heard from Pepper in a week. Pepper was just leading a life that didn't include her, things changed so completely when they changed. Although so far as the duplex went practically nothing had changed except that Myrtle had bought another lawn chair so Jessie could keep her company in the shade of the garage.

When the cab dropped her off there they were. Jessie had just done her nails and was watching them dry, and Myrtle was stirring her drink with one finger and trying to write an ad for a going-out-of-business sale. Holding garage sales had begun to depress her and she was hoping to get rid of the rest of her stock of secondhand clothes and imitation pearls.

They watched her get out of the cab as if it was the big event of the day, which might be the case. Apparently Monroe had gotten discouraged and wasn't really trying anymore and Wendell worked all day, not a lot happened around the duplex.

"Hi, I'm back," Harmony said.

"Why, was he unfaithful?" Jessie asked. She had a thing about men being unfaithful.

"Sure, give 'em time, they'll all cheat," Myrtle said.

"I can't talk about it, I'll cry," Harmony said, which wasn't true, she felt pretty good. She just didn't feel like explaining that not only did Giorgio not cheat he even neglected his business in order to continue making up for lost time. Earlier on in life it might have made her love him, but this time it didn't, she just mainly wanted to get along home and sit under the umbrella with her peacocks.

So that was what she did, not only that day but for the next week, spent a lot of time under the umbrella, drinking a few rum Cokes and feeding the peacocks. When it got real hot in the middle of the day she would put on her bikini and go back to the umbrella, it was very peaceful with just the peacocks.

Jessie and Myrtle had become fast friends. They sat in the cool of the garage most of the day, talking about men, how unfaithful they were and dishonest and not too sensitive and hard to understand. They had enough complaints to get them through the day. Harmony didn't take much part, she didn't care to hear complaints and had none to make particularly, men weren't perfect but neither were women, much as she loved Myrtle and Jessie it was obvious they were a long way from perfect.

The big scene with Giorgio never happened. It was such a blow to his vanity when she just moved out that he dropped the jealousy issue and all other issues too, he chose to pretend it never happened. Harmony took the Buick and went to the bar once to show him there were no hard feelings, they could still be friends, after all it had only lasted six days. But Giorgio acted like she was someone he had maybe only been introduced to casually once or twice, he wouldn't look at her and definitely didn't rush over to refill the peanut bowl. It was pretty plain he would rather she found another bar to drink in, she had to give up on still being friends.

"Well, I told you it was a mistake to switch him on," Gary said. He came out often before going to work, to see how she and Jessie were doing.

"I didn't mean to but it was my birthday," Harmony said. "How's Pepper doing?"

"Fine," Gary said. "She knows the routines. Monique could leave now, as far as that goes."

It seemed peculiar, Pepper was at the Stardust every day and she wasn't. It had all happened so quickly she couldn't even figure out what she felt about it, except definitely it didn't feel so good not going to work. She had always kept herself in shape and already she was beginning to feel not in such good shape.

Gary was worried, he didn't like her just sitting around with the peacocks.

"You gotta look for a job, Harmony," he said. "Two hundred dollars isn't going to last forever."

"I know, besides I owe Madonna," she said. "I always like to pay for Pepper's lessons first."

"You don't owe Madonna, Mel paid her," Gary said. "He knows you're out of work. It wasn't that much money. It's like small change to someone who's rich."

She knew Gary was right, she ought to be job hunting. But Jessie read the want ads out loud constantly and none of the jobs available seemed like things either one of them could do. She had only been a showgirl and a waitress, maybe she could get a job as a waitress but she kept putting it off, hoping a girl would drop out of one of the shows and a producer would call. Everybody in town knew she was fired, if a girl dropped out surely they would call her.

7.

So FOR a week she mainly sat under the umbrella, not so much thinking bad thoughts or good thoughts either, just sort of sitting, watching the days get hot, and then cool again, as the evening came. When the sun sank the sky got very clear—she loved the evenings. Sometimes just before sundown she would stand by the fence and look across the desert to the Strip, the lights were beautiful above the desert shadows. It was not a hurt exactly, to be watching the lights from across the desert, it was peaceful even, just different from being over there where the life was, putting on her makeup and getting ready for the show.

It was not easy to believe it was over, it had been her life since she was seventeen and she had taken care of herself. She wasn't in really bad shape yet, maybe she had just gained a pound or two since being laid off. Looking over at the Strip in the evenings she just felt like it was a vacation, a little time to be with the peacocks. She would probably be back on the Strip any day, as soon as a producer who knew her had a girl drop out.

Only the problem was the money, it was running out fast. Even if all she did was go down to a bar and have a few drinks or maybe take Myrtle and Jessie to Wendy's for dinner it used up money. There wasn't enough to pay the phone bill, for one thing—any day the phone was going to be cut off.

"You should have took your real estate license," Myrtle said. "You could be as rich as that guy Pepper's marrying if you knew how to sell real estate."

It was not a helpful complaint. It was true that a lot of girls went to the university and took real estate courses but

Harmony had just never had any urge to, real estate hadn't interested her that much.

Then just when she thought she was going to have to call a guy she knew named Big Ben who owned a couple of restaurants, she practically knew he'd give her a job but she kept putting it off, a sort of miracle happened, which was that Ross called.

Harmony had about given up on Ross. Her guess was that he was wrong about Linda's attitudes, probably Linda wanted to keep him to herself while she was pregnant at least. She didn't think it was realistic to count on Ross to come through with anything, after all it was fourteen years, he probably didn't really want to try getting back together.

Then one morning she was sitting at the kitchen table drying her hair with Jessie's blow-dryer when the phone rang. She started not to answer, probably it was the Visa people, they were pretty persistent, not that you could blame them, but then she thought who knows, so she answered and it was Ross. He wasn't calling from a pay phone, either, he was calling from his own apartment.

"Oh Ross, how are you?" she asked, he didn't sound too great.

"I've been missing you a lot," Ross said. That was surprising, Ross almost never came on that strong, even when they were first married he hadn't. She had had to do most of the coming on.

"Is Linda there?" she asked, that was the crucial question, and it turned out she wasn't. Linda had decided it was time to go to the commune and get settled in with her friends. One of her friends was a midwife and she planned to have the baby right there in the commune so it would feel at home right from the start.

Ross seemed to feel like talking, so Harmony let him, after all the phone might disconnected any day. It turned out Linda hadn't exactly been the best girlfriend in the world, she had a violent temper and a couple of days before had hit Ross in the face with a mop and had broken one of his front teeth. One reason he was missing her so much was because he had just been to the dentist to get the tooth fixed. Ross didn't like pain any better than Jessie did, he definitely needed someone around to take care of him when things like that happened.

"How could she break your tooth with a mop?" Harmony asked, that was hard to imagine but it turned out that the handle of the mop had actually hit the tooth. The reason for the fight was that Ross had gone to a party with a girl who was a friend of Linda's and Linda hadn't liked it.

Then Ross said, "So how you doing?" and Harmony had to admit she was hardly doing at all, no job and no guys either. She just decided to be frank about that, it might give Ross a little encouragement.

"Well, I got a big empty apartment," Ross said, plus he said he could definitely get her the job as hospitality hostess if she came right away, they had hired a girl who hadn't worked out, she had only worked a week and then ran off with one of the junketeers. So the job was open. And of course it might lead to a job in a show—he had shown the producer some of her pictures and he had sounded impressed.

"Oh Ross, I was younger in those pictures," Harmony said. "He might not be impressed if he saw me now."

"I would, though," Ross said. "I bet you're still as beautiful as ever." He had used the line before but the sweet way he said it made it a good line. Ross definitely sounded a little down, it was pretty obvious he could use someone to take care of him, so Harmony thought well, why not? What do I have better to do? Before the conversation was over she agreed to go to Reno, she said maybe in two days, she had a few loose ends to tie up, if she didn't get him she would leave a message with Martin, probably she would come on the bus.

242

Then she went out to the garage to tell Myrtle and Jessie the good news—she practically had a job in Reno—but both of them were such pessimists they didn't even consider it good news.

"How do you know he'll be faithful?" Jessie asked, she was sort of obsessed with that issue. Harmony never had been obsessed with it, after all humans were humans, if there was some kindness in the relationship a little slip now and then could be overlooked, and actually in most cases she had been the one prone to the little slips.

Myrtle didn't care about faithfulness unless Wendell was the male in question, she was more interested in who paid for what. She said if Ross was serious he ought to have offered to buy the bus ticket.

"If I was gonna ride all the way to Reno just to let somebody get in my pants they could at least buy the bus ticket," Myrtle said. She was not a very sentimental person most of the time.

Harmony had not even been thinking of Ross in that way, she had mainly been thinking of taking care of him a little. Jessie and Myrtle were getting to be less and less help. It was almost just as well she was leaving, maybe they would miss her when she was gone.

But then she hit it to town and got Gary just as he was waking up and he thought it was a great idea. He said a change of locale might do her all the good in the world. But then he went to shower and when he came out of the shower he was crying, Harmony didn't know whether it was because of his unrequited love or what.

"No, it's you," Gary said. "You're one of the most wonderful people I've ever known, I don't know what I'll do without you.

"You're just always so cheerful," he said. "You're not a depressive, like everybody else around here."

It was sweet that he thought that of her. For a moment she wished Gary wasn't gay, something might have happened, but what happened was that they went for a long walk and held hands. Harmony was thinking that their friendship could never be hurt. At that point she didn't feel too sad to be leaving Las Vegas. She and Gary talked about what might happen. Gary said, "Well, maybe Ross is grown up now and will make you a perfect husband. Or if not maybe some wonderful guy will show up with one of the junkets and you'll marry him and live happily ever after."

Harmony didn't know about that, but she didn't feel sad. Maybe they would need two hospitality hostesses and Jessie could come to Reno too. When she got home she asked Jessie if she'd ever consider such a job and Jessie got a little excited too, she was definitely ready to consider it. Jessie's only worry was that Francois wouldn't like it in Reno, the winters were supposed to be a lot colder there.

Then Myrtle became disturbed, she hadn't counted on everybody suddenly moving out of the duplex, after all Harmony had shared it with her for fifteen years. Once Myrtle got disturbed she tended to get very disturbed, she began to walk up and down the driveway drinking—finally Harmony had to take her to Wendy's to get her to stop and even that didn't work, she hardly touched her food. It made Harmony realize it was a little complicated, just suddenly moving away.

"I depend on you like a daughter," Myrtle said, which reminded Harmony her own daughter was getting married. Ross said she had to hurry if she wanted the job, which meant she would probably miss the wedding. It was a very upsetting thought, it worried her all night. The next day she called Mel's house, hoping to get Pepper, but got Mel instead.

"Thank you for paying Madonna," she said. "I didn't mean for you to do that."

Mel just said forget it, so she asked about Pepper.

"Oh, she went off with Woods, I think they went to an arcade," Mel said, he sounded quite friendly.

It was a surprise about Woods, Harmony had supposed that was over although she had never been quite sure if it was a romance or what. Mel was quick to realize she was puzzled—he just laughed.

"Pepper's still a child, you have to remember," he said. "She has to go play with her friends once in a while."

Then she told him she was going to take the bus to Reno, probably the next day, she had a prospect of a job, and before she could go any further Mel said, "Harmony, you don't have to take the bus, I'll be glad to buy you a plane ticket. Why suffer?"

Harmony said no thank you, being in the air was suffering as far as she was concerned, if God happened to be mad at you being in the air was sort of giving him a good chance to show it. She said she had just called to find out about the wedding.

Mel said it could be another month, his father was recovering very slowly, but they would certainly fly her down for it. Or if she couldn't stand flying, he would send a car, he wouldn't think of letting her miss the wedding.

Harmony thought it was wonderful that Pepper had found such a considerate man. She didn't have much more to say so she thanked him and hung up. Then she decided she'd just go on and leave the next day, why wait?

8.

THE PEACOCKS were the sad part. When she went out in the early morning to feed them she realized she was leaving them too. Somehow that hadn't gotten into her mind. Of course Myrtle and Jessie were staying, but they didn't love the peacocks. Jessie hardly ever looked at them. The only thing to do was call Joy, the friend she had got them from in the first place. Joy had been the lead dancer at the Dunes and had married an architect who was quite successful. They had a big house on the edge of town and a lovely yard with trees in it. It was kind of a peacock farm, actually—Joy bred them.

Joy said sure, she'd be glad to take them back, and she wouldn't sell them or anything, she'd just keep them until Harmony saw how Reno was working out. Maybe a little later they could go and live in Reno too.

It was a relief, Joy had a wonderful place and the peacocks would have more space to walk around in, and trees for shade, they wouldn't have to huddle under the little shade Wendell had built them.

Only when Joy came to get them in her big pickup with the camper shell it stopped being a relief. The peacocks didn't like being put in the dark pickup. They got very anxious and screeched and looked miserable. Joy rushed right off so they wouldn't have to stay in the hot pickup very long, she told Harmony not to worry, they'd calm down in no time once she let them out in her yard. Then the peacocks were gone. It made her feel horrible, she went in her bedroom and shut the door. Jessie probably got an instant migraine just from the sight of her face but Harmony couldn't help it. She felt like she had betrayed the peacocks, maybe they wouldn't like it at Joy's even if it did have more shade.

For a while she thought it's not worth it, I'll just be a waitress, at least the peacocks will be happy. She was on the verge of calling Joy and telling her to bring them back. The thought that they would never understand why she had done it to them was the terrible part.

Jessie didn't help. When Harmony finally came out of the bedroom and told her how she felt Jessie said, "Oh well, peacocks probably have a terrible memory, they'll forget you in five minutes." She was trying to be cheerful but it was the wrong thing to say, it was a little like suggesting that Francois would forget Jessie in five minutes. Harmony pointed that out and Jessie got upset and hobbled into *her* bedroom and shut *her* door.

Anyway, there was Ross to think about—she would just have to keep in mind that the peacocks would have a much more beautiful yard. Joy even had a sprinkler system, the yard was real nice. Harmony decided to take the late-afternoon bus. It would put her in Reno about three in the morning, which would be a good time for Ross, he would be off work. She called him and got him, he sounded a little drowsy but denied having been asleep.

"Ross, I'm coming tonight, will you meet me?" she asked.

Ross seemed a little startled. He said he definitely would meet her but he still seemed a little startled.

"Is it okay or what?" Harmony asked, she didn't have time to be subtle.

Oh sure, Ross said, he could hardly wait to see her. The problem was that Linda hadn't liked it at the commune and was on her way back, she had changed her mind about the commune life.

That was a shock, what was the point if Ross and Linda were getting back together? But Ross said oh no, she had misunderstood, Linda was bringing a girlfriend back from the commune and they were going to live together. The thing was Linda had demanded the apartment, so he didn't have a big apartment to offer anymore—Linda had demanded it.

But Ross said not to worry, he had a friend who owned a little motel. It had a pool but wasn't expensive. Maybe they could stay there for a few days until they got another apartment.

"It could be our second honeymoon," Ross said, sounding a little shy about it.

"Okay," Harmony said. The part about the second honeymoon cheered her up. She had been developing a few worries about Linda but if Ross wanted a second honeymoon there was probably no reason. Their first honeymoon had been to the Grand Canyon and they had even ridden down into it on mules.

It didn't take long to pack. Upon close examination she decided she only had one suitcase full of clothes that she actually liked, which was sort of lucky since she only had one suitcase anyway. While she was packing it she began to feel bad about Myrtle and decided as a parting gesture just to give Myrtle all the rest of her clothes—maybe it would revive her garage sale business.

So she hauled out an armful of slacks and blouses and even a few dresses—Myrtle was beside herself with gratitude. It occurred to Harmony after it was too late that she should have offered a few to Jessie, even if Jessie had hurt her feelings about the peacocks. Myrtle said forget it, she would make Jessie a good price on anything she wanted— besides Harmony was leaving Jessie the duplex, not to mention the furniture and all the kitchen stuff.

It turned out Jessie would rather have been left a particular black dress that Harmony had decided didn't fit her anymore, it had always been tight and the pound or two she had gained sort of tipped the balance. Jessie and Myrtle immediately started haggling about the dress, Jessie was a little hurt that Harmony hadn't remembered she liked it, so before the haggling was over they all began to cry—it was not so much the dress, it was that she was going away and everyone was emotional.

So when Gary suddenly drove up with Pepper in the car they were all in Myrtle's garage crying, amid Harmony's old clothes. Maude and Francois were there too. They had learned to tolerate one another, although in Harmony's view Maude was just waiting for her chance, her main interest was in the dry dog food Jessie was trying to get Francois to learn to eat. So far Maude had eaten several pounds and Francois about one nibble.

"Well, you're a cheerful bunch," Gary said.

Pepper looked wonderful and didn't comment on the tears. She just said hi and played with Maude a little. She was wearing a white silk blouse and some slacks that looked quite expensive. While they were talking she went in the house and got a few record albums she had forgot to take when she moved out.

"That house looks like a slum," she said, when she came back. "Don't you guys ever clean up?"

Harmony decided that Pepper had grown up—she had a lot of presence, it was a cool presence, but a lot of presence. She was so beautiful and well dressed that it made everyone a little uncomfortable, even Gary. He had been drinking too much due to his unrequited love and had put on weight. None of them looked that wonderful, they were all sitting around in a garage full of dusty costume jewelry and worn-out tires. Maude had eaten the bottom out of both the card tables, so that things kept falling through, so in a way Pepper was right, it *was* sort of slumlike, actually.

Jessie asked Pepper about her job at the Stardust and Pepper was casual about it. When Jessie asked if Bonventre had done anything mean Pepper just looked scornful and said, "No, and he better not." She seemed to think she could make sausage out of Bonventre if the need arose.

"Well, we gotta move it," Gary said, he was quite nervous, so Harmony got her suitcase and her little traveling bag.

"Be good to Wendell," she said, as she was hugging Myrtle. Of course they all cried again, and Pepper informed Gary that she would drive since she was the only one around with enough self-control to steer a car.

"Oh, Pepper, you're so self-possessed," Gary said. "You

ought to give courses in it, you'd make your fortune in this town."

He was a little biting, he thought Pepper ought to be more sentimental, but Harmony wasn't upset that Pepper wasn't sentimental, Pepper had a right to be the way she was.

As they headed on down toward the Stardust Harmony was mainly just looking at Pepper—it was wonderful to have a beautiful grown-up daughter. She decided that Pepper was going to have a lot more success in life than she had. Pepper sort of glanced at her once in a while, she wasn't totally cool. It was hard to tell exactly how sorry Pepper was that she was going away, but not hard to tell that she was a little nervous, she honked at people who made very slight driving errors, which made Gary nervous too. He hated a lot of honking.

When they got to the bus station Harmony gave Pepper a hug and a kiss. She knew adolescents didn't much like being hugged by their parents, particularly not Pepper, but at least she didn't seem too revolted.

"I know it's going to be wonderful for you, Pepper," Harmony said. "You're so talented, you'll have a real career."

Pepper had killed the motor. They were sitting in the parking lot behind the Stardust—the lights had just come on.

"That's the nice thing about Las Vegas, though," Harmony said. "I was never talented like you are, I was just pretty. Nobody would have known what to do with me anywhere else, but here I got to be a feathered beauty."

She didn't let them wait—didn't like people sitting around feeling awkward while she got her ticket. People ought to get on with their lives, particularly people like Pepper and Gary, who had jobs.

Pepper didn't say anything while Harmony was giving

Gary a long long hug, Gary was quite upset—Pepper sort of stood by the door of his Datsun, watching the hug. Harmony thought for a moment she would say more, explain to Pepper that it was silly to be jealous any longer, she had never been talented and now wasn't even a feathered beauty anymore—probably in a few more years she'd dry up like Myrtle and not be any kind of beauty, the jealousy was pointless—the few years would pass soon enough, then maybe Pepper would remember how hard she had tried to be a good mom, giving the birthday parties every year and reading stories and things. But she didn't say any of it, she didn't want to be a demanding parent, and anyway it would be better if Pepper just remembered it sometime.

"Will you say hello to my father?" Pepper said. She sounded rather formal but it was interesting that she said it, she hardly ever mentioned her father.

"Oh sure, he's been so proud since he heard you were dancing the lead, maybe we'll come down and see you sometime," Harmony said. Then she blew her daughter a little extra kiss and went on in, it was time those two were getting on with their lives.

She didn't feel so bad, waiting. The bus station was full of interesting-looking people, and it was sort of exciting to be getting on a bus and going someplace new, she hadn't really done it since that time in Tulsa when she was seventeen, and the bus then hadn't been nearly as fancy.

While she was waiting she struck up a conversation with a man who didn't tell her his real name. He just told her his nickname, which was Boston. He said he was a professional semipro softball player and he was going to Seattle, where he said a professional could always get by playing semipro baseball. Harmony didn't quite grasp the distinction between pro and semipro, but it didn't really matter, it was nice to have someone friendly to talk to. She told him she had been a showgirl and maybe still was, it depended on whether any producers in Reno happened to need one. Boston was optimistic, he said he didn't doubt she could get on with a show right away. It cheered her up even though it was obvious he didn't know the slightest thing about it. He even offered to buy her coffee but they called the bus about that time.

It was getting dark when they pulled out. The sky in the west was still blue, over the lights of the Strip—she still loved seeing those lights. The big dome was flashing in front of Caesars Palace and the Flamingo was lit up.

Since Boston didn't know much about Las Vegas she pointed out the MGM Grand and told him about the fire. They were nearly to the Trop when they passed the Amoco station. Harmony happened to glance out and see Wendell. There were no cars in the station, Wendell was just standing there by the pumps in his clean uniform, looking sad, she wanted so much to throw him a kiss. It would be quite a while before he got her windshield again, like forever probably, and she was remembering Pepper and being a parent and the problems and all and it broke her heart that Wendell's son was actually dead and could never remember that he had been a good dad, or stop being jealous or whatever.

She began to cry for Wendell, as they went on past the Tropicana. Boston was pretty upset by the sight of her tears, he thought maybe he had made a wrong move, offended her in some way. Harmony shook her head no, but she couldn't tell him the reasons, about Didier being dead in their room at the Trop and her not admitting it, about that or about any of her life—but it wasn't any wrong move, it was just the sight of Wendell, his sadness would go on forever even if Myrtle did let up about the jealousy.

The tears were too much for Boston though. Ten minutes later he had to go to the bathroom and on his way back he stopped and started talking to a black girl who was traveling alone except for a transistor radio. Boston sat down with the black girl and that was that. Once she stopped crying Harmony thought it was probably for the best, if she had got off the bus talking it up with Boston Ross might have got the wrong idea.

Soon it was quite dark, just now and then a light far out in the desert or the wink of an airplane far up in the sky. Harmony had kind of supposed it was all just empty and they would zoom along and there Ross would be, but in fact there were quite a few stops. Behind her she could faintly hear Boston telling the black girl about the life of a professional semipro, but she wasn't really listening, it was just sounds in the background. After Tonopah she got really drowsy and went to sleep. Reno was where everybody changed buses, so there was no danger of her sleeping right through it. Ross knew how to tease and would tease her for months if she did something as dumb as that.

But she didn't, she woke up while they were still in the desert and freshened up a bit as they were coming into town. Reno seemed bigger than it had when she had come as Miss Las Vegas Showgirl. It had its share of lights—nothing to equal the Strip, but quite a few.

As they wheeled on into town Harmony got nervous all of a sudden. One moment she had her optimism and felt very hopeful, but then in a second the optimism went away and she began to think like Jessie thought. After all, it had been fourteen years, it was definitely sort of crazy what she was doing. It even occurred to her that Linda could have showed up during the day and decided to keep Ross instead of just living with the girlfriend. It was hard not to be a little nervous, if Linda had come back it could be all off.

She was just as glad Boston had settled in with the black girl, one complication was enough, but then she stepped out into the cold bus station and Ross was right there.

"Oh, Ross, Pepper said hello," she said, didn't want to forget that important information. Of course she gave him a big hug but seeing him was sort of a shock, Ross seemed to have shrunk—not that he had ever been a giant, but definitely he seemed to have shrunk. He had always had a kind of potato face, only the potato had shriveled a little and the bald spot had definitely taken over. Ross had hair on his temples but only maybe about ten on the top of his head. She was thinking I shouldn't have thrown away so many sweaters, it's cold up here in Reno. Then she got over the shock a little, after all looks weren't everything, she had probably changed too.

She noticed that Ross was sort of watching Boston, who had his softball glove buttoned around the handle of his little bag. Boston was moving right along with the black girl and her transistor.

"How come that ballplayer didn't take up with you?" Ross asked. "Don't he know the most beautiful woman in the world when he sees her?"

"Oh Ross, he did, but I cried and scared him away," Harmony said, then she grabbed his arm, forget about the potato face, he still had the soft little Kansas voice, plus best of all Ross still had the sweet eyes.